Island Endgame

Rebecca Hodge

Paperback ISBN: 979-8-9991130-0-9

eBook ISBN: 979-8-9991130-1-6

Cover Design by 100 Covers

For Deb

Contents

Chapter One

Kenzie - Tuesday

A heavy June mist clung to my tiny, hired boat and shrouded the view ahead, but I leaned forward anyway, hoping to spot solid ground. A cold breeze chilled my face, and the uneven rattle of the motor plucked at nerves already stretched past their limits. The surly teenaged boy at the tiller slowed the boat, and a short wooden pier on a rocky shore came into view. Beyond it, dense forest loomed.

Salish Island, one of the smallest islands in Puget Sound, my home for the summer. A refuge where I hoped to piece myself back together.

I gripped the side of the boat, inspecting my new home, and grim reality hit. No buildings. No cars. No people. No anything. Not even the caretaker who was supposed to meet me. The island appeared ominous, nothing like the idyllic retreat I'd expected. I shouldn't be surprised. My life had been disintegrating for months. Why should this be any different?

The boy slipped the motor into neutral, and we drifted to the dock.

"Are you sure this is the right place?"

He snorted and gave me a side-eye. "Yeah, lady. This is it. You're on your own from here."

That sort of rudeness would have earned me a week of double chores when I was his age, but I swallowed a cutting reply. At forty and childless, kids were not my specialty, but I'd be surrounded by teenagers all summer. I might as well get used to bad manners.

He grabbed a cleat and held the boat steady while I heaved my duffel bag onto the dock and scrambled after it. "Do you bring people here often?"

The kid shrugged and pushed off. "Good luck." The words hung in his wake, as if emphasizing the fact that I needed every bit of luck I could get.

The boat dissolved into the haze, leaving me surrounded by endless water, dense trees, and unsettling silence. A cormorant splashed into an awkward landing, unperturbed by my presence. A light breeze sent ripples dancing toward shore, and goose bumps raced up my arms, ending in a shudder. Moisture coated everything. This speck of an island was an impudent invader in a world of wet.

I tried to shake off the creepiness of being so alone. *Come on, Kenzie, shape up. You agreed to come here.*

Back in Seattle, this job as resident nurse at a summer camp had sounded like the perfect escape, a needed change from the exhaustion of swing shifts at the hospital. I'd be far away, in a place without trauma, without memories, without people who knew about my nephew's death.

I would treat sunburns and headaches and the occasional skinned knee. I'd have peace and quiet and time. Not to recover—I didn't ever hope for that—but maybe I could get my emotions back under control so I could keep my hospital job. Assuming the isolation here didn't drive me totally nuts.

Stop. This was a fresh start, and I *would* embrace it. I grabbed my cell and punched in the phone number for the caretaker but got a *mailbox full* message.

If Tim were still alive, he'd tell me to chill. But just thinking about him ripped me apart.

I lugged my duffel off the dock and dumped it on a rock that appeared drier than the rest. A rutted dirt road led through a mix of madrona and fir trees, and I crossed it to check out a faded wooden sign that had fallen off its post.

Camp Madrona. No Trespassing.

Not exactly welcoming, but at least I was on the right island. An ancient VW van, purple with a camp logo of a twisted madrona tree, sat tucked into the trees a little farther in, and I walked over to check it out. No keys in the ignition. But at least someone was here. Or had been.

The camp's colorful website had included a map of the island. Its twelve hundred undeveloped acres formed a crescent more than three miles long and a half mile across. I was standing at the southern end, the end closest to Guemes Island and civilization. If my bad luck held, the caretaker probably lived far away at the northern end.

My phone chimed with a text. I saw who it was from and deleted it, unread. I should have blocked my sister months ago, but the daily scourge of her too-kind, too-understanding, too-painful texts and voice mails was a punishment I deserved. Caustic salt in an unhealed wound.

I could stand here and hope for the best, or sit on a boulder and sob, or suck it up and get going. The sobbing option had its draw, but a walk would let me pretend I was proactive. I hoisted the duffel and started down the road. Surely, I'd meet up with someone before I walked the whole three miles to the north end.

An hour later, the road grew narrow, and its ruts grew deep. I was hobbling. My bag had magically doubled in weight, and my new tennis shoes had rubbed blisters on both heels. I'd been phoning the caretaker every five minutes but never reached a human.

The mist thinned, then disappeared. The sun took full advantage, and the day grew warm. I dropped my duffel in a patch of shade and pulled my hair back in a scrunchie. Then I fished out my water bottle and gulped the last stale swallow.

Something rustled close by. Something sounding far bigger than the occasional blackbird or sparrow I'd seen along the way.

I stepped back. The sound came closer. "Who's there?" My shaking voice matched my trembling insides.

A boy stepped onto the road, a boy maybe nine or ten years old.

My stomach and chest clenched so hard I could barely breathe. I'd been careful to check the ages of the campers. Thirteen to sixteen, no exceptions. I couldn't face a summer surrounded by children who would remind me of Tim. But here stood a child about his age.

He had tangled, black, shoulder-length hair, wore a mud-splattered T-shirt, and a muddier pair of ripped jeans. His tennis shoes dangled from his backpack. Dirt clung to his bare feet.

He inspected me from head to toe, then glanced into the underbrush behind him and gestured. A small brown dog appeared, a fluffy-haired mix of heaven knows how many breeds. He trotted to the boy's side and sat looking up at him with devoted eyes.

"Who are you?" My words came out fast and sounded harsher than I'd intended.

"I'm Chris." He said it like I should have known. He pointed at the dog. "This is Skagit. Who are you?"

"Kenzie Adams. I'm the new nurse. Have you seen the caretaker?"

"Sure. That's my mom." He checked me out again. His small nod of approval had the air of royalty conferring favor on a commoner. "Want me to show you where she is?"

"How far?"

"Not very. Come on."

He turned, and Skagit fell into step beside him. Tim would have loved a dog like that. I grabbed my bag and started walking. My blisters screamed but the tenseness that had overtaken my body wasn't quite as bad. I could deal with this boy. "You live out here with your mom?"

"Yep."

"You'll be around all summer?"

"Yep."

"With the other campers?"

"Nope. Skagit and I do our own thing."

The feeling in my stomach eased even more. I shelved the rest of my million and one questions and tried not to twist an ankle on the uneven road.

Chris's definition of *not far* didn't match mine. But after another twenty minutes, the road reached the end of the forest. Wildflowers dotted a broad meadow of knee-high grass that led downhill to a pebbled beach. The same beach I'd seen in the website photographs. At least one thing on the island was the way I'd expected.

The snow-capped silhouette of Mt. Baker on the mainland pushed other thoughts out of my mind. I'd read that its slopes were more than sixty miles away, but standing as I was at sea level, its ten-thousand-foot peak claimed a huge swath of sky. This view, I could get used to.

We kept walking toward the water, and I checked out the five buildings scattered along the road. On the left, a small cedar-shake cottage with a wooden shed behind it. On the right, a padlocked, metal storage shed and a pavilion stacked with clutter. A small cinderblock building near the beach had doors labeled *Boys* and *Girls*.

No cabins. No dining hall. No infirmary.

No pier off the beach, no range marked for archery practice, no obvious space for arts and crafts.

And no matter how hard I looked, no cabins anywhere.

Now that I thought about it, the camp website showed smiling campers and striking scenery but not much else.

"Where are the other buildings? The cabins for campers?" Heck, where was *my* cabin?

Chris looked puzzled. "What other buildings? This is it."

What the hell had I gotten myself into? I'd trained my replacement at the hospital and sublet my apartment. And I'd promised my boss I'd have my shit together when I returned at the end of the summer. I couldn't leave now.

I was stuck.

Served me right. I'd taken this job on impulse, an easy gig that I hoped would let me escape constant reminders of Tim. I'd regretted the impulse at once and mentioned it to my supervisor as a joke, a *you-won't-believe-what-I-did-last-night* story that I assumed would make her roll her eyes. To my astonishment, Betsy had heard of Camp Madrona and thought it would be a fabulous idea for me to spend a summer away from the hospital.

But she didn't mean sleeping outdoors, did she?

She'd taken me by the arm with a firm grip and led me to her office. "You took no time off after the funeral. You need to heal." She usually barked orders like an experienced drill sergeant, so her sympathetic tone caught me off guard. "Losing a nephew the way you did would be tough on anyone. But you're second-guessing yourself. Making mistakes."

She pulled a form from her drawer and wrote while she talked. I strained to see it from the other side of the desk.

Leave of Absence Request.

I'd been a nurse for twenty years. I'd embraced the long hours and shift work, focused only on my career. Taking a leave had never occurred to me.

Betsy handed me the form. "Anyone would need a break, and that includes you. Don't beat yourself up. You used to be kind and empathetic, but now we're getting complaints."

People had complained? About me?

I searched through my memories of the past few months, but I couldn't recall a single specific patient. Not one. That realization sat like a jagged boulder in my stomach. Maybe Betsy was right. I'd walled my patients out.

I snapped back to the present and took another look at the primitive conditions that surrounded me. *You need to heal.* Yeah, right. Sort of like saying *you need to grow that limb back.* As if erasing those memories and setting aside the guilt was remotely possible. But something had to change, and now that I'd arrived, it was obvious that Salish Island would be a bigger change than I'd expected. I had to make this work. I had to reclaim myself. I had to get my job back.

Chris ran ahead to the cottage, and I followed, although a bit slower with my throbbing blisters.

"Mom! Someone's here!" His yell echoed across the entire meadow, then he headed toward the woods.

The screened door opened at once and a woman in her late twenties or early thirties waved me over. "Hi there! You must be Mackenzie. Come in. I'm Leah Kenner. I'm sorry you had to walk so far. Erik told me you weren't coming until Tuesday, or I'd have met you and given you a lift."

She spoke quickly, her words merging into a river of sound that took a moment to navigate. She had waist-length brown hair pulled back in the sort of loose braid I'd always envied. No makeup. Triple piercings in each of her ears held a mix of studs and dangly silver earrings. Her loose denim sundress fit her earth-mother vibe. No shoes, like her son, but cleaner feet.

"Yes, I'm Kenzie."

I considered pointing out that today actually *was* Tuesday, but her not knowing told me plenty about what I'd walked into. I followed her inside, dumping my duffle on the floor as soon as I crossed the threshold. I stood in a small living room, cluttered with a couch, two easy chairs, a small television, and a large bookcase crammed with dog-eared paperbacks. An open door on the right led to a bedroom. The cottage smelled like baking bread, and my stomach rumbled. "I didn't realize this place was so isolated."

"Quiet, off-season. Chaos, when the campers arrive." She led me across the living room into the kitchen and picked up a knife from the counter. The kitchen had basic appliances, a table, and four chairs. A second bedroom opened from the side. The place had a relaxed, homey feel to it, but if Leah and Chris lived here year-round, it must be a lonely existence. Anyone who would volunteer for this kind of isolation had to be a little odd.

She finished chopping an onion on a large, wooden cutting board, tossed the bits into a large pot, and rinsed celery in the deep iron sink. Silver rings set with semiprecious stones flashed bright colors as she worked. "I hope soup suits you for dinner."

"Sounds good. I've got lots of questions, but first, could I use your bathroom?"

"Sure. Cinderblock building down the way."

No bathroom here? I took a closer look at the cottage. It didn't take long. A rectangular box, about twenty by thirty, divided into fourths by walls that didn't quite reach the ceiling. Every room had two interior doors, so if I'd wanted, I could have circled through all four rooms in a tight loop. No bathroom.

I tried to hide my dismay. "Be right back."

The bathhouse turned out to be not as gross as I feared. A few spiders and dead moths, but I'd braced for worse. Five toilet stalls. Five sinks. A communal shower with a half-dozen nozzles. High windows let in light, but there were no electric outlets. And the water from both taps was icy cold, which didn't bode well for taking showers.

When I returned, Leah was peeling potatoes. "Can I help?"

"I'm almost done."

"Fill me in about the camp. I'm excited to be here." I kept my tone all happy-happy and hoped she didn't suspect a lie. I settled into one of the kitchen chairs. "Camp starts in a little more than a week?"

"Yes. It's good of you to come early to help with the set-up. There's a lot to do. We expect seventy-two campers plus the rest of the staff. It will be a crazy zoo, but I love it." She diced the potatoes, tossed them in the pot. "I've been here for ten of the camp's sixty years and it's a good life despite the limitations. For example, there's no electricity except when I kick the generator on here at the cottage."

"You mean nowhere? Anywhere?"

She laughed. "It's not worth running power lines to an island this small. The stove, fridge, and the furnace here in the cottage are propane. I usually click the generator on for a few hours in the evening to let Chris get some TV, computer, and video game time, and I charge a bunch of storage batteries. Feel free to charge your phone in here when it needs it."

She still spoke as fast as a whirlwind, but I was getting better at deciphering. No electricity. Guess my hair dryer was pointless. "Where do the campers sleep?"

"In tipis. The biggest part of set-up is pitching them all."

"You're kidding." I was supposed to sleep in a glorified tent for three months? My disbelief elicited another laugh. "But there's an infirmary somewhere, right?"

"You're sitting in it. Truth is, you're the first real nurse we've ever had. Mostly, you'll be dealing with cuts and scrapes or offering TLC to a new kid who's homesick. If someone needs real tending, we put them in Chris's room. There's a spare bed there, and I can move him in with me. We've got a cupboard full of basic first aid supplies. We'll put your tipi in the Puffin group, which is closest. That way you can tend to patients without having to traipse all over."

I looked away, trying to hide my dismay. I hadn't expected luxury, but I *had* envisioned a solid roof over my head.

My misgivings must have been more obvious than I hoped because Leah frowned. "How did you hear about this job anyway?"

"I met Erik at a Mardi Gras party." Fifty people packed into a room designed for twenty. I'd gone, hoping to whittle away some of my depression, but it proved to be an opportunity to drink too much while pretending my life wasn't in shreds. When a bearded guy in a flannel shirt, hiking boots, and a serious tan kept his eye on me, I flirted right back. He looked ten years younger, but I was game for anything that would dull the ache. "He said he heard I was a nurse. Refilled my wine glass and settled in to talk."

Leah laughed. "Let me guess. The conversation wasn't what you expected?"

"It took me a while to realize his questions weren't a typical pickup routine. Did I like to camp? Hike? How would I like to take a break from the hospital? Low pay but beautiful scenery, interesting people, and plenty of time on my own." The more he talked, the more tempting it sounded. Or maybe that was the wine talking. All I could think was no demanding patients, no computer screens, no night shifts.

"Erik could sell Christmas trees in January. It makes him a great lead counselor, but you're not the only new arrival who's surprised at what they find here. I take it he didn't tell you that he'd been struggling for months to line up a nurse for the summer?"

"That didn't get mentioned. And I think I forgot to ask a few key questions."

She shook her head. "Don't worry. You'll figure it out. And this place will grow on you. Wait and see. You can sleep in Chris's room tonight, and we'll put up your tipi first thing tomorrow so you can get settled."

I mumbled something I hoped sounded polite and moved into the living room to claim a comfortable chair. My head was spinning, but my body felt numb. I'd landed on an alien planet, and the culture shock hit hard. In self-defense, I dozed while dinner simmered, and Leah had to shake me awake when it was ready.

The bean and vegetable soup, loaded with fresh herbs and served in dark blue pottery bowls with an intricate flower pattern, would have commanded a premium price in town. The homemade bread made me wonder why I paid money for the bland, store-bought stuff. At least my stomach found contentment. Chris and Skagit materialized in time to eat in silence, then disappeared outdoors again.

"He knows these woods better than most kids know their own house." Leah stood to fix big mugs of tea. "I've homeschooled him so far, but I need to decide what's best for this coming year. He's far ahead in his studies, and he's been so independent here that, in a lot of ways, he acts older than his age. But he needs friends. If I have to take him to school in Anacortes every day, it means a lot of boat time."

Tim would have been scared to even step foot in this forest, much less travel to school by boat. "You've been here for ten years?"

"Yes. Settled in soon after Chris was born. I'm a potter." She gestured toward the crockery. "My wheel and kiln are in the shed out back. I teach the kids basic clay techniques in the summer along with a handful of other crafts, then the rest of the year is mine to make ceramics full time. I sell to a few galleries and do mail order through my website. The camp doesn't pay much, but it gives me a beautiful place to live and work and garden."

"Your pottery is amazing. And it sounds like this place suits you." I still couldn't imagine staying even the three months I'd committed to. So isolated. So backward. So foreign compared to my normal life.

I'd signed up for the postcard version of a summer camp—outdoorsy fun followed by smiling singalongs around a campfire. This full-text version of tipis and a communal bathhouse, dirt and damp and daily challenge, had caught me off-guard. I wouldn't be able to rely on normal distractions like computer games and television, and no city lay at my doorstep offering unlimited, mindless diversions. What if being here simply gave me too much empty time to think about Tim?

I had another sudden urge to turn around and go home, but I shoved it aside and arranged my face into what I hoped was a believable smile. "It's been a long day. Let me help you with the dishes, then I think I'll head to bed early."

We finished, and I stepped outside. I'd focused on the layout of the place when I arrived, but now I paused to soak in the atmosphere. With the sun low in the sky behind me, Mt. Baker shimmered as if sprinkled in fairy dust, and the Puget Sound sparkled, restless and alive. The air carried the scents of dozens of flowers without a hint of car exhaust or fast-food grease or other random city stink. When it grew fully dark, I'd probably be able to see stars.

The extreme quiet stunned me. Meadow grass rustled in the breeze. My clothing whispered when I walked. Each one of my breaths made tiny sounds I'd never noticed before.

A shame, really, to waste all this on me. Some people embraced this sort of thing, but as far as I was concerned, the place would be infinitely improved with bright lights, a Starbucks, and fast pizza delivery. Tim would wish for a proper soccer field and a McDonald's, then wonder where to plug in his game console.

On the other hand, my sister Paige would pull out her camera and angle for the best composition of light and shadow, wondering what time she should get up to capture the sunrise.

But no. Not anymore. The last time I saw her was at the funeral, catatonic with grief. People surrounded her—neighbors, friends, fellow PTA moms. She didn't need me. I stayed in the background, not belonging, turning away from offers of sympathy. In the months since, I pushed aside friends who tried to lure me back to normal life, and I couldn't face Paige. She called. Texted. Left notes on my door. She said she didn't want to lose me too. Claimed Tim's death wasn't my fault.

But she was naïve. I was responsible. *Do no harm.* That phrase wasn't part of the Nightingale Oath, but as a nurse, it had been my personal promise. Until I broke it.

Even here, on this remote spit of land, I couldn't escape the burden of that knowledge. I slid my hand into my pocket and touched the small painted stone that lived there. Tim had given it to me years before. A pet rock, he claimed, with blue eyes and painted-on fur. Usually a source of comfort, but not today.

I walked downhill to the bathhouse, my steps slow, weighted by memories. Chris and Skagit were hanging out on the beach. I looked again and froze. Chris wasn't on the beach. He stood in the water, knee-deep and wading deeper.

Ice filled my veins, and my heart seized. "No!" I shouted. The scene blurred, and for a moment, all I could see was Tim, floating face down in a backyard swimming pool. A wave of panic rose to swamp me.

I blinked, and my vision cleared. Chris, not Tim. He looked my way but made no effort to return. I forced my rigid legs into motion and raced toward him, dodging the driftwood logs that lay heaped along the transition from meadow to pebbles.

"Chris, be careful! No swimming! Come back. Please. Come back now." My voice shook, and I fought a swell of nausea.

He took two giant steps deeper into the water. "You're not the boss of me." His voice held the same tone of disdain Tim used when I tried to be the tough aunt instead of the fun one.

"Chris. Please." I reached the edge of the water. Pried off my tennis shoes and waded in. My socks offered little protection against the rough bottom, and the breathtaking chill of the fifty-degree water stunned me. I'd read the warnings in town. Full immersion in the sound meant unconsciousness from hypothermia in ten to fifteen minutes. Chris must be made of titanium.

He stopped, but I suspected it was more from surprise than obedience.

"Please." I held out a hand.

He ignored it, but after a moment, he shrugged and waded back to shore to join his dog. Toes already numb, I followed more slowly. By the time I reached shore, the pair had walked farther down the beach. I pulled off my socks and forced shoes onto my frigid feet. Chris and Skagit disappeared into the trees.

He was safe for the moment, this odd feral child. But that didn't make me feel any less a failure.

Chapter Two

Kenzie – Wednesday

E arly the next day, the sound of a man's voice startled me from an unsettled sleep. I crawled from under the covers and fumbled my way into a pair of jeans and a sweatshirt. Sounds carried freely over the partial walls of Leah's cottage, and the voice and laugh sounded like Erik. My watch said six a.m. He must have left town in the middle of the night to arrive so early.

Chris slept on in the bed across the room, curled into a tight ball, and Skagit lifted his head to look at me but showed no inclination to get up. I needed to pee, brush my hair, and clear my head before I faced my new boss. I eased open the door to Leah's room, ducked through it and the living room, and slipped out the front door. Middle of nowhere or not, this was still a job, and I didn't want to start off looking like a derelict.

The thought pulled me up short. I still had more doubts and hesitations than I could count, but overnight my subconscious must have made up its mind. I would stick it out for a few days. See how things went. I squared my shoulders and quickened my pace.

If I were home, I'd be stepping into a hot shower about now, then pulling on scrubs and hustling out the door. I'd read email while I waited in line for my caramel macchiato, then I'd walk five blocks to the hospital, wondering what cases I'd be assigned that day. I used to follow that routine on autopilot, but these last few months, every step had been a struggle. Here, a new sense of purpose brought a glimmer of hope.

Patchy clouds drifted overhead, the grass and trees glistened with dew, and scattered beams of sunlight glinted off the calm water of the sound. The water's surface formed a perfect mirror, reflecting the silhouette of Mt. Baker in crystal detail. I took a deep breath of Christmassy evergreens mixed with an energizing floral scent. By the time I finished in the bathhouse and headed back to the cottage, I was fully awake and managed to pull up a patched-together smile.

Such a smile could be a good omen. Maybe to earn it, I could even live out of a duffel bag and sleep in a tipi.

The purple van I'd seen yesterday at the pier now stood beside the cottage. I rubbed my aching shoulder, still sore from hauling my duffel, and went in.

Erik, at the kitchen table, raised his coffee mug in greeting. "Good morning." A half-eaten stack of pancakes and a sliced apple filled the plate in front of him. "Glad you made it okay."

"A bit of a hike, but Leah has made me welcome." This was the first time I'd seen him since the night of the party. He looked thinner now, with fine lines of strain etching his face and a nervous twitch in the hand that held his fork. Leah watched him carefully, and she added two more pancakes to his plate without asking.

"Eight days until the little grunions arrive, and we have plenty to do before then. Have a seat. Eat." He gestured to the empty chair across from him as if this was his house and he was the host. "The rest of the set-up crew won't arrive until later today, but the three of us can get rolling."

Leah filled a second plate and set it in front of me.

I ate, studying the two of them while Erik scrolled through his phone and Leah ladled more batter onto the griddle. In his initial pep talk at the party, he'd mentioned he worked ski seasons in Utah as an instructor and had been lead counselor at Camp Madrona for the past five summers. That meant he and Leah had worked closely together, but instead of catching up, I sensed a silent wariness between them. He glanced in her direction when she was focused elsewhere, but I couldn't read his expression. When she came close to refill his coffee, she took care not to brush against him.

"It's nice that you could come earlier than you originally planned. Extra hands are always appreciated." Erik's words sounded right, but he didn't look at me when he said them. And when I'd emailed him to let him know my arrival day, his response had been lukewarm. Not a big deal, but it was a contrast to the more genuine welcome I'd gotten from Leah. I shifted on my chair and failed to come up with anything to say.

"Chris! Breakfast!" Leah called over the wall and flipped a final set of pancakes. In seconds, the bedroom door opened, and Chris stepped in wearing an oversized T-shirt and rubbing his eyes. He'd scrubbed off yesterday's mud, but his legs still had an orange tint. I resisted the urge to grab a bar of soap and a washcloth.

"What's for break—Erik!" All sleepiness gone in an instant, Chris zoomed around me and launched himself at Erik, who spun in his chair to seize the boy in a bear hug that lifted his feet off the floor. Skagit bounced beside the chair, beside himself with excitement.

"Who's this? What have you done with the little kid I kept tripping over last summer?"

Chris didn't loosen his hug. "It's me. You know it's me."

Erik laughed and eased him back to the floor. "Yeah, yeah, fair enough. How've you been? You ready to help with setup?"

"Can I use the axe to trim new poles?"

Leah jumped in before Erik could answer. "Not this year. Maybe next."

"Come on, Mom. You never let me do anything fun." But Chris's protest sounded half-hearted, and I got the impression that when Leah vetoed something, he knew he was sunk.

She distributed more pancakes, then joined us at the table. Chris dove into his breakfast while filling Erik in on everything that had happened over the winter.

It was a ten-year-old's version of *Pilgrim at Tinker Creek*: two pairs of eagles returning to their nests, a lone seal spotted sunning itself near the beach, a frozen wellhead in January, a new trick that Skagit would be happy to demonstrate after breakfast. Erik responded to each snippet of news with solemn consideration, attention never wavering. Chris paused occasionally to stab a chunk of pancake as if he expected it to escape. The same way Tim used to. I blinked hard.

Tim used to be like this. Moments when his excitement sky-rocketed out of control. His enthusiasms didn't involve animal tracks or weather updates, but he'd fill me in excitedly on his newest video game, his soccer coach, the exact model of bike he'd added to his Christmas list. Chris had the same light in his eyes, the same restlessness in his body. They both grabbed so much joy out of tiny things, taking for granted that they had endless time ahead for adventure.

My heart seized, and I bit back tears. I stood and began clearing plates, turning my head so the others couldn't see my face. Leah had heated a large pot of water on the stove, and I mixed it with cold water from the tap to wash and rinse the dishes. She joined me, drying each item and putting it away.

I did my best to steady my hands and appear normal. I could take almost anything in stride as a nurse, but I sucked at hiding personal distress. Leah looked my way, brows furrowed, then rested her hand on my shoulder for a long moment when we were done. She gave it a supportive squeeze, though she couldn't know what had sideswiped me. I made sure not to meet her eyes.

Erik stretched, stood, and slipped his phone into his back pocket, then waved Chris out of his chair. "Okay, kid, go find some clothes, and we'll get to it." He looked at Leah and me. "Let's start with the tipis so we all have somewhere to sleep tonight."

Chris disappeared into the bedroom, and Erik walked outside. Leah leaned in. "Are you okay?" She kept her voice low.

I made the mistake of looking at her, and the sympathy in her eyes slipped through my armor and lured the truth from its hiding place. "The past catches me sometimes. It blindsides me when I least expect it. Sadness. Guilt. Anger at myself." I stopped. I'd given away too much.

Her breath caught, and she blinked a few times. "I know something about that. But even the sharpest edges soften with time. Would you judge a stranger as harshly as you're judging yourself?"

She paused for a moment, as if expecting an answer. She may have lugged around some serious history of her own, but even so, she didn't understand my situation. Some things couldn't be forgotten. Or forgiven. And some things couldn't be shared. I shook my head.

She gave me one of the saddest smiles I'd ever seen. "Come on then. Let's get to work. Maybe this island will work some of its magic on you."

I had my doubts, but I followed her out of the cottage and across the drive to the large open-sided pavilion I'd noticed the previous day. Large cracks crisscrossed its concrete floor, and a few chunks canted at strange angles. At one end of the structure, a long counter stood across from an oversized propane cookstove, an extra-large propane refrigerator and freezer, two giant ceramic sinks, and a network of storage cupboards. A dozen graffiti-etched wooden picnic tables and benches crowded helter-skelter beside the counter.

"We call this space the Lodge." Leah gestured with a broad wave of her arm. "But it functions as dining hall, meeting hall, dance floor, craft center, and pretty much anything else we need it to be. We keep meals simple and kid friendly. Calories and lots of them, that's the key. The campers burn through mountains of food, living outdoors and staying busy all day."

Stacks of odd-shaped bundles wrapped in blue plastic tarps covered the rest of the floor. Erik headed for a group at the end, pulled off the tarp, and dragged a tied bundle off the top. More than a dozen wooden poles stuck out of the ends, each appearing more than sixteen feet long, wrapped in rope and heavy white canvas.

"Give me a hand," Erik called. Leah and I paired up on one end, and he took the other. Chris materialized and did his best to help. We lugged the hundred-pound bundle to a cleared patch of meadow fifty yards from the cottage.

"The campers are grouped into units by age," Erik said. "The youngest girls, thirteen- and fourteen-year-olds, are called the Puffins, and their tipis go here. So will yours. Which way do you want yours to face?"

The next hour proved to be a crash course in how to properly set up a tipi. Three stout primary poles formed the key tripod, then we bound in secondary poles and positioned the canvas. This resulted in a large structure, fifteen feet in diameter at its base, complete with a circular entrance door, a smoke hole at the top, and smoke flaps that could be adjusted in bad weather.

"We'll drive a few stakes to anchor the bottom edge." Erik hefted a hammer. "But these things are incredibly stable. Close the smoke hole when you expect rain, and you'll stay dry in the roughest storms."

Leah and I stepped inside. We'd carried in a wire-framed cot and mattress before putting the canvas up, and the bed sat opposite the door. I'd be able to lie there and look out over the sound.

"We've got some spare canvas if you want to cover the grass," Leah said. "And you'll want to dig a trench outside to route rainwater away. Living in a tipi is more comfortable than you think."

I wasn't convinced. The canvas gave out the dank, musty smell of long storage, and no matter how I looked at it, a tipi did not have four walls and a roof. But a breeze off the water filtered under the bottom edge of the canvas and passed up through the central smoke hole, creating a pleasant cooling effect. And a diffuse light filtered in, making the space cozy. If I collected stones for a central fire pit and lined up some dry wood, the smoke from a fire would draw well. Somehow the idea of a pleasant evening fire made the place a little more homey.

"This should work out okay." I tried to sound sincere, and maybe I meant it. The tents I'd used in the distant past for camping had all been cramped, with low ceilings and flapping nylon sides. I'd spent as little time in them as possible. At least this version had space.

But Erik gave me no time to sit and contemplate my new home. "Come on, you two," he called. "Let's hustle."

The rest of the morning flew past. We built a circle of five tipis next to mine for the Puffins, then followed a nearby trail through the trees to a clearing that would be home to the fifteen-year-old girls, the Herons. Small volunteer saplings and tall weeds dotted the space.

Erik surveyed the overgrowth and shook his head. "We'll need to scythe this down before we can do much here."

By noon my shoulders ached, and blisters on my hands competed for attention with the blisters on my feet. Erik gave no sign that he planned to break for lunch, but I was saved when he glanced at a text message. "Hey, the others will be here in ten minutes." He ruffled Chris's hair. "Want to ride with me to pick them up at the pier?"

"Yay!" Chris and Skagit raced for the van, and Erik gave a wave and followed.

Must be nice, getting a ride in. I walked toward the cottage with Leah, trying not to limp. "How do the campers get here?"

"They assemble in Anacortes. We have a boat we use to shuttle back and forth on the first and last day of each session. It's in Anacortes at the moment for an engine overhaul. Then we use the van to haul their gear from the pier. The campers walk."

I'd wondered how parents reacted to the bare-bones appearance of Camp Madrona, but this explained it. All they ever saw were the carefully curated photos on the website. If they got a happy camper back at the end of the summer, it must work.

Leah and I assembled a giant platter of turkey sandwiches, and she gave me a quick rundown on the new arrivals. We were finishing when the van returned, and in moments, the front door of the cottage flew open and two new people tumbled in. Chris ran from one person to the next, talking nonstop, and Skagit barked in excitement. Absolute chaos.

"How was the winter here?"

"Have you heard from Eliza? Is she coming back this year?"

"Erik, how's your leg? Any more problems?"

"Chris, what's your mom been feeding you to make you grow so fast?"

The questions flew, but nobody paused to give answers. Both new arrivals were in their late twenties, which surprised me. I'd assumed the camp's counselors would be college students.

Drake Corder turned out to be a short, muscular guy with a scraggly beard and sleeve tattoos featuring colorful marine mammals. His gruff voice, harsh laugh, and abrupt manner reminded me of a wrestler I'd dated in college. That relationship ended when the guy stole all the money I'd saved for a beach vacation. I didn't want to judge Drake based on the resemblance, so I did my best to act extra-nice when he said hello. The smile he gave me in return used the fewest muscles possible, a lip twist over clenched teeth, more of a snarl than a greeting. So much for acting nice.

On the other hand, I instantly warmed to Bree Bennet, who had short blonde hair, blue eyes, and a calm, even voice. She walked like a dancer or maybe a gymnast, light on her feet, poised and balanced and strong. She touched each person she spoke to, resting her hand on an arm or a shoulder and looking directly at them as if nothing else mattered in that moment. She gave me a kind smile but kept her distance.

Leah hugged Bree as soon as she saw her but kept distance from Drake, as she had with Erik.

Everyone wore ratty T-shirts and torn jeans, making the new ripstop pants and Patagonia hoodie I'd picked up at REI on my way out of town look too crisp and out of place. Leah introduced me, and everyone made welcoming noises, but their skeptical expressions gave me a new-kid-at-school awkward feeling. I was conscious of being the oldest one there. They belonged. I didn't.

The sandwich platter made the rounds, and the group spread out, half in the kitchen, half in the living room. I sat in a corner, ate my fill, and hoped the conversations buzzing around me would delay the start of the afternoon work session. What I really needed was a nap.

No such luck.

"Okay, folks, time to get cracking." Erik stood in the doorway between the kitchen and living room to claim everyone's attention. "We've got plenty to do this afternoon. Drake, Leah, and Kenzie, you'll work on setup for the Otter group. Bree, come with me to help clear the undergrowth for the Herons."

"What about me?" Chris stepped close to Erik, looking hopeful.

"You're sticking with your mom."

The boy's face fell, and his shoulders slumped. "Okay." The word dragged out in five syllables.

We all stood, stretched, and got to it. The three of us on the Otter team went to select the next tipi bundle, while the others unlocked the metal storage building and lugged out scythes and clippers.

"What's the deal on the names for the camper groups?" I asked.

Drake forced a lopsided grin that didn't mask his impatience at having to answer. "The girl groups are birds—Puffins, Herons, and Eagles, youngest to oldest. They're all at that end of camp." He gestured toward the north side of the meadow, where we'd erected the Puffin tipis that morning. "The boys are the Otters, Dolphins, and Orcas, and they're spread out to the south. Youngest live in the meadow, where it feels less isolated and they're closest to the bathhouse. Middle-aged groups are further out in the woods, and that's where Erik and Bree are headed. The oldest groups have tipis tucked next to the water. The stairs at each end of the beach lead to boardwalks. The one to the north leads to the Eagles, and the one to the south leads to the Orcas. We'll set them up last."

We grabbed the next bundle and headed out.

"The group names date back to the earliest days of the camp." Leah didn't even pant as we hefted the poles and canvas uphill. "Each group sleeps and eats together, does activities together, develops a tight camaraderie. Each group picks their colors, chooses a theme song, designs a flag. Does a skit on Talent Night. Stuff like that."

I nodded, too out of breath to respond. Now that tipis were going up and other people were here, the place looked more like a proper camp. And talk about skits and songs had me envisioning the island full of happy campers. The setting still felt strange, but if I could find a way to fit in, maybe a summer here wouldn't be so bad.

We worked hard. I kept my head down and my complaints to myself, except for one exchange when Drake and I were lugging a tipi to the Dolphin unit.

"Hurry up, will you? There are more important things to do." He didn't even look at me when he spat out the words.

I dropped my end of the bundle, stopping him cold, and took a few gasping breaths. "Give me a break. I'm a nurse, not a weightlifter."

"You came early for set-up. That means you work." Still no eye contact.

Spiked anger surged up my throat, and I gritted my teeth to hold it in. These last few months, my temper lived just under the surface, and that was part of what had gotten me in trouble at work. I couldn't ruin this too.

Leah rejoined us, and she seemed to assume we were just taking a break. "Ready to go?"

She and I lifted one end, Drake lifted the other, and we hustled forward at double speed. Drake said nothing to me the rest of the afternoon, which suited me just fine.

We finished setting up for the Otters, got a start on the Dolphins, and scrubbed down the kitchen area in the Lodge. Despite his crusty personality, Drake's strength came in handy and he proved to be a steady worker. Leah never let up, and Chris darted in and out, helping where he could.

Erik and Bree didn't return until late in the afternoon, and we all called it quits. After a dinner of the rest of the vegetable soup, we settled in the living room, bringing in enough kitchen chairs to seat everyone. Beer, weed, and edibles made the rounds and the mood mellowed. I stuck to beer and hoped I could stay awake. An occasional question came my way when someone noticed me in the corner, but it was primarily a reunion of four old friends focused on catching up.

Erik, Leah, and Bree had been patient all day, explaining the million things I didn't know. They didn't laugh when I fumbled a hammer or had trouble positioning an awkward fold of canvas. But I still felt like an outcast, and the few moments of optimism that had buoyed me in the morning seemed imaginary now.

The others didn't have to highlight my faults. I took care of that myself. Incompetent, that's what I was. I'd lost my confidence at the hospital, and it was clear I couldn't function here either.

I shook myself and finished my beer. That lack of confidence was the Seattle me talking. Here, I had a chance to put all my problems behind me. I would stand up to Drake's snarls and reach out to the others for friendship. I would look forward, not back. Chris wasn't my nephew, and I wouldn't let his presence push my buttons.

I stood and stretched. My back and shoulders ached, and tomorrow's work wouldn't be any easier. I walked through the kitchen into Chris's room. Small stones lined one of his shelves, organized into groups by size and color. Another shelf held sea glass, odd shapes worn smooth by the ocean. Photos of distant galaxies from the Webb telescope papered the walls, and a star chart hung by the window. He lay on his bed reading but set his book aside when I entered.

I gave him a smile. "My tipi is ready. I'll grab my stuff and get out of your way."

"Okay. Or it's all right to stay here another night if you want." The tough, almost regal attitude I'd noticed when I first met him had vaporized, leaving a ten-year-old boy who needed friends.

But that wouldn't be me. "Thanks. I'd better unpack."

I took a moment to check out the cabinet of medical supplies. A shelf of over-the-counter products to treat common ailments. Lots of Band-Aids, bandages, and antibiotic ointment. Stretch wrap for sprains and even some splints and casting tape. Major injuries would need treatment off-island, but this should be enough for me to manage what I hoped would be a quiet summer.

I turned back to Chris. "You were a big help today." Once he'd resigned himself to the job, he always popped up in the right spot at the right time, bringing stakes, passing a hammer, circling the tipi with its tie rope. He seemed to have forgotten, or at least forgiven, the episode at the shore when I'd panicked and yelled at him to get out of the water.

"I like summer best, when everyone is here."

"What are you reading?"

He lifted his book so I could see the cover, and a quick kick in the gut caught me off guard. One of the Olympians series, Tim's favorites. I'd read the books aloud to him at many bedtimes.

"You okay?"

Like his mother, Chris noticed things I wanted to hide. I composed my face. "That's a good one, where Artemis gets kidnapped."

"Yeah. I've read it before."

"I like the labyrinth one the best."

He sat up straight. "I don't have that one. Maybe some time you could tell it to me?" His face lit up. "Or maybe some time you could read to me?" He gestured to a shelf that contained all the Harry Potter books as well as the Tolkien and Narnia classics. "Mom gets too busy in summer."

No way. It was bad enough that Chris served as a constant reminder of what I'd lost. Telling stories, reading books, tucking in a sleepy child with a kiss on the forehead—those were things I needed to forget.

But he looked at me with those innocent puppy-dog eyes, and I could no more refuse him than I'd been able to refuse Tim when he begged for one more chapter. "Maybe after we finish the setup work." Chris gave me an incandescent smile, but I hated myself for caving.

I stuffed my nightclothes into my duffel and scooped my hairbrush from the bedside table. "May I borrow this pillow? I only brought a sleeping bag."

"Sure. Mom has extras." He settled back on his bed and picked up his book. "Night."

"Good night."

The conversation in the living room had switched to movies and music, and Leah came into the kitchen to fetch more beer.

"I'm going to take my stuff to my tipi and get settled before it gets dark."

"Good idea." She balanced a mix of cans and bottles in her arms. "Come back when you're done. I'm sure we'll keep going for hours."

"Thanks, but it's been a long day. I think I'll read for a while, then crash."

"Do you need a light?" She set down her load, rooted in the cabinet below the sink, and pulled out a battery-powered camping lantern. "I've got spare batteries when these give out."

"Thanks, that's great." Such a simple kindness, but it meant a lot. Maybe I'd been too eager to cling to the role of outsider tonight. At home, I pushed aside anyone who tried to offer sympathy. Here, no one knew what had happened. I didn't need such thick walls to protect me.

"Tomorrow afternoon, we'll build a fire under the bathhouse water tank. Give everyone a chance to clean up with hot water."

Relief at the prospect cheered me at once. "Thank goodness. I'd envisioned three months of cold showers."

She laughed. "We're not quite that cruel. Once the campers get here, it's their job to keep the fire going, so as long as they don't forget, you'll have hot water every day. Sleep well. Tomorrow will be another backbreaker."

Trying not to sigh, I said goodnight and headed out. Leah had the makings of a friend, a possibility that wrapped me in warmth. A step, I hoped, in the right direction.

I walked past the pottery shed and scuffed through the thick meadow grass to the doorway of my tipi. There was still enough light to see by, and I spread my sleeping bag on the thin mattress. I reached for my phone to check the time, then remembered I'd plugged it in to recharge in Leah's kitchen after she cut the generator on.

It would take a while to get used to new patterns. I headed back to the cottage and slipped in the back door. I grabbed the phone and turned to leave, when I heard my name mentioned in the living room.

"Where's that Mackenzie girl? Is she still here?" The voice sounded like Drake.

"No, she turned in for the night." That was Leah.

"Good."

"Come on, now," Erik chided. "Kenzie's nice enough. I know she's clueless, but she'll fit in over time." I crossed the room to hear better over the hum of the generator.

"Why do we need a nurse? We never needed one before." That was Bree.

"Liability. You remember the appendicitis mess with the Jackson kid last summer. The insurance people said they'd shut the whole place down if we don't have someone with medical training here this year."

The comment generated multiple murmurs of concern.

"But how are we supposed to search the island with her here?" Drake's question pierced the air, part complaint, part challenge.

"We need to keep this between the four of us. I can't believe you let her come early."

Any qualms I had over eavesdropping evaporated.

"I know, I know." I pictured Erik holding up his hands, trying to calm things. "She wasn't supposed to get here until next week, but something came up about the timing of her sublet. I couldn't very well refuse. It took me forever to find a nurse willing to take the job. Don't worry. We'll work things the same way we did today—split into groups with some of us staying with Kenzie doing setup and the others working the search pattern. She won't suspect anything. And it's not like we could spend the week doing nothing but searching anyway. We still have to get ready for campers."

"I get it." Drake still sounded sour. "But we keep her out of it. Dividing four ways is bad enough. I don't want to divide by five."

"Relax." Leah was using her soothing Mom-voice. "This entire search is a gamble. Maybe we find the cache, maybe not. The notes Edward Allman left behind in his journal are vague. It's far too soon to worry about dividing spoils that may not even be out there."

"We *have* to find it." Drake's voice rose, and it sounded like he slammed his hand on the coffee table. I pictured him red-faced, almost frantic. "I *need* this money. I need it now. This week."

"Don't be ridiculous," Erik said. "Gordon has assured me it's ours if we find it, but there's no guarantee we can locate it that fast. If we can locate it at all."

Drake spluttered to a halt. "My god, Erik, if I don't get this money, I'm a dead man."

"You worry too much. I've got this under control." Erik's voice sounded firm, but then he laughed. "Enough about the search. Tonight, we party. Pass that bottle, will you?"

I turned toward the back door, then froze. Chris stood in the doorway to his bedroom, watching me. I hadn't heard his door open, but he must have seen me eavesdropping. For that matter, with the rooms partitioned only by partial walls, he could have been listening as well.

I couldn't read his expression. I lifted my finger to my lips, and after a moment, he gave a nod. Maybe my willingness to read to him had tipped the scale. Or maybe he, too, was ticked off at the others, excluded from these mysterious search plans. For the moment, he appeared to be on my side, and even a ten-year-old ally was better than nothing. I eased out the back door, stomach churning. I could still hear the frantic desperation in Drake's voice.

What in the world could they be looking for? Pirate treasure? Loot from a bank heist or a drug-runner's cache? Remnants of a wrecked boat or a crashed plane? My ideas got wilder with every step.

I didn't like what I'd overheard, but in one respect, it was a relief. Yes, I was an outsider, but not just because I was older or clueless or incompetent. Something more was going on. I quickened my pace.

The last thing I needed was a mystery. If I had any sense, I'd ignore the whole thing. Let the others waste their time on what sounded like a search with poor odds of success.

But not knowing would drive me crazy. I had no idea what was going on here, but I sure as hell planned to find out.

Chapter Three

Jon - Thursday

The moment I stepped onto the Salish Island pier, the Seattle tension that knotted my lower back floated away. My lungs filled with the island's clean, salty air, as soothing as aloe on a burn. I was home. I'd been away for nine months, and that was nine too many. I hadn't told Leah I was coming early, but I knew she wouldn't mind. I belonged here.

I waved good-bye to the skiff that had dropped me off and stepped onto land. Wavelets lapped against the shore. A cool breeze rustled leaves. A western tanager called in the distance, and the forest embraced me.

I had no need to phone for a ride. I'd packed light, and the road to camp was an easy three-mile walk. After a day of bus, ferry, and skiff travel, it felt good to stretch my legs. And the walk gave me a chance to see what progress had been made in getting ready for summer.

Initial signs didn't look good. The camp boat wasn't moored in its usual spot at the pier. The camp sign had fallen off its post.

The road had deteriorated into a mass of ruts and random holes. Leah usually hired maintenance crews for heavy work off-season, but it didn't look like anything had been done this year. Salal and huckleberry crept in from both sides of the road, and sword-fern fronds brushed against my jeans. My to-do list got longer the farther I went.

I swallowed my irritation, but it left a bitter taste. Special places like this island needed to be loved.

I walked for forty-five minutes, rounded a curve in the road near camp, and came close to colliding with a woman who stood peering into a grove of madrona. The trees' deep red trunks were in a shedding phase, paper-thin bark hanging in long, curling strips. The puzzled expression on her face while she fingered a long shred of bark told me she wasn't a native. She jumped when she saw me and looked for an instant like she considered screaming for help or disappearing into the woods. To her credit, she stood her ground and did neither.

"Sorry. Didn't mean to startle you. I'm Jonathon Griffin." She looked older than our normal staff members, maybe forty or forty-five, fit-looking, but with some middle-aged softness. She tipped her head back to look at me with hazel eyes. Her faded-blonde hair was dripping wet, and a peeling sunburn marked her as someone who usually spent most of her time indoors.

She crossed her arms and narrowed those eyes, acting tough even though she was shaking. "I'm Kenzie Adams. I work here. Who are you? What are you doing here?"

"Most people call me Jon. And I work here too." I stuck out a hand.

She hesitated, then gave it a tentative shake. She grimaced, and when she let go, I noticed blisters on her palms.

Her shoulders relaxed. "I didn't realize they expected anyone else today. You're one of the counselors?"

"King of the Orcas, that's me. I didn't tell anyone I was coming early. Sort of a last-minute thing." I took a step, and she fell in beside me as we headed toward camp. "Are you a new counselor? Maybe a former camper?"

"Camp nurse. And no, I've never been here before."

I'd heard rumors we were required to have a nurse this year and that Erik had been scrambling to find one. Camp staff usually fell into two categories—old salts like me who'd been coming for so many years it had become embarrassing to admit, or college kids lured by the romantic myth that three months on an island would be more vacation than work.

Kenzie didn't fit either group. She limped a little, like she wasn't used to walking very far, and she jumped every time a finch or warbler rustled the undergrowth. New shoes and high-end clothes meant money. If she could pull down a proper nursing salary, why would she sign up for this gig?

But then, she wouldn't be the only one here with a backstory. The camp took pride in the fact that the average age of its staff was twenty-five. Parents assumed the added years ensured both maturity and intelligence. They never suspected that we returnees were broken somehow and needed an island fix.

As a kid, I used to envy the families I saw on TV. My parents weren't dysfunctional. They were invisible. With unlimited cash, a love of travel, and zero interest in a quiet, introverted son, they let me grow up with a series of nannies, then shipped me off to the isolation of boarding school. When I was thirteen, they discovered that Camp Madrona would keep me out from under foot for an entire summer, and they jumped at the opportunity. A wilderness experience? Learn about woodcraft, botany, and the local marine life? They didn't care. They only wanted to know if they had the option for early drop-off and late pick-up.

I went without complaint, expecting the same stagnant boredom and alienation of my previous dumping grounds. Instead, Salish Island turned out to be the one place where I was accepted. The one place where I could rest and breathe. I had friends here, which I valued, but I could also disappear into the forest whenever I wanted. I trusted nature. People? Not so much.

"Who else is here?"

She rattled off the names. Erik's little in-group, the cadre that spent winters as ski instructors at various resorts and summers here on the island. I'd always wondered how people like Erik, Bree, and Drake managed to scrape by. The money rolled in during ski season, but camp salaries were minimal, and months-long gaps loomed between the two jobs. Erik lived with his sister part of the year. Bree taught yoga, both online and in person, so maybe that helped. Drake seemed to always be scrambling for cash, sometimes in ways that didn't stand much scrutiny.

Erik's crowd typically arrived last minute and complained about the poor-quality set-up work completed by the younger peon counselors. Odd to find them here this early. Erik must be up to something.

He always had some scheme up his sleeve, but his ideas usually tanked. The bargain boat he bought to fix up for resale, sank. The shuttle service he envisioned for Bear Valley Mountain Ski Resort went belly-up. I'd always stayed clear of his projects.

"How'd you end up stuck on setup crew?"

She shrugged. "I sublet my apartment for the summer and needed to clear out. Erik had mentioned the date he was arriving, so I told him, if he wanted me as an employee, I needed to come ahead."

"You know Erik well?"

"No. Met him at a party, and the idea of a different sort of summer sounded good."

So, not part of the inner circle. Good. It'd be nice to have a new person around.

We walked in silence for a time. Kenzie glanced my way. "So, what's your story? Are you another ski instructor?"

I laughed. "I'd break my neck. I'm a freelance software engineer. For nine months a year, I hit impossible deadlines and charge outrageous fees, then I come here for an internet-free change of pace. It clears my head, then I dive back into the frenzy." She gave me the same incredulous look my Seattle friends always did, and I laughed. "Hey, why grow up if you don't have to?"

We reached the meadow. Nobody had mowed, and nature had reclaimed the space. Red currant and dwarf dogwood bloomed along the edges, and scattered wildflowers added extra color—the purple of camas, the pink of tiny shooting stars, and a few white clusters of chickweed. In a few weeks, the campers would tramp the grass flat, but now it stood tall and shaggy. Farther down the hill, the planned repairs for the Lodge hadn't happened, and random piles of driftwood, brought in by winter storms, lined the beach. My poor island was in sad shape.

But the sound was still a deep blue, the breeze was still cool and calming, and Mt. Baker anchored the horizon in regal splendor. The madrona trees were in full bloom, and their sweet lilac scent added an exotic tone to the rest. Some things were eternal. Everything else could be fixed. It was good that I'd come early to help.

I looked at Kenzie. "Guess I'd better announce my presence. Everyone hanging out at Leah's?"

"Yep. We had actual hot water in the bathhouse this afternoon, so we quit early for cleanup." She checked her watch. "Just about time for dinner."

I headed through the front door of the cottage, and she followed.

Drake was sprawled on the living room couch, Erik and Chris sat at the kitchen table playing cribbage, and Leah and Bree were busy cooking. We stepped into the living room, and Kenzie cleared her throat. "Look who I found."

I expected a moment of mild surprise, but when people looked up, they froze with identical deer-in-the-headlights expressions. Erik, Drake, and Bree exchanged glances as if trying to gauge what their reaction should be, and only then did they paste grins in place and act somewhat normal. I'd been right. Something was definitely up. Within moments, people surrounded me. A hug from Bree. Backslaps from the men. But the cadence seemed off, and the welcome felt fake.

I went into the kitchen, where Leah stood by the stove.

Her smile lit the room, a warm, genuine welcome that contrasted with the strange one I'd gotten from each of the others. Leah's smile would weaken the knees of far stronger men. I'm sure, if I dug out old photos, I'd see that she'd aged over the years, but to me she was changeless, the fixed center that kept the rest of us in balance.

"Good to see you," she said. "How has your year gone?"

No hug—Leah always guarded her personal space—but my heart lifted. I'd always thought that expression was stupid when I read it in books. Hearts don't budge. They're anchored in place. Then I met Leah, and the description seemed apt. "It's been busy. Sorry I didn't let you know I was coming early. I finished my last project ahead of schedule and couldn't stand the city any longer."

A low mumble came from behind me but I didn't turn to acknowledge Erik. I should've directed my apology at him since he served as lead counselor, but he could wait. "How did the winter play out here?"

"Peaceful. Pottery sales are keeping me hopping. I can't thank you enough for the new website. It's made a huge difference. It showcases my work in a whole new way."

I would have been happy to talk forever, and I wanted to ask her about the camp and its ragged appearance. But the back door banged open, and Chris raced in. "Jon! You're here!" He gave me an uninhibited hug. Skagit bounced at his heels, his tail a wagging blur. "You won't believe it. I saw them. I really did."

I refrained from telling him how much he'd grown—I always hated that as a kid—and tried to figure out what he was referring to. We'd traded emails all through the off-season, but the topics ranged from snails to stars. It could be anything.

He bounced with excitement. "Orcas. A whole pod. A little off the Point, close to shore. Six of them."

I had complained to Chris that, although I led the Orca group, I'd rarely seen the whales outside of an aquarium. "Fantastic! I'll have to take you with me when I hike the shore. You might be my good luck charm."

"Really? I can go with you?"

"As long as your mom agrees. I know there's plenty to do around here, but maybe we can sneak out after dinner tomorrow."

You would have thought I'd offered a round-trip ticket to Disneyland instead of a walk on trails he followed every day. For most of the year, Chris only had a mom and a dog for company. I'd been lonely at his age, too, but it was loneliness in the midst of others. Lonely alone would be a different beast entirely.

Leah announced dinner, and people queued up to assemble tacos, grabbing seats wherever they could find them. Bree took the chair next to Leah in the kitchen, so I ended up beside Erik in the living room.

"Sorry to just show up like this."

His jaw tightened, but he swallowed his annoyance along with a bite of taco. "Not a problem. We don't have the Orca tipis up yet, but you can crash in one of the others until yours is available."

"Looks like there's a lot left to do."

"We'll get there. The weather is supposed to hold. Maybe you can take the lead in finishing the boys' tipis tomorrow? The work there is lagging behind."

A movement behind Erik caught my eye. Kenzie had taken a seat on the floor, and she must have overheard the comment because she frowned.

"Sure. I'm here to help."

"Great."

He went on to list the other projects we needed to take care of in the next week, but none of that was news to me. I chatted with the others for a time, finished a beer, and said my goodnights. I had another few hours of daylight to work with, so decided to check things out instead of waiting for morning. This end of the island was as familiar to me as my Seattle townhouse, and I hiked in a loop through the sites of all six camper groups.

Lagging behind? No shit. What they'd accomplished wasn't anywhere near two days' work for five people. The Heron clearing was a tangled mess, the Orca site stood empty, and nothing had been done at the Eagle site, perched on a high outcrop above Nesting Cove. I cut through its clearing, overgrown and looking sad, and took the shore path that led toward the island's northernmost tip.

Erik and his hand-picked group. Camp prep falling behind. The uneasy reception I'd received. It added up to something underhanded.

Along this path I found plenty of evidence of recent activity. Someone had overturned boulders in random places near shore, leaving craters of raw earth behind. They'd even dug sizeable holes beside two large madrona trees that grew on either side of a rocky outcrop. I walked on and found a dozen more holes. None of the excavations were deep, but the sheer number reflected a lot of effort. I could find no sense or pattern to their location.

I reached the Point, where a stone foundation and tilting chimney marked the site of one of the houses built during the years of the Baytree Community back in the thirties. During the early 1900s, the sound had been home to at least a half-dozen utopian communities. They each had their own flavor, ranging from the socialist Equality Colony on the mainland to Pastor Gourley's religious sect on Lopez Island. The only thing the communities had in common was their eventual failure.

The Baytree members had followed a single charismatic leader, Edward Allman, who had worked to create a utopia based on peace and a strong dedication to the land. The group prospered at first, but after his death, the colony dispersed. Remnants of their occupation were scattered throughout the island, but vegetation had overgrown most sites, so they were easily overlooked.

Here, too, someone had been busy with pick and shovel. A shallow trench of freshly dug earth started at one corner of the crumbling cottage foundation and ran thirty feet toward the edge of the steep cliff that dropped into the water. I poked around the rest of the area, but nothing else had been disturbed.

A sea otter whistled in the distance. A fish broke water, arced through the twilight, and landed with a splash. I breathed in the salt air, but the pleasure I'd enjoyed when I arrived on the island had faded. What the hell was going on?

Island visitors tended to be curious picnickers out boating for the day, not destructive diggers. Leah kept a gun locked away in the cottage, but at most, she occasionally waved it around to shoo away drunken partiers. Outsiders seemed unlikely.

And these holes appeared recent. The overturned soil was still moist, and the wind hadn't yet smoothed raw edges.

I headed back to camp. I would wait a day. Keep my eyes open and see if I could figure out what was going on. I had no authority, but if the others meant to abandon setup and let the camp go to hell while they dug a bunch of random holes, I would have plenty to say about it.

Chapter Four

Kenzie - Friday

I woke Friday morning from a restless sleep in dim morning light, bone-tired, confused, and uncertain about the where and when of things. The where came as I scanned the canvas surrounding me, then I sorted through the rest. When I stretched, my aching muscles were proof that my group had worked hard the day before. Damn hard. Pitching tipis, clearing underbrush, constructing firepits. Struggling to get a massive amount accomplished before the campers descended in less than a week. Meanwhile, the other work group had done nothing at all.

I'd checked. *We'll clear the overgrowth from the Heron's site and set up those tipis.* Thick weeds still choked the clearing and not a tipi in sight. *We need to check out the trail system, make sure they're all accessible.* Ridiculous. The woodland paths were practically concrete, worn smooth by generations of campers. If a fallen tree needed to be cleared, even I knew that shouldn't be a priority.

Erik and his groupies thought I hadn't caught on, and I resented being considered so brainless. I hadn't yet figured out what they were searching for, but I hadn't given up. The possible wildcard was this new guy, Jon. A techy nerd with an outdoorsy overlay, he listened well and spoke little. He kept an interested eye on Leah, seeking her out whenever possible, and his face lit up each time they spoke. She gave no obvious sign of noticing, but she had to know he had a thing for her. The others didn't appear happy to see him, but he seemed a possible ally.

A possible ally. Was I seriously thinking of the situation as *me versus them*? I couldn't spend an entire summer at odds with the people around me. If I were one of those strong, determined heroes in a book, I'd tap into my inner Wonder Woman and demand to know what was going on with this weird search. But the isolation of the place and my newbie status made me hesitate. I hated the idea of creating a stir. Maybe it was better to find a quiet moment with Leah and insist she tell me their secret.

I squirmed out of my sleeping bag, reached for fresh jeans and a T-shirt, already damp from the thick morning air, then ducked out the tipi door. Mist hung low over the sound, cutting visibility to only a few hundred feet. Nearby trees stood like ghosts, wreathed in white wisps of cloud. My tennis shoes squelched through the grass on the way to the bathhouse, where I brushed my teeth and ran a comb through my hair, blessedly clean after yesterday's shower.

I'd come here to heal, not to solve a mystery, but it wouldn't hurt to explore a little. Maybe I could figure out what was going on. If nothing else, it kept my mind from dwelling on Tim.

No one else wandered around, so I headed toward the beach. Gentle wavelets lapped the shore, and a tall heron froze, watching my every move. I turned left, north, toward the girls' end of camp, passing Leah's lone canoe on the long wooden rack designed to hold a dozen, and crunched my way across the uneven pebbles to the end of the cove. Here, the beach ended, and large boulders edged the shoreline. A set of wooden steps led to a boardwalk that paralleled the water's edge for a hundred yards, and I followed it.

The walkway ended at a large clearing, surrounded on one side by forest and on the other by a rocky expanse overlooking the sea. This must be the space designated for the oldest girls, the Eagles. They certainly commanded a premium view. I could see no sign anyone had been working here, despite Erik's claims. It gave me one more piece of evidence for when I spoke with Leah.

Several trails led into the trees, and movement along one of them caught my attention. Shapes materialized in the fog, solidifying into Chris and Skagit. Chris waved and joined me.

"Good morning." I bent to give Skagit a pat. He licked my hand and wiggled all over, eager for attention.

"Hi." Chris gave me a quick glance, then inspected the clearing. "Looks like *our group* will have plenty to do today." He paired the emphasized words with a pointed look my way. He and Leah had been part of my group each day, the three of us the only consistent members of the group that got work done.

It didn't seem fair to share my worries with a kid, but his comment cemented my decision to speak up. After all, even a ten-year-old could tell things weren't right. "I don't think we'll run out of things to do." I turned to head back. "Come on. Let's see if your mom wants help with breakfast."

We walked in a companionable silence, much as Tim and I used to do, and I reminded myself to stay uninvolved. Nice advice, but I wasn't convinced it would stick.

Breakfast. Dishes. Sleepy conversation about ordinary topics without hidden meanings. Jon sat by himself, silent and watching. Erik once again assigned work groups. Leah, Jon, and I would continue working on the boys' sites, with Chris along. Erik, Bree, and Drake would work on the Heron clearing. At least that's what they claimed.

Our team straggled to the Lodge to select the next tipi bundle, but Jon looked around in surprise. "You're lugging these things by hand? Where's the tractor?"

A tractor. Of course. No one had mentioned a tractor before, but my aching back agreed that engine power was long overdue.

Leah shook her head. "It gave up the ghost the end of last summer when we took everything down."

"It hasn't been fixed?"

"Hopeless. We need a new one."

The blisters on my palms had popped, leaving throbbing patches of raw skin. I was in no mood to be understanding. "Why didn't you buy a new one?"

After an awkward silence, Leah didn't meet my eyes. "This camp always runs on a shoestring. Fees are high, but so are costs—the boat to get everyone here, food for the summer, equipment, staff.

There were additional budget items this summer, so some things couldn't be replaced."

This sounded like pure bullshit. The Lodge was falling apart. Patches covered some of the tipis, and others were too ragged to repair. I'd seen no piece of equipment younger than Chris. "What additional budget items could possibly be more important than getting a cheap tractor to save us from this misery?"

"You." Leah was usually so kind that this single barbed word struck hard. "You're the new budget item. A nurse for the summer. I'm sure you're not being paid anything like what you're used to, but I can guarantee you're getting a hell of a lot more than the rest of us."

It took me a moment to recognize that my mouth sagged open, and I closed it with a sharp click. I wasn't just an outsider. I was a burden. I was the reason the others probably ached as much as I did.

"I'm sorry. I didn't realize." Heat crawled up my neck, and my cheeks burned.

Leah shrugged. "Not your fault. We know that." She laughed. "Think what good shape we'll be in by the time we're done."

I kept further complaints under wraps and forced myself not to flinch when I grabbed the next bundle. My determination to demand answers dwindled like the mist. I would wait and see how the day played out.

The morning moved on. The sun came out, and tipis went up. Jon's strength and efficiency made tasks easier. We finished the Dolphin tipis before lunch, then started on the Orcas after a quick round of sandwiches. The location for the oldest boys mirrored the one on the girls' side, a clearing edging the sea, and the biggest challenge was hauling the bundled tipis down the beach, up the stairs, and along the boardwalk. By the time we finished driving stakes for the final Orca tipi, my legs and back ached like they belonged to an out-of-shape ninety-year-old.

We had chili for dinner, spicy and delicious, warming from the inside out. Jon, Leah, Chris, and I chanced to sit together at the kitchen table. Chris and Jon kept up a steady discussion about climate change and its ongoing impact on the area's fish and wildlife. Leah and I were content to listen. I'd moved to Seattle from Albuquerque to be closer to Paige. Closer to Tim. I still had plenty to learn about the local environment.

A lull in one of Chris's stories made me realize that things had grown quiet in the living room. Jon, too, looked toward the doorway.

Quiet, but not silent. We could hear whispering. Then Drake's voice rang out. "I don't care about setup. We need to focus on what's most important."

Bree and Erik made shushing sounds, and Jon tossed his napkin to the table and stood, his face tense. "This is ridiculous. It's time to get things straight."

He headed for the living room with Chris on his heels, and Leah rose to follow. She waved me forward. "Come on. It's past time you were in on this."

By the time I reached the doorway, Jon was standing in the middle of the living room, facing the sofa where Erik and Drake sat. Bree lounged in the easy chair. Jon squared his shoulders. "We need to talk."

Everyone in the room leaned forward. Expectant or combative? I couldn't decide, and I stayed in the doorway. The air vibrated with tension, as if the room held dynamite and Jon held a match.

Erik frowned and began to say something, but Jon gave him no chance. "I explored the north end of the island last night, and someone's been digging. The old foundation at the Point looks like a construction zone, and the damage is recent. Your team is getting no setup work done. What the hell's going on?"

The question sliced into the scene with a scalpel's precision, but its impact varied from person to person. Erik sighed and gave a half-hearted shrug. Drake's fists clenched, and he muttered under his breath. Bree lifted her can of beer in a salute. "Welcome, friend. We need your brain on this. You know this island better than anyone."

Her amiable comment prompted glares from Erik and Drake, but Leah spoke before they could start. "Don't give Bree nasty looks like that. She's right." Her voice could have cut glass, and the two men flinched. "I'm tired of hiding this. We need to tell Jon and Kenzie about the treasure."

Treasure? That was one of the possibilities I'd considered but tossed aside, thinking it was too crazy to seriously consider. But crazy or not, I was in no mood to be odd woman out any longer. "What in the world are you talking about?"

Erik's clenched jaw hadn't relaxed a millimeter, but he cleared his throat and shrugged. "Treasure. Relics. Gold."

Gold. The word hung in the air as if painted in ornate italic script and surrounded by glittery sparkles. The single most unexpected thing he could have said.

Jon looked as stunned as I was. The others simply watched our reactions.

Jon found his voice first. "*Treasure?* What the hell?"

Erik gestured to Leah, and she stepped forward. "It all started because Camp Madrona is in financial trouble. Gordon is threatening to close us down and sell the island for vacation condos."

"No way. He promised." Jon appeared more energized by this news than he had about the idea of treasure.

I still didn't have a clue. "Who's Gordon?"

"One of the Microsoft billionaires," Jon said. "He was a camper here as a kid and loved the place. When the camp got in financial trouble ten years ago, he bought the island as a sentimental investment."

"Well, the investment has appreciated, and the sentiment has dwindled. This summer may be the last." Leah twisted her long braid. "At any rate, I wondered if there might be other well-heeled former campers who had a soft spot for the place. Figured we could ask for donations. Maybe set up a foundation. I sorted through the old camp records, looking for rosters, seeing if I recognized names."

Not a bad idea. I'd heard of historic buildings saved through community donations, so why not an historic island?

"The records were jumbled," Leah said, "and in one box, I found a bunch of stuff dating all the way back to the Baytree Community.

It included Edward Allman's journal from 1938, the last year he led the group."

Drake had been fidgeting through all this detail. "Gold and jewels. Precious stones. He found them, hid them, then died before he could retrieve them."

Erik smiled, but it looked forced and brittle, as if he'd lost patience with Drake's persistence. "That's the short version. It's not quite that simple."

If it were that simple, Leah could have simply gone out and retrieved it. I leaned forward. "Why in the world would anyone hide gold and jewels on this tiny island? I assume this Allman guy found it by accident?"

"Where the gold originally came from is a mystery," Erik said. "Allman described it as Russian treasure. He claimed it included thousands of gold rubles dating from the 1820s."

Jon had acted highly skeptical to this point, but now he looked interested. "That's possible. There was a big fur-trading boom in this area in the early eighteen-hundreds. Russia owned Alaska then, and their ships worked all over this sound, as did Canadian and U.S. traders. They paid Native tribes for furs with trade goods. Hudson Bay Company even minted their own coins, redeemable at their trading posts. But if a Russian ship wanted to buy directly from one of the big companies, they would have needed more than fabric and axes in their hold. It's conceivable they could have brought gold and jewels. That doesn't explain how or why it would end up hidden here on Salish, but it makes Allman's tale believable."

"Hot damn." Drake leaped to his feet. "I knew it. Millions of dollars. We'll be rich."

His excitement kicked off a general buzz.

It sounded sketchy to me, but something about the words *millions of dollars* set my heart fluttering. I'm no gambler. Vegas is a waste of time. But when the Powerball tickets hit stratospheric numbers, I usually bought one. You never know, right?

Jon stuck to the essentials. "Even if you find something, could you keep it? I don't know anything about treasure-hunting laws."

Erik waved his concern away. "We've looked into the legal side, and we've got written permission from Gordon. If we find it, it's ours."

That set off another flurry of excitement. Jon left his stance in the middle of the room, sat cross-legged near the door, and waited for the others to wind down to a standstill. "Look, maybe there's treasure hidden here, maybe there isn't. I'm sure none of us would pass up free money if it landed in our laps, but this sounds pretty farfetched. You've been digging based on signals from metal detectors?"

That got a few nods.

"And your holes are all over the place. So whatever information you have can't be very specific. A broad search like you're doing is a total crapshoot. Even if such a cache is here, it could take years to find, and campers arrive late next week. You're spending all your time hunting, and setup isn't getting done."

He held his hands out, inviting response. Everyone began talking at once.

"We have to look for it now. Once the island is full of campers and other counselors, there won't be—" That was Erik, getting in first, making sure he didn't let Jon take over.

Drake was right behind him. "You need to stay out of this, Jon. We came up with this idea. The four of us. You can't—"

"I wish you'd take a look at what the journal says. I'm tired of digging holes and finding crap." Bree's soft voice got swamped in all the crosstalk.

In the midst of the furor, Jon's eyes met mine, and he gave me a do-you-even-believe-this grin. At least he was being sensible, reminding the others of what the camp needed.

"Enough!" Leah reined in the noise. "I'm sick of secrets, with some people knowing what's going on. Some not." She gave me a pointed glance and mouthed the word *sorry*. "Jon is right. If we don't keep the camp solvent, we'll all lose something we love. We can't just drop everything on the off chance we'll find what Allman left here."

This got supportive nods from Jon and Bree. Erik didn't look so enthusiastic, but he sat back on the couch and appeared willing to listen. Drake, on the other hand, remained tense, red-faced, and frowning. With a temper that lurked so close to the surface, I had a hard time picturing him as a camp counselor.

He started to say something but stopped when Erik held up a hand. "I admit, our initial search hasn't panned out. Leah and I believed what Allman wrote would lead us there. But that hasn't happened yet. What do you propose?"

Jon shook his head. "Hey, I'm not trying to take over." But everyone continued to look at him, and after a minute, he shrugged. "Okay. What if we finish essential setup tasks as quickly as possible—everybody working—then if you still want to hunt for this thing, we spend the time we have left before the campers arrive studying whatever the journal says and launching a coordinated search? If we don't find anything, we keep searching through the summer and refine things as we go."

Nicely done. He made sure his top priority—the camp—got taken care of first.

"Hold it." Drake's voice, tense and impatient, stopped Jon cold. "Are you talking a six-way split now? That's not fair. This was our idea. And what happens when the rest of the staff gets here? Do we divide twelve ways? Twenty? I'm not giving up my money!"

His dismay kicked off another heated discussion. I pulled a chair in from the kitchen and took a seat out of the way. Chris materialized and sat at my feet. Leah disappeared into the kitchen, returned with a notepad and pen, and scribbled notes.

In a momentary lull, she spoke. "Shut up a minute." She used a no-nonsense schoolteacher voice, and everyone looked her way. "Here's what absolutely has to get done before campers arrive." She read from her notes, a surprisingly short list of final tipi set-ups, Lodge assembly, and miscellaneous other tasks. "The rest we can delay. Things like pulling the canoes from storage, assembling firewood for the hot-water tank, and clearing deadwood from the trail system will wait. We'll put the campers to work when they get here. Call it camp community service."

That got a laugh. "Oh, yeah, they'll love that." Bree rubbed her hands together.

Leah shrugged. "If all six of us focus on the priority items, and we work through every daylight hour, I think we can finish in a day and a half. Then we'll have Sunday afternoon through Wednesday evening to focus on the search. Thursday morning, the camp boat returns from getting its overhaul, and we'll need all hands to go into Anacortes and pick up the food and supplies. The rest of the staff arrives Thursday night." She looked up from her notes. "Makes sense to everyone?" That got a few nods. "Then let's sit down after lunch on Sunday when we've worked through this list. We'll review the information we have and go from there."

A sensible plan, and nobody objected. Erik had given Leah a narrow-eyed look when she began—after all, he was theoretically in charge—but when she finished, he stood and took back the reins. "Okay. That settles it."

"But—" Drake tried to jump in again, but Erik held up a hand.

"The split will be five ways. One share to each of the original four, and one to divide between Jon and Kenzie."

Drake's face still reflected a flickering mix of anger, impatience, and frustration, but the others didn't protest. Leah handed him a cold beer, and he settled back, drumming his fingers against the arm of the couch and grumbling.

Conversation turned to what all that money could buy. Jon crossed the room to join me. "You okay with all this?"

"I'm surprised to be included at all. Millions of dollars? It sounds surreal. What are the odds we actually find anything?"

He held up a hand and tapped on his palm with a finger as if entering invisible numbers. "My precise calculation, based on zero current data, is that we're looking at odds of roughly a zillion to one." He dropped his hands and laughed. "But, hey, I'm willing to look."

His cheerful attitude made me forget my aching muscles and the prospect of working even harder the next day. "Fair enough. I'll add *treasure hunting* to my list of unexpected summer activities. And I owe you one for forcing some honesty out of this group. I knew something was off, but ..." I quit there. I knew, but I didn't have the nerve to confront anyone. Incompetence strikes again.

"You're welcome. Just don't blame me if this ends up a complete waste of time."

If nothing else, it would certainly spice up the next few days. And the idea of shifting work off to fresh, eager campers had a definite appeal. I looked around the room and soaked up the vibe. Chris reminded Jon of his agreement to go on a post-dinner walk, Erik and Leah huddled together as they double-checked her lists, and Bree was stretching her body into an impossible-looking yoga pose.

But when I turned toward the couch, a quick chill raced up my spine. Drake sat glaring at Erik, his jaw clenched and his shoulders stiff. He took a final swig of beer and crushed the can with a single vicious squeeze of his fist.

I couldn't escape the unsettling impression that he would rather have his fingers around Erik's throat.

Chapter Five

Chris

J on kept his promise. Not every grownup does. After everyone quit talking about treasure, he and I walked to the Point on the coast path. Skagit ran ahead to check out the smells he found along the way. Skagit and I usually did this walk alone, but having someone along to talk to made it better.

Jon showed me the places where Erik and the others had been digging. I'd already seen them, but I didn't let on. I'd found holes along the western shore, too, lots of them, one big enough to hide in, but I didn't say anything about that either. Mom didn't like me to play on top of the steep cliffs on that side of the island, and I figured what she didn't know wouldn't hurt anything.

The sun got low. The time I saw the pod of orcas was a little before sunset, so I had hope. Jon and I stood on the Point and looked hard. Really hard. But no killer whales.

I picked up Skagit and gave him a hug, but he wiggled until I set him back on the ground. Digging holes was stupid because if there really was treasure on the island, wouldn't Skagit and I have found it already? But I asked Jon anyway. "Do you think there's really gold here?"

He didn't say anything for a while. I like people who think things over first, not just saying something to get me out of their way.

"I can't think of any reason Edward Allman would make something like that up in a journal he kept only for himself. I've read a lot about the Baytree Community, and he sounds like an honest man who did his best to create a place of peace and fairness on this island." He leaned over and scratched Skagit behind the ears. "But even if what he wrote is true, that doesn't mean we'll find gold. Think about this hunt like a game. It's something fun to puzzle over, but don't count on finding anything."

He patted me on the shoulder. Mom hoped it was real—I could tell by her voice when she talked about it. "Mom says the reason he hid it was because he knew he should share it with the others but wanted to keep it for himself."

"He put that in the journal?"

"Yeah. Something like that."

"Big money can change people. And it can cause trouble. Maybe he took it all for himself and didn't write that part down."

"Maybe. But Mom looked it up. He died the day after he wrote the journal entry. He wouldn't have had time to move it, would he?"

"I don't know what to tell you. Sounds like the stress of it all might have done him in."

I guessed I'd have to wait and see. It might be fun to look. And it sure would be fun to have all that money. A new Nintendo Switch. A mountain bike. Maybe even a trip to Seattle.

We didn't talk about treasure anymore after that. Jon quizzed me on tree names, and I knew them all. I showed him a screech owl nest and a new place along the cove to find mussels. He told me I was becoming a true naturalist.

I liked it when Jon came to the island. Mom did too. She smiled and laughed more, and she made sure to make those peanut butter brownies with tiny chocolate chips that he liked so much. I asked her one time if he was my dad, and she laughed and said she didn't even know Jon until after I was born. Sometimes I pretended I knew who my father was—maybe it was Jon, maybe Erik, maybe one of the other counselors. But that was sort of like pretending about treasure. A fun game, but not real.

The sun set and darkness closed in by the time we got near home. The sky was clear, and I found Vega and Altair, but it wasn't dark enough to see the Big Dipper yet. "In a few weeks, Jupiter, Mars, and Saturn are all going to line up with the moon."

Jon looked surprised. "Sounds neat. We'll have to get out the telescope." He stumbled over a rock and pulled out a tiny flashlight on his keychain to light the path. "Can you still see?"

"It's not dark. There are enough stars." Even if there weren't, I'd be okay. Mom said I knew every rock and tree root on the island. Not really, but maybe almost true.

He laughed. "Starlight's decoration, not enough to see by. I think you must be part bat." We reached the front door. "Get a good night's sleep. Tomorrow will be a long day."

"Okay." I opened the door. "Thanks for going with me."

"Any time, kiddo. I enjoyed the company."

He waited until I stepped inside and closed the door. Erik sat at the kitchen table, rolling a joint and checking his phone. He didn't look my way when I told him good night. Drake and Bree and Kenzie had gone to their tipis, and Mom sat in her bed reading. I gave her a hug.

"If we find all that money, can I get a mountain bike?"

She marked her place with one finger and gave me one of those looks that meant *no*. "Don't spend money we don't have. And if we do end up with treasure, we need to put most of it in the bank. Start a college fund for you and get a larger kiln." But then she reached over and squeezed my hand. "Okay. We'll put a mountain bike on the list too."

Good. But I had one more worry. "Jon says big money can change people and cause trouble."

She laughed and picked up her book. "Don't worry. Everyone on this island is sensible. Even Drake is sane enough when he settles down and thinks. Maybe we find the money. Maybe we don't. Either way, I don't expect any trouble over it. No trouble at all."

Chapter Six

Jon – Saturday/Sunday

The next morning dawned in a steady drizzle of rain, and a grumpy group gathered at the cottage to chug quick cups of coffee and grab handfuls of granola. Leah had estimated a day and a half to complete essential tasks, but I had my doubts, even with six of us tackling the list. I shrugged into a rain slicker and headed outside, but I would have been happier sitting by a fire in Leah's cottage. Preferably with Leah beside me.

Drake sought me out, carrying two scythes, a rusty limb lopper and a set of garden clippers. "Want to work on clearing out the girls' camps?" He said it like a challenge, not a question.

"Sure. We can make short work of it."

I'd known Drake for more than five years, but I'd never been able to figure him out. His sandpaper personality kept me at a distance, but the kids loved him despite his rough edges. He worked as one of the Dolphin counselors, partnered each year with a calm and empathetic counselor. The combination of one gruff, rough-and-tumble leader with another far more soft-spoken had worked well, and the Dolphin group thrived every summer. He must have qualities I couldn't see.

But when it came to this treasure, he acted as if his internal brakes had failed. His voice shook with desperation when he talked about it, and the prospect of getting this money seemed to gnaw at him with sharpened teeth. He didn't try to hide the fact that he didn't want me involved, and the air between us crackled with tension.

Despite the resulting unease, we worked steadily, first hacking through the wet undergrowth that had taken over the Heron and Eagle sites, then hauling in and setting up the tipis. Most of our conversation related to the tasks at hand, but when the rain stopped, we paused to take off our cumbersome rain gear and face the sun for a moment.

"This would have been a hell of a lot easier if we'd done it before." Drake wiped sweat off his face.

"Before?"

"Yeah, when things were dry. Right after we got here, Erik and Bree carried scythes and tools this way as if they planned to clear these sites. Then they dumped the gear and headed off with the metal detectors to dig holes instead. We faked it so Kenzie, and maybe Chris, wouldn't know what was going on. Seemed stupid at the time and even stupider now. If we're going to find this thing, we need to get going and do it."

"How'd you get roped in to all this treasure stuff?"

"Erik called, full of talk. Got me all excited. I thought he had a specific idea where it was hidden. You know, a map with an X or a set of specific coordinates." He glanced my way, but only for an instant. "Look, I know I sounded like an asshole yesterday, and, okay, I was pissed at Erik. I don't have anything against you and Kenzie. It's just ... that kind of money ... I could really use it. And fast."

The corner of his mouth twitched, and his hand tightened on the scythe. "It's different for you. You've got money and a great job, and when you come here in the summer it's more like a vacation for you. Leah's not much different—she doesn't have cash like you do, but she doesn't have to worry about rent, and she does alright with her pottery. But for Erik, Bree, and me, it's different. We're all past thirty with empty bank accounts. All it takes is a broken leg on the ski slopes and we're screwed. You don't get that. It's not your world."

The accusation stung because it was truer than I liked to admit. I wasn't mega-rich, not like Gordon and the Microsoft crowd, but I'd grown up with money and I earned well now. I could try to empathize with Drake's desperation, but I'd never known the stomach-churning fear of not having the month's rent or not being able to put dinner on the table.

For me, finding treasure would make a great story and maybe give me a chance to help care for this island. For Bree and Erik, it would mean security. And Drake? For him, apparently this treasure must mean a whole lot more. Fear and anxiety rolled off him in waves.

I faced him. "Look, I'm not trying to screw you over. I'm involved in this by chance."

Drake shook water off his coat and gave a slow nod. "I thought about it overnight, and I'm glad you're involved now. Maybe you can talk some sense into the others. Those metal detectors beep over the tiniest bits of crap. Erik would have us digging holes from now to doomsday without a clear plan."

It was as close to an apology as I would get. "I'll do what I can."

"You know what all that digging got us?" He unzipped a pocket of his sweatshirt, pulled out a handful of store receipts and empty power bar wrappers, then dug again. This time he came up with an object about five inches long that gleamed dully in the sun. "Found this by the cottage at the Point. Some treasure, huh?" He dropped it into my hand.

It was one arm of a small pair of scissors, possibly silver but tarnished and crusty with dirt. One side of the blade had curling scrollwork engraved along its length, the sort of decorative tool that might have been part of a woman's sewing kit.

"Not sure it's worth much, but it's a nice souvenir." I reached to give it back, but he picked up the clippers, ready to go back to work.

"Toss it. I don't know why I bothered to keep it."

I didn't want to throw it aside—with my luck, some barefoot camper would step on it—so I stuffed it in the back pocket of my jeans. If this was all they'd found after so much digging, I didn't have high hopes.

Our discussion cut the strain between us, and we got back to work. We took a half-hour break for cold sandwiches at lunch. Took another break for cold sandwiches at dinner. The others had paired off to work on their own setup projects, and we saw them off and on through the day, but nobody had any inclination for talk, and nobody gathered at the cottage. I looked for a chance to talk to Leah, but she was working on the other side of camp. She had tacked her to-do list to the bulletin board in the kitchen, and one by one, we lined through the completed items. Drake and I quit when it got too dark to see, and I tumbled straight into bed in my Orca unit tipi.

Sunday started the same but without the rain. Since we'd achieved a fragile truce, I paired again with Drake, and we tackled the kitchen equipment in the Lodge, scrubbing and scouring, the Pine-Sol smell artificial and irritating. We powered up the appliances, making sure everything still worked after the winter's hiatus. The stacks of tipis and other gear that had filled the far end of the Lodge had all been distributed. Bree and Kenzie mopped the concrete floor and dragged the picnic tables into rows.

Drake didn't strike up more conversation with me, and I noticed he stared off into space at times, body tense, shoulders bowed, brow furrowed. Atlas carrying far too much weight. Whatever financial mess he'd gotten himself into must be serious. He worked steadily, eager to get chores done so we could move on to what he really wanted to do.

A little after one, I wrung out my sponge and stepped back to survey all we'd accomplished. "Looks good. All we need are six dozen teenagers, and we can call it a camp."

Kenzie pushed a strand of hair off her forehead. "When I got here, I couldn't imagine how this would work, but with all the tipis set up and ready, I finally believe."

Bree wiped down the last table. "I'm calling this done. I think I saw Erik head to the cottage half an hour ago. Let's go see what's happening."

"That's got my vote." Drake dumped the mop water, and the four of us headed in.

Erik, Leah, and Chris were already there. I checked the posted list. Every item had been checked off. "We did it."

"We sure did." Erik lifted a beer in salute. "Grab some lunch, and we can talk about what comes next."

Leah had put ingredients for yet another round of sandwiches on the counter. She must have seen my face because she gave me a quick one-armed hug that meant nothing to her but sent my spirits soaring. "Spaghetti casserole for dinner. I promise. I've already pulled it out of the freezer along with a couple home-baked loaves of bread, and I'll whip up a batch of peanut-butter chocolate-chip brownies later this afternoon."

"I'll hold you to it." I'd never mentioned they were my favorite, but I liked to pretend they were for me when she made them for Chris.

I sank into a chair, grateful there was nothing left to haul, as-semble, or clean. Nine months in front of a computer screen had sapped my stamina. It would take half the summer to get back in shape.

The break proved short-lived. After lunch, Drake herded everyone into the living room, assembling the entire group for the first time since our Friday night discussion. Six adults plus Chris and Skagit packed into a room better suited for half that number. The harsh smells of sweat and damp dog overwhelmed the lighter scent of the violet water Leah used to rinse her hair, and I missed that comforting smell. The crowd was too much, and I fought a wave of claustrophobia. A shame I had no excuse to flee outdoors.

"Okay. We've worked our asses off. Camp is ready for campers." Drake glared at Erik. "Now what?"

Erik and Leah were ready. He cleared books, ashtrays, and beer cans off the coffee table and spread out a detailed map of Salish Island. We provided simple maps to each camper when they arrived, and I taught the older ones how to use a compass each summer, but this map included far more detail than any I'd seen before. Handwritten notations labeled each cove, beach, and inlet.

I looked closer. It didn't show any of the camp buildings. "Did this come from the Baytree Community?"

Leah nodded. "It's been sitting in the camp files all these years." She tapped several places on the drawing. "Every one of the original Community cottages is marked with the name of its owner."

It was a roll call of the long-departed. Some of the names sounded familiar from gravestones in the tiny cemetery that overlooked the southern shore. Others were new to me.

The hidden history of this place had fascinated me from my first summer here. I'd spent countless hikes exploring the island and had learned to keep watch for signs of the island's former inhabitants—overgrown foundations, collapsed chimneys, stacks of stones cleared for a garden plot. Sometimes a cluster of daffodils or a hardy rose bush marked a former house, non-native plants that had once graced a doorstep, thriving long after the house itself had crumbled.

Whole families had sold all they had in the east and moved here to Salish to follow Edward Allman's dream. They built simple homes, then gardened, fished, and raised their children in quiet isolation, surrounded by the island's beauty. As a kid, I'd envied the tranquility they created. As an adult, the idea of such a life still tugged me here each summer.

Leah shared my interest in the island's past, and we'd explored obscure parts of the island together, looking for remnants that might tell us more about the old community. She must have been thrilled to find this map, hidden away for so long.

Kenzie, the person least familiar with the island, studied the map, but Erik forged ahead without glancing at it. "Here's what we've got. Over a thousand acres of undeveloped land. We tend to stick to the main camp and the established pathways, but that leaves hundreds of acres that are rarely touched. There could be a million treasure troves hidden here, and we'd never know it."

Discouraging. Bree and Drake grimaced and exchanged glances. If we couldn't narrow things down more than that, we were screwed.

Drake made impatient keep-going motions with his hands. "Don't tell us what we don't know. Where do we look?"

Leah rustled a stack of papers. "All we know for sure is what Allman recorded." She handed me three pieces of paper and gestured for me to look before passing them around. "He wrote that he was clearing brush to expand his garden and had to dig deep to uproot a small tree. He found a wooden box buried there. He described it as a foot long on each side and packed solid with gold coins, jewelry, and gemstones. He estimated a value of over a million dollars, and that was almost a hundred years ago. In today's market, we'd be looking at four or five times that."

"Four or five *million*?" Bree always sat with perfect posture, but now she straightened even further, eyes wide.

"You're assuming his estimate was right." I scanned the pages and passed them on to Bree. Drake scowled at my skepticism, but I saw no point in getting our hopes up based on notes from a long-dead utopian.

"Right. We're taking his description on faith." Leah continued. "He goes on for a few paragraphs debating what he should do. It's obvious he felt obligated to share it with the full community, but it's also clear that he was severely tempted to keep it all for himself. He says in the journal that he needed to give himself time to make a decision. Then he says he told no one else and buried the contents in a more secure box in a new place. *A shallow hole on a promontory.*"

A long silence followed. A silence that spread its tentacles through the room and tightened around us. A silence that emphasized how little we knew.

"That's it? That's all the detail you have?" Drake's voice held a frantic edge. "No wonder we haven't found anything. You should have told us from the get-go that the directions were crap." He lunged around the coffee table, snatched the pages from Bree's hands, and flipped through them. "Leah, you said a journal, but this is your handwriting."

"I made the copy. Sent it to Erik to see what he thought."

"And I called Gordon," Erik said. "Told him some of us planned to search. He checked out the legal side with his attorneys. It sounds like what we find would probably belong to us in the eyes of the law, but to make sure, I got him to sign a document saying we had permission to search as long as we used reasonable care not to damage the property. And the agreement states clearly that what we find is ours." His jaw clenched for a moment. "He laughed at me. Said we're on a fool's journey. But that's his problem."

"Then you generously reached out to Drake and me. Asked us to help." Bree watched Drake when she said it, trying to calm the waters, but he was pacing now, the turbulence that had hovered just under the surface surging into the open.

"I thought this was more definite. I'm counting on this money. Leah, you shouldn't have raised everyone's hopes without knowing exactly where to search!" He stepped closer, looming over her with his reddened face and loud voice. She flinched.

Her tiny reaction ripped something loose inside me. "Back off, Drake." I pushed myself between them, my fists so tight, my fingers ached. "Back. Off. Right. Now."

I wasn't a fighter and didn't usually give orders, but he glanced at my face, backed away, and sat. My heart clogged my throat, beating triple-time, the flash of anger burning my chest and catching me off guard. I took a moment to steady myself. "Let Leah finish."

She mouthed a silent *thanks* that helped center me, then lifted her notes. "Erik and I made a list of the places on the island that could be called a promontory. Unfortunately, there are so many coves and inlets, so many zigzags in the shoreline, the list is long."

She gestured toward the map, and we crowded around.

But we had no chance to study details. The sudden sound of a racing engine interrupted, and we all looked toward the open front door. The sound grew louder, fierce and out of place. Erik and Drake rushed outside, and we all hurried after them.

The noise came from a boat roaring past the cove, but this was no ordinary boat. All kinds of fishing and pleasure crafts frequented the sound, everything from commercial salmon boats to fancy yachts to small skiffs like the one I'd taken to get here. This boat was a sleek, open-cockpit cigar boat designed for speed races, not open water.

Chris stood close to Erik, and Leah joined them. "What the hell is that idiot doing?" She sounded puzzled but not yet worried.

Erik shook his head. "Idiot is right. A boat like that shouldn't be out here. It's a runabout with barely enough room for two people, and it can go over a hundred miles an hour, but it's not designed for open water. Do they have three people crammed in there?"

I squinted, and sure enough, I could spot three heads. None of them had helmets. Foolish. Possibly deadly. "They look low in the water."

Erik nodded. "Too much weight. At the rate they're burning fuel, they'll end up with an empty tank soon. Those boats aren't equipped for distance."

Bree used one hand to shield her eyes from the sun. "It looks like they're turning. Heading straight toward us."

"Yeah, but they're not slowing." Erik walked down the road toward the water, but after only a few strides, he ran. The rest of us followed. Chris grabbed his mother's hand, and Skagit stuck close to his heels.

Erik positioned himself in the center of the beach and waved his arms. "Slow down! There are rocks offshore!" He shouted, but the scream of the tiny boat's oversized motor drowned his voice.

I stood transfixed, wanting to help but powerless to move. It was like watching one of those horrible slow-motion replays of a traffic accident, where you dread the moment of impact but have no way to stop it. The boat charged toward the beach without making any effort to slow or turn.

When it was twenty yards out, it gave a sudden jolt. The piercing screech of tearing fiberglass ripped into my eardrums and set my teeth on edge. The engine stuttered for an instant, then the propeller caught, and the craft roared forward again. Erik dodged to the side to avoid being hit. The boat shot onto the narrow band of beach at full speed, spraying pebbles in all directions, crunched into the canoe and its rack, then slammed to an abrupt halt, its bow buried in one of the driftwood tree trunks that lined the edge of the meadow.

Two of the figures in the cockpit must have been belted in because they jerked forward on impact but stayed in their seats. The person crammed into the middle wasn't so lucky. He flew out of the boat as if propelled by a slingshot, a tumbling kaleidoscope of blue jeans, black sweatshirt, dark hair, and horrified eyes. His body soared in a shallow arc, landed hard on a boulder, and rolled onto the meadow grass, slack and unresisting. I fought a swell of nausea, too stunned to even shout.

The boat's engine died. The outboard's propellers spun for a final few seconds, then stilled. Total silence hung over us for one second, maybe two. Then Bree screamed, Drake swore, and we all surged forward to help.

Chapter Seven

Kenzie

I raced toward the demolished boat, my eyes on the man who lay sprawled on the ground. Voices came from all directions and frantic movement centered on the wreckage, but I blocked it all to focus on my patient.

No helmet. Had his head hit that rock? Right arm horribly bent below the shoulder where no joint existed. I got closer. Thank God, his chest was moving. I dropped to my knees, seized his left wrist, searched for a pulse. Strong and racing, which was more than I expected.

Male, maybe eighteen or nineteen. Normal weight. Good musculature. Pupils dilated. Gums slightly pale. Bad teeth. Nicotine stains. Breathing, shallow but adequate. I gingerly palpated his head without lifting it. Swelling already evident on the right side, but no obvious skull fracture.

I skipped an examination of his neck—*too dangerous, too dangerous*—and forced my mind to back away from memories of Tim. Checked the man's left arm, both legs. No other long-bone fractures. Internal bleeding? Possible, but his color was reasonable. If he landed on his right arm, it may have absorbed the brunt of the impact and saved the rest of him from the full force of the crash. The fracture looked nasty. A slow seep of blood through his sweatshirt meant it might be an open break, but at least it wasn't the massive bleeding of a severed artery. Overall? I'd seen worse.

I pulled myself back to the world around me. Jon crouched on the other side of the unconscious man with Leah at his shoulder. Beyond them, the rest of our group clustered around the other two boaters. Injured? Maybe, but they'd climbed out of their wrecked craft and were on their feet. They'd have to wait.

"Leah, I need my stethoscope. It's in my tipi, left side of my duffel. There might be a neck brace in the first aid cupboard. We can't move him until his neck is stabilized. I can't examine his broken arm until it's safe to roll him over."

My throat closed, so small and tight I could hardly force out the words. When they pulled Tim from the water, I'd been so focused on CPR, so desperate to get him breathing, I hadn't considered a possible neck injury. *Stop it ... Concentrate ...* All I had to do was stabilize this man, then EMTs would take over. If I had any hope of reclaiming my Seattle job, I couldn't screw up.

Leah was already moving.

"Bring bandages and scissors too."

She broke into a run. The others left the wreckage and hurried our way. Chris and Skagit trailed behind.

"What can I do?" Jon reached toward the injured man but pulled his hand back before touching him.

"He needs a hospital."

He stood, tugged his phone from his back pocket. "I'll call 9-1-1. See if we can get a helicopter from Bellingham for medical transport."

He thumbed his screen open, but a huge hand snatched the phone away. "No emergency call. No chopper." The words came at us in a menacing growl.

I twisted to take my first good look at the other two new arrivals. The man who was stuffing Jon's phone into his coat pocket was enormous, six-three, maybe six-four, broad shouldered with a weightlifter's muscles pulling his shirt taut. Older than the others, younger than me, maybe in his late thirties. Square face, square jaw, shaved head. Flat ears with ragged edges, as if they'd been chewed, and dark, deep-set eyes. Spidery tattoos of black ink crawled up his neck and down his arms, stretching below his sleeves onto the backs of his hands.

My insides turned to ice, and I pressed my hands against my sides to hide their sudden tremor. Compared to this hulk, Erik and Jon looked small and ineffectual, better suited for desk jobs. Even Drake watched this guy with a wary look.

The other stranger, younger, mid-twenties, with blond shaggy hair, shoved Jon aside and dropped to his knees beside the injured man. "Ryan! Ryan, wake up!"

He reached as if to shake him, but I grabbed his wrist. "Stop. I'm a nurse. His neck may be injured. Don't move him. It could make things worse."

He shook off my hand and looked back, not at me, but at the scary guy. "Sonny, we've gotta call. He's unconscious. He needs—"

"No." Sonny's voice rang out hard and flat, and he glared at the others. Erik had his phone out, not calling, just staring at the man, slack-jawed, but Sonny grabbed the phone from his hand and added it to Jon's. He reached into his other pocket and pulled out a gun, took three steps back and aimed it in a slow arc to cover us all.

It was so quick, so unexpected, that everyone froze, stunned. My mouth dried in an instant, and my breath came quick and shallow. The day suddenly felt twenty degrees colder. I looked from face to face, but all I saw was the same dazed panic that roiled my insides. I knew nothing about guns, but this one looked big and black and bulky. Sonny held it, not as a weapon, but as if it were an extension of his hand, a familiar friend.

Chris waved Skagit away.

Bree tugged Chris to her side.

Erik took a step back.

Drake took a step forward, hands outstretched in appeal. "Sonny, come on. No need for this. I'm the one you want. Don't involve these others."

"You know this guy?" Erik's voice rasped.

Drake gulped, his eyes on the gun. "Yeah. Sort of."

Sonny laughed. Relaxed. In control. "Drake and I go way back, don't we? We need to complete a small financial transaction, Drake and I, then we'll be on our way. Looks like our boat is out of action, so I'm afraid we'll need to borrow your camp boat. I saw it at your pier when I was here before."

Nobody commented on the boat. All eyes stayed glued on Drake, who rocked back and forth, taking quick, gasping breaths. He looked two sizes smaller, his shoulders drawn inward. "Sonny, look, I told you I'd get you your money. And I will, honest I will. But we haven't found it yet."

The gun, which had continued to move in a relentless arc, giving all of us equal attention, settled on Drake. My instantaneous relief—*yes, please aim at someone else*—was crowded out at once by a wave of guilt. *How could I wish someone else in harm's way?*

Sonny's eyes narrowed. "Haven't *found* it? What the hell are you talking about?"

"Just a minor delay. Give me a week. I'm sure by then ..." Drake stopped. If Sonny had given me a look like he was giving Drake, I would have stopped too. Stopped and huddled on the ground and prayed for salvation.

Sonny's partner watched this back-and-forth while twisting his hands. "Sonny, forget the cash. We have enough to make Canada. We need to call for a doctor. Come on, man. He's my brother. I promised him this would all go down easy. We can't let him die."

"Shut up, Tremaine. Get the other phones."

Tremaine gulped but went from one person to the next, gathering phones, even checking Chris's pockets. Bree snarled and handed hers over. Drake didn't budge, and I could see his inner debate flit across his face. He took another look at the gun, then fished out his phone and thrust it into Tremaine's hand.

Tremaine tapped me on the shoulder, and I shook my head. "Mine's in the cottage." He grabbed my arm, pulled me to my feet, and checked the empty pockets of my jeans. Not a cruel grip and not an invasive search, but he had control, and I had no options.

Leah returned, stumbling in her haste. Sonny's back was toward her, so she must not have seen the gun. "Kenzie, I couldn't find a neck brace. I brought—" Sonny spun her way, and she skidded to a halt, eyes wide. One arm clutched bandage material. My stethoscope dangled from her hand. "What the hell?"

Tremaine plucked her phone from her back pocket. Chris ran to her and buried his face in her side. She wrapped her arm around him and crushed him close.

Sonny aimed at Chris's head. Jon stepped forward to intervene, his face so pale, it redefined the word *white*, but his glance fell to the gun, and he stopped. Bree gasped, and Erik let out a moan. Leah was shaking so hard, Chris's hair trembled. Her fingers turned white where they dug into his shoulder.

"You're the caretaker here." Sonny made it a statement, not a question.

Leah cleared her throat. "You were with that group of partiers I chased off a few months back. You tied up at the dock and tried to get a bonfire going on shore."

"I thought you lived here on your own with your kid. That's what the guy I was with told me. I knew Drake would be here, but who are all these other people?"

He looked around for a moment at the rest of us, but his gun never wavered. I was afraid to move. Afraid to blink. *Not Chris. Please, not Chris.*

Leah pulled her son even tighter against her. She looked to Jon, her face pleading, but all he could do was lift his hands in a helpless gesture. She then glanced at Erik, who gave her a go-ahead nod.

"I'm the only one here off-season, but this is a summer camp. We're here to get ready for campers."

"Sonny, you told me there'd be nobody—" Tremaine gulped. Sonny's glare would snatch anyone's words from his throat.

"Who else is on the island?" Sonny focused again on Leah.

Lie. Please lie. Tell him there are dozens of others, expected any moment. Tell him we called the Coast Guard before the boat hit land. Tell him anything to get him to leave us alone.

But the gun remained steady, and Chris's small head was the target. Leah would tell the truth. I would have done the same.

"This is everyone."

"When do you expect more?"

"Thursday."

"You're sure? Wrong answers will shorten your son's life expectancy significantly."

"Thursday." Her voice shook as hard as the rest of her. "The camp boat will be delivered Thursday morning. More counselors arrive Thursday afternoon."

"Very good. Now, the camp boat. It was tied to the pier when I was here before, and I thought it was always here. What other boats do you have?"

She glanced along the beach, where the wrecked speedboat sat on top of the remnants of her canoe. "There are more canoes in storage. That's it."

Tremaine looked down at his brother. "You mean we're stuck? Ryan needs help."

The gun swiveled my way, and the chunk of ice inside me doubled in size.

"You're a nurse?"

"Yes." I tried to sound tough, but the tremor in my voice gave me away.

He pointed to Erik and Drake. "You two. Pick him up. We're all going to head into that cottage over there, and this nice little nurse is going to patch up our friend."

I braced for a bullet but forced words up my throat. "You can't do that. His neck—"

Erik and Drake both hesitated, but Sonny shifted the gun back to Chris. "You heard me. Pick him up. Now."

No choice. A wave of nausea surged, and I swallowed hard. *No choice at all.*

Tremaine fluttered around us, focused on his brother as if he expected his head to fall off as soon as we lifted him. Nothing that dramatic would happen. The risk lay in the delicate, invisible spinal cord. If damaged, it could mean paralysis. Worst case, it meant loss of enervation to the chest muscles, which led to cessation of breathing and death.

I'd seen it once. I relived it daily. Even at gunpoint, I prayed not to see it again.

I positioned myself at Ryan's head, grasped his shoulders, and created a cradle with my arms to keep his head as stable as I could. *Do no harm.* Drake and Erik squatted on either side and struggled to figure out handholds. "Don't pull on his broken arm."

Each of them wiggled one hand under Ryan's back to grasp the other man's wrist, then grabbed a thigh. We stood at the same time, the two of them carrying the weight, me trying to maintain a balance. It was awkward, and Ryan's head and neck shifted despite my best efforts.

One stumbling step after another, we made it to the cottage. The others followed. Sonny kept Leah and Chris beside him, his gun trained on them. Jon stayed as close to Leah as he could, but Sonny gave him no chance to fight.

I had envisioned taking Ryan to Chris's room, but passage through one doorway was tricky enough. "Put him on the couch. His right arm toward the room, so I can look at the fracture."

We got him settled. I was soaked with sweat despite the cool day, and my arms trembled from the strain of trying to hold Ryan's head still. Maybe I'd done enough. Maybe I'd prevented further damage.

But I was fooling myself, and I knew it. If Ryan's neck was broken, we'd made things worse. *Exactly like Tim.* I sank to the floor by the couch, utterly exhausted. Sonny scooped up my phone from the end table, then bolted the front door and ordered everyone to sit on the floor in a tight group. With the gun still directed at Chris, they obeyed.

"Is he okay? Is he going to be okay?" Tremaine stood close, twisting one hand in his hair.

"How the hell should I know?" My words came out hard, my doubts soaring. I had been sure I was doing the right thing when Tim drowned, but I'd been wrong. I could still feel his thin body under my hands as I gave CPR. I could still see my sister's face contorted in fear and panic as she watched. The memories sliced through common sense and released my inner demons. "Ask your friend over there." I spat the words. "He's the one who forced us to move your brother. If Ryan ends up paralyzed, it's his fault."

Tremaine shook his head, and I thought he was disagreeing, but then he flexed one hand in a small, dampening gesture only I could see. *Back off.* The next moment, a powerful arm shoved him aside, and Sonny stood in his place.

I had a split second to register Sonny's calm, relaxed face. A face with the flat unemotional eyes of a predator. Then the cold muzzle of his gun buried itself in my left breast. Bree cried out, but I couldn't have spoken even if I'd been able to draw in enough air. My back pressed hard against the couch. My fingernails dug into my palms. My eyes bored into his. *Now I'll never get the chance to make up with Paige.*

One second. Three. Five.

It felt like weeks, not seconds. I tried not to picture the path the bullet would take, all those textbook illustrations of the thorax far too vivid in my mind. My heart stopped. The blood in my veins turned to sludge. The edges of my vision grew fuzzy, and all I could see were those black, black eyes, digging into my soul.

Behind me, Ryan moaned and shifted one leg. Sonny broke our staring duel to look at him. He pulled the gun back, and a choking sob escaped my chest before I could swallow it.

"Take care of him. Now. Fix his arm so he can be moved. And watch your mouth." The command crackled with stark brutality. He twisted away, grabbed Leah, and jerked her to her feet, the gun buried in her side. He pulled her with him to check out the other rooms in the tiny cottage. He returned in seconds, then issued commands to Tremaine, who dragged the kitchen table to block the back door.

Jon caught my eye and gave me a shaky smile, but it changed nothing. None of the others could help. I was on my own.

I bent over my patient and dragged my thoughts back to the task at hand. *Get him ready to move.* Maybe they would leave when I finished. Maybe I needed to forget about paralysis risks and focus on getting these men out of here. I checked Ryan's pulse, but my hand shook so badly, I couldn't find it. He was still breathing, so his heart must still be beating. Pulse could wait.

He wasn't conscious, but he shifted his head and moaned again. He wiggled both feet this time. At least he wasn't completely paralyzed. I checked his eyes. Both pupils remained dilated, a sign of concussion. "We should elevate his head. There are cinderblocks out front edging the flower garden. We need two of them to lift this end of the couch."

I spoke the request to the air, not looking at anyone in particular, but after a moment Tremaine stepped outside and returned with the blocks, shedding dirt on the floor along the way. He lifted the end of the couch, and I slipped the blocks under the legs without looking up. Not ideal, but it might minimize some cranial pressure.

I focused next on the fracture. Leah had dropped her armful of supplies beside me, and I found the scissors. I cut through Ryan's blood-soaked sweatshirt and the T-shirt beneath it and pulled the wet cloth back to expose the broken humerus.

Bad. But not as awful as I'd feared. The proximal end of the jagged fracture had pierced the skin, triggering the bleeding, but it was a relatively small wound. I palpated both sides of the break and couldn't feel loose fragments.

Hot breath blew against my neck, smelling stale. It was Tremaine, hovering. "Oh my god. I can see the bone."

"He needs antibiotics. And a metal pin to repair the break."

"Fix it." Sonny spoke from farther back, and I twisted around to see that he still had his gun pressed to Leah's side. He held her arm wrenched high against her back, forcing her onto her toes. She leaned hard to the side with a look of pain mixed with revulsion on her face, putting as much space between her body and Sonny's as she could manage. When she caught my eye, she gave me a look of pure desperation.

I gulped, tasting bile. "I need to set the break, bandage the wound, and strap his arm to his chest to hold the fracture still. I need a towel, a bag of sterile saline, and two or three Ace bandages from the cupboard in the back bedroom. And I need more hands."

Sonny gestured to Tremaine, but he backed away. "No way."

Sonny's eyes narrowed. "You're a wimp. Go get the shit." He gestured at Jon and Bree, who sat closest to me. "You two. Go help."

They scrambled to their feet. Jon stepped beside me and rested a comforting hand on my shoulder for a moment, but it barely registered.

Tremaine brought the saline and the towel, and I did the best I could, flushing the exposed bone while stopping the liquid from flowing back inside the wound.

Then I stiffened my spine and tried to assemble whatever scraps of inner strength I still possessed. I touched Tim's stone through the cloth of my jeans, not daring the risk of reaching into a pocket. Setting that bone was going to take brute force, not finesse, and I'd never done anything like it before. Panic squeezed the air from my lungs. Sweat chilled my skin. I couldn't screw up. I. Could. Not. Screw. Up.

"Jon, stand at Ryan's head and hold his shoulder still. Bree, take hold of his hand and wrist." My voice came out wrong, too high-pitched and squeaky, as if I spoke through a tiny tube.

They both looked pale and shaken, but they obeyed.

I rested one hand above the break and one below. "Bree, start pulling. Use steady, hard pressure. You're fighting spasmed muscles."

She pulled. Jon leaned back against the drag. I guided the bones, helping the proximal end of the break swing back where it belonged. Bree pulled harder, and the two jagged ends of bone interlocked with an audible click, the sound almost drowned by Ryan's heartrending moan.

"Don't let go!" I'd seen casting materials in the supply cupboard, but I couldn't put a cast on top of an open wound. I slapped a rough bandage coated in antibiotic ointment in place, then bound the fracture in a tight compression wrap. "Okay, Bree, ease off gradually, and let's see if it holds."

The three of us let go. I half-expected the fix to fall apart, but at least for the moment, the pieces of bone behaved. My heart still beat triple-time, but I could breathe again. "Can you sit him up?" I'd abandoned my concerns about a neck injury. I had to get these men out of here.

Jon braced Ryan's shoulders, lifting his back off the couch, and I used rolls of Ace bandages to bind the injured arm to Ryan's chest, wrapping it tight to keep it immobilized. "Okay." Jon eased him back onto the couch. I wiped the sweat off my face and gave him and Bree a shaky nod of thanks.

I faced Tremaine, taking care not to look at Sonny. "This is a temporary fix, but it will hold for now. The big risk from the fracture is infection from the open wound."

"When will he wake up?"

"He's stirring, and that's a good sign, but there's no way to know how long he'll be out. He's got quite a lump on his head and a likely concussion. But if you're careful, you can take him with you now."

That's what Sonny had asked for—make him mobile—and that's what I'd done. Now, if only they'd leave. Sonny had been to the island before. He could call someone for a boat, load Ryan, and we'd be free.

Tremaine looked at Sonny, eyebrows raised, but Sonny only shrugged. "Not yet."

My heart plummeted to my toes and wedged there.

"Okay, nurse lady, we'll keep you around a little longer." Sonny tossed Leah to the floor, and Chris scrambled to her side.

This time, instead of clinging to her, he gave her hand a squeeze and positioned himself in front of her, facing Sonny. His face was rigid, and his eyes never left the big man.

It wasn't fear I saw there. It was hatred.

Chapter Eight

Jon

Kenzie sat beside me, and I gave her arm a reassuring squeeze. Her face still looked bloodless, but she no longer trembled as if ready to fall apart. The terrible sound of Ryan's jagged bone crunching into place echoed in my head, and I kept replaying the sickening way his body had jerked in my hands as I tried to hold him still. I always got a kick out of horror movies, but real-life horror hit home like a swift punch in the gut. I would flunk as a nurse.

On my other side, Bree settled cross-legged on the floor and shifted into one of those weird yoga breathing patterns—slow inhale through the nose, slower exhale through the mouth. Her hands rested loosely on her knees, palms up, and her eyes were closed.

How could she look so calm? She appeared to be *elsewhere*, and I wanted to be there too. Some place where adrenaline didn't pound through my veins. Where my heart didn't skip a beat every time

that oversized gun pointed my way. Where I didn't keep envisioning bruises and blood and bullets.

Sonny swung an upholstered chair around to face us, leaned
back, and crossed his legs, a picture of arrogant ease. He cleared
his throat, and the room's tension tightened. "Here's the deal. We
don't want to be here. You don't want us to be here. Nobody wants
to get hurt. Let's see what we can do to make that happen."

"You shouldn't have come." Drake tossed the words down like
a gauntlet. The rest of us stiffened, bracing for a quick reaction.

A small muscle beside Sonny's left eye twitched, but the rest of
his face didn't react. "You owe me. I'm here to collect."

"But—"

"Save it." Sonny turned to Leah, who sat huddled with Chris off
to one side. "You said your boat is expected Thursday."

She gave a miniscule nod, but there was no energy in it, and
my heart tightened into a concrete lump. She didn't even look in
Sonny's direction. I wanted to take her into my arms, and I almost
stood to do it. But that sort of damn-the-consequences impulse
didn't belong to me. I needed to wait until the odds weren't so
lopsided.

Sonny sorted out her phone from the half-dozen he'd collected.
He flashed it in front of her face to unlock it. "Who's doing the
boat work?"

Leah tensed, and Erik answered. "Jackson Marine Services. Anacortes."

"What's the name of this place again?"

"Camp Madrona."

Sonny waved Tremaine closer and handed him the gun. "Shoot first, ask later."

Tremaine took the weapon, but he let it hang at his side. Even such a tiny improvement let me breathe easier.

Sonny squinted at the phone screen, entered something with his thumbs, and held the phone to his ear. The distant rumble of a lengthy recorded message echoed through the silent room, and his face tightened. The message ended. "Hello. I'm calling about the Camp Madrona boat you're servicing. We've had an urgent change of plans and need the boat returned to the island at once. I'll call again soon for an update."

He used a professional voice, and the local suppliers were used to hearing from multiple people as camp geared up each season. They wouldn't question the call. Maybe the marina would deliver the boat fast, and these creeps would go away.

Tremaine gave Sonny a questioning look.

"Closed on Sunday. They probably won't even get the message until tomorrow."

"Then what are we going to do?" Tremaine's voice carried a jagged edge of panic.

Sonny shrugged. "We wait." He stood and stretched. "Sit here. Keep the gun aimed at them. I'm going to check things out."

Tremaine raised the gun again, more alert now that Sonny had left him on his own. Sonny disappeared into the kitchen. Cupboard doors creaked open and slammed closed. The refrigerator whooshed open, then the freezer. The sounds shifted as he searched Chris's room, then Leah's. We all sat still. I couldn't force down a swallow. The air filled with the acrid smell of fear.

Sonny returned carrying a toolbox, Leah's satellite phone, and a rectangular metal box with a touchpad on its top.

Leah's gun safe.

Sonny set it beside her. "Open it."

Leah shook her head slowly. Sonny stepped back, took the gun from Tremaine, and aimed at Chris. "Open it."

Chris pulled back, eyes wide and fixed on his mother. Leah squeezed his hand. She punched a six-digit code into the touchpad, released the latch, and opened the lid. She pushed the box away without looking inside.

"Good girl." Sonny handed the gun back to Tremaine and squatted before the box, removing a pistol, a magazine, and a box of bullets. He inspected the gun briefly, snapped the magazine in place, and set the extra bullets on the end table by the couch. "Smaller than I like. These bullets won't fit my gun, but it will still help to have two."

He traded guns with Tremaine, the larger one a better fit for his giant hand. Two guns pointed our way now. My spirits plummeted so low I couldn't imagine them ever rebounding.

He handed the satellite phone to Leah. "Activate it."

She didn't even protest this time. Once Sonny got it back, he spent a moment changing the password, then forced it into his pocket, its square bulk and short antenna bulging the fabric. He gave a self-satisfied grin and surveyed the group. "Drake. Get up. Come with me."

He grabbed the toolbox and waved Drake into Leah's room. Tremaine, now with his own weapon, kept watch from the chair. Steady hammering sounds began, followed by a pause. Then more hammering echoed from Chris's room. Next came noise from something heavy dragging across the floor. The two returned to the living room from the kitchen.

Sonny walked to the couch, jabbed Ryan hard in the ribs with his thumb, and got no response from the unconscious man. Kenzie's shoulders stiffened, but she had enough sense not to protest. Sonny grunted, poked again, then gave up. He pulled down a cloth bag that hung on a hook by the door and dumped all of our phones into it. "Tremaine. Drop your phone in."

"What? I turned it off before we got on the boat, just like you said. They can't track it if it's off."

"The satellite phone is better because nobody knows we have it. Drop your phone in. Ryan's too. Come on. I'm getting rid of mine as well."

Tremaine's eyes narrowed, as if he wanted to keep pushing back, but another glare from Sonny changed his mind. He added his phone and his brother's to the collection.

"Okay. You." Sonny pointed again to Drake. "We're going outside. I'll have this gun on you every minute. If Tremaine hears me fire, he starts shooting people, starting with the kid and working down the line. Understand?"

Drake's jaw jerked as if he were grinding his teeth, but he left when told to exit. Sonny followed close behind, leaving the door standing open.

Tremaine sat forward in his chair, the gun grasped in both hands, pointed in our direction. I had hoped, with Sonny gone, he might relax, but instead he twitched when anyone made the slightest noise.

We were all seated on the floor. He stood fifteen feet away. I caught Erik's eye. Raised my eyebrows. He frowned. Gave a micro shake of his head. Too risky. By the time we scrambled to our feet and got across the room, Tremaine would shoot, and in these tight quarters, he couldn't miss. We had to wait.

But perhaps I could learn a few things. "So, Tremaine." I sat back and kept my voice neutral. "Sounds like things didn't go as you planned today."

"Shut the fuck up." He glanced toward the open door. "Sonny knows what he's doing."

"That's good. It's important to trust your leader. What's the deal on your racing boat? I've never seen one like it out here in the islands."

He looked again toward the door, but seemed reassured when no one appeared. "We had a line on easy money, but a nosy night watchman got in Sonny's way. Things didn't play out so good."

"You mean the watchman's dead?" The words fell out of my mouth and hit the floor like a series of lead weights. If Sonny had already killed once ...

Tremaine tensed. "Looked like it. I didn't exactly check for a heartbeat."

Leah gasped.

Graphic images flew through my head. Fist fight, knife fight, gun fight. Bruises, stab wounds, worse. Things might not play out so well here either.

After a moment, Tremaine continued. "Cops were on alert in Anacortes. All of them with Sonny's photo on their screens. Had to get out any way we could, and that classy little boat was sitting there, ready to go with nobody around. Sonny figured it would get us this far, then we could pick up the cash Drake promised, take the boat from your pier, and head north into Canada."

I'd wanted to learn more, but now I regretted the attempt. He'd said too much, confessing to murder and letting us know their escape plan. Could they afford to let us live to share all that with the authorities?

Tremaine must have also worried because he cast an apprehensive look at the door. "Coming here was supposed to be easy. Nobody supposed to be here but Drake and the caretaker. Sonny roared around the island searching for the boat, fuel gauge blinking like crazy. Saw the buildings and you people running out, so we headed in. Then he couldn't cut the engine."

The story poured out the way water jets out through a hole in a dam. But when he got to that point, he looked at his brother and gulped. He rubbed his right shoulder, the side with the gun. Bruised in the crash from the shoulder harness? The impact must have been rough, even strapped in.

His focus snapped back to us. "Enough. Shut up. No more questions."

Saw you people and headed in. The words soured my stomach. If we hadn't heard the engine ... Hadn't run out to see ... Maybe they would have tried a different island to find a boat. Then again, maybe not. Drake and his debt. Easy money. Too tempting.

Small rustles sounded as one or the other of us shifted position on the hard floor, but fear kept us from anything more. Tremaine showed no sign of relaxing, still plenty alert to pull a trigger.

Ryan moaned. Turned his head. Shifted his unbandaged arm.

Tremaine turned his way for a second, and Kenzie tapped me quickly on the knee.

"He's waking up," she said. "A critical moment. I need to examine him."

A statement, not a question. She didn't wait for a response, just rose to her feet, hands out in an *I'm harmless* gesture. She stepped to her patient.

Tremaine kept the gun pointed at the group, but his head swung toward Kenzie and Ryan. I gathered myself. Bree tensed beside me. Erik pulled his feet beneath him. Leah tucked Chris behind her.

Tremaine, sensing a shift, pivoted our way, but Kenzie cried out. "Oh no! Look!"

Tremaine looked. The muzzle of his gun dropped. Erik, Bree, and I surged forward as if we'd rehearsed it. I grabbed Tremaine's sore shoulder in one hand and his wrist in the other, twisting hard. Erik and Bree went in for scrambling, clutching tackles. The gun hit the floor and skittered out of reach. Tremaine's body slammed to the floor between the chair and the couch, all three of us sprawled on top of him, pinning him down.

Two shots rang from the doorway behind us, the noise simultaneous with Leah's scream. The bullets shattered the overhead light, and glass shards rained on my head and shoulders, a glittering badge of defeat.

"Don't move." Sonny sounded more lethal than ever. He and Drake stood just inside the door. The gun's muzzle hovered inches from the back of Drake's head.

Sonny shoved him aside, approached, and plucked the loose gun from the floor. "Tremaine, what the hell? I can't even leave you for half an hour?"

Tremaine struggled to his feet, red in the face. "Sonny, I—"

"Forget it." Sonny glared at the rest of us. "Enough. All of you. Get in there." He gestured toward Leah's room.

One after another, we obeyed. Leah looked close to collapse, and I took her arm. Chris still appeared defiant, and I ruffled his hair. Leah let go of me and pulled him close.

We packed in, too many people in too small a space, the smell of sweat and fear overpowering. Sonny grinned from the doorway. "Nice and cozy."

Bree faced him. "You can't keep us here. We need food. And water. And I have to pee."

For the first time since his arrival, Sonny appeared uncertain, glancing around as if only now registering the lack of plumbing. *Good job, Bree.* Trips to the bathhouse might give us another opportunity for action. But Sonny recovered fast. He said something to Tremaine, who fetched the bucket from under the kitchen sink.

"Here you go. All set." Sonny tossed the bucket into the room, where it landed on its side and rolled. Bree opened her mouth, but he cut her off. "I don't want to hear a peep out of any of you. You're not going anywhere."

He slammed the door, and we all stared at each other.

"Shit," Erik whispered. "We're in trouble."

Despite that truth, a wave of relief washed through me. The constant threat of those guns had knotted every muscle and turned every heartbeat into an insistent presence. My entire body hummed with adrenaline. Now I could draw the first full breath I'd taken in hours. Safe for the moment, I inspected our prison.

The room held a bed, one chair, a wardrobe, an end table, bookcase, and chest of drawers. Every drawer stood open, and clothing hung over the edges as if scrambled in a hasty search. The wardrobe doors stood ajar, a jumble of clothing and hangers on the floor. An enlarged photo of a younger Chris in a thick silver frame hung crooked near the window.

Leah let go of Chris, straightened the picture, then went to the dresser and searched through the top drawer.

"No use," Drake said. "Sonny found your hunting knife." He kept his voice low. Sonny had cranked on the rumbling generator, and as long as we talked softly, our voices wouldn't carry into the living room.

She clutched a wad of socks. "What about my pocketknife? It's in the end table."

"Not anymore."

"Damn it, Drake, why didn't you stop him?"

"Hey, what choice did I have?" Drake's voice spiked. "Don't give me shit I don't deserve."

I stepped forward. "Stop. Both of you. We can't be arguing with each other."

Leah's shoulders slumped. She sat on the edge of the bed and dropped her head into her hands. "What are we going to do?"

Chris stood beside her, watching, his lips tight. I needed to get them both out of there, but how?

Erik peered at the frame of the only window, and I joined him. A long row of large nails had been driven through the lower sash into the upper, making it impossible to open. Thick storm glass remained in place outside, a double barrier blocking escape.

"Drake, did you have to do such a good job with the hammer?" Erik crossed the room and pushed on the door to Chris's room, but it wouldn't open.

"It's nailed shut from the other side, and the spare bed is pushed against it." Drake twisted his watch back and forth on his wrist and looked from one of us to the next. "This isn't my fault. You know that, right? I told him I could pay next week ... I never thought ... I didn't imagine ..."

He swallowed hard and stopped.

I forced myself not to yell. Not his fault? Of course it was. Leah and Kenzie glared at him. Erik's fists tightened and he took a step backward as if forcing himself not to punch Drake then and there. The air in the room shimmered with anger.

"What else have you done?" Bree snapped the words, a too-loud whipcrack in the small space. "What exactly did you tell him when you went outside? Did you tell what Allman wrote?"

Drake closed his eyes and turned aside.

Bree snarled, Kenzie sighed, but I held up my hands. "Enough. We can waste time later. Drake, how do you know these guys? What should we expect?"

At first, he didn't answer, but after another minute, he turned back to us. "Sonny's the only one I know. We weren't exactly friends in high school, but he knew who I was. He used to be an okay guy and a pretty good student, but his dad shot himself during our senior year, and Sonny fell apart. Gave up a spot at UCLA. Dropped in and out of work. Did a few years for possession, but I heard he was actually selling." He twisted his watch again. "Look, I needed cash and heard he could lend it. It was the first time I'd seen him in years, and he'd changed. He's tougher now. Colder. And today? Something's riding him. He seems desperate. And not just about money."

Erik glanced toward the living room. "Tremaine said something went wrong. A night watchman hurt. Maybe killed."

He spoke the words slowly, and a cloying silence wrapped around the room, making it hard to breathe or think or move.

Drake broke the spell. "You asked what to expect? I'd say, expect the worst."

Leah gave a quiet sob that caught in my own throat.

"We'll be okay. Don't worry." I made my voice as reassuring as I could, and she wiped her eyes.

Erik shook himself. "We need a plan. Time to get our shit together. Come in close." He sat on the bed beside Leah. Chris sat on the floor at her feet. Kenzie, Bree, and I shifted over to stand nearby. Drake stayed behind us, pacing back and forth in the tight space, managing only three shortened steps in each direction. His fists clenched, and he exhaled in short, audible snorts.

"When we were outside," Drake whispered, "Sonny had me drag driftwood to cover the boat wreckage and scuff through the track it left on the beach. He tossed all the phones into the sound. The only one left is Leah's sat phone."

"Tremaine told us a few more things while you were gone," Kenzie said. "They'd planned to steal the camp boat and make it to Canada. The police were already looking for Sonny before they left the mainland."

She twisted to face Drake, as if trying to make him feel included. Me? I could hardly look at him. How could he have been so reckless?

He chewed on Kenzie's words for a minute. "I can't believe you worked so hard to take care of that Ryan guy. If he recovers, we'll have three of them to deal with."

Kenzie flinched but said nothing.

"Stop it. We're all walking a fine line here." I didn't like giving orders but couldn't let things escalate. We'd get nowhere sniping at each other. "You helped hide the boat. Kenzie set a fracture. Leah opened the safe. It's not like any of us have much choice."

Drake picked at one of the nail heads that pinned the window closed. The air grew heavy with apprehension, and I fought another wave of claustrophobia. Too many bodies. Too much emotion. Too little control. I fought a sudden urge to pound on the door in panic and instead forced my breathing to slow.

"Do you think the marina will deliver the boat early like Sonny wants? Can we get rid of them that way?" Bree sounded hopeful, but Leah shook her head.

"I spoke to Jeff—the lead mechanic—last week. They're rebuilding the entire powerhead. The whole thing's in pieces while they wait for a replacement part. He promised they'd get it to us on Thursday, but I don't think it can be ready any sooner."

So much for the easy solution. Most of the group looked just as discouraged as I felt, but Drake left the window and faced off with Erik. "Why are we even talking about Thursday? We need to take action *now*."

"And what exactly do you suggest we do?" Erik hissed. "We can break out this window, but we sure as hell can't do it silently. That's a guarantee that someone gets shot. We don't have tools or weapons. No phones. No way to signal the outside world for help. Sonny didn't hesitate to pull the trigger when we tackled Tremaine. We're lucky he aimed at the ceiling."

"He's full of threats, but so far, none of us has been hurt." Drake said it as if risking a bullet was nothing to worry about.

Chris was following the conversation with focused attention, and Leah rested a hand on his shoulder. "We need to keep it that way. Once they shoot somebody, it takes the brakes off. After you shoot one person, why not two? Or three?"

"I agree." My voice was firm, and Leah gave me a grateful glance. "If Sonny did kill that night watchman, he may already feel like he has nothing to lose. We can't aggravate him further."

There were nods all around, but Drake glared and said, "So, what do you want us to do? Tiptoe around like wimps, piss in a bucket, and call these pirates *sir*?"

His voice rose, and Sonny's response from the other room came at once. "Quiet in there!"

Everyone huddled tighter, and Erik and Drake began arguing in a whisper. Not about next steps, but about who should have done what sooner to avoid this whole situation. Then Drake went off about the treasure, worried Sonny and Tremaine would find and take it all.

Too idiotic. I stopped listening.

Bree walked to the bookcase, which stood against the wall shared with the living room. She removed a half-dozen books from the second shelf, set them on the floor, then did the same to each of the higher shelves. A decorative basket sat on the very top, and she put it aside.

I realized her intention and joined her, bracing my arms against the bookcase frame to hold it steady. She nodded her thanks and scaled the case, using the gaps she'd created as ladder steps. She ended up stretched on her stomach on top of the bookcase, her legs hanging off the side.

The interior walls of the house looked like they'd been added as an afterthought. Vertical studs, spaced every twenty-four inches, went all the way to the ceiling, but the wallboard on both sides of the studs stopped short, leaving a gap between wall and ceiling of about five and a half inches. Propped on her elbows, Bree could peer through the gap. She looked for a moment, then cocked her head as if listening.

One by one, the others turned to watch, waiting to find out what she'd learn, clinging to the slim hope that it might provide a clue to our fate.

Chapter Nine

Chris

My stomach hurt, but not as bad as when we were in the other room and Sonny was pointing his gun and Mom was so white and shaky I thought she was really sick. We needed to escape, but nobody was doing anything except arguing and sitting around and staring at Bree, who was eavesdropping like Mom always told me not to. At least she was doing something that might help.

Jon looked my way. "Where's Skagit?"

"I sent him away. Into the woods, where he'll be safe." Easier to hurt a dog than a person. Even I knew that.

I was glad he was outside, but I kept turning to look for him, reaching out to pet him. I'd gotten him for my fourth birthday, a tiny puppy scared and whimpering without his brothers and sisters. Mom told me he had to stay in his box at night, but he stopped crying when I tucked him under the covers, warm against my stomach. From then on, he stayed with me like my shadow.

Everyone agreed he was smart. Smarter than most people. When Sonny pulled his gun and I told Skagit to go, he cocked his head and gave a little whine. But he obeyed, ducking into the thick grass and staying invisible, even though I knew he kept watching. It had only been a few hours without him, but I wasn't sure how long he'd stay hidden once he got hungry.

He was my best friend. I couldn't let Sonny get him. We had to do something.

Erik waved to get everyone's attention and whispered, "What's in your pockets? And Leah, is there anything else in this bedroom that could help us?"

Pockets were pretty much empty. Bree handed down a quarter and two nickels. Jon had a tube of lip balm and half of an old pair of scissors. That caused some excitement, but when Drake tried to use it to pry a nail out of the front window, the metal bent. Jon took it back.

I had a black mussel shell and two dog biscuits. Drake had half a pencil and an open pack of peppermint Life Savers, fuzzy with lint. Kenzie had a painted rock and nothing else. We piled it all on the bed. Everyone kept mentioning things in their tipis—pocketknives, hammers, screwdrivers, extra tent stakes—but it was obvious none of that helped.

Mom circled the room, putting clothing back in drawers and adding things to the pile. A pair of stone bookends, maybe heavy enough to hit someone with. An extension cord, which Jon said was long enough to tie someone up, hopefully Sonny. Wire clothes hangers, which I couldn't think of a use for, but Drake grabbed one.

He straightened the wire, took it to the front window, and used the end to scrape at the wood around one of the nails. In that old movie, it took the Count of Monte Cristo and the **Abbé** years to dig out of their prison, but Drake was trying anyway.

"The medical supply cupboard has more scissors," Kenzie said. "And scalpel blades. I saw several packets of casting material. You could use it to make whatever shape you wanted, then let it harden."

Drake pulled at his bottom lip. "How strong would that casting material be? Could it dig through wood?" His wire hanger must not have been doing much good.

"Maybe." Kenzie's face wrinkled like she was thinking about it. "It's strong enough to hold a person's weight, like in a foot cast, but it's not designed as a scraping tool."

"If we're considering the impossible," Mom said, "why don't we imagine we're in the kitchen? Knives, mallets, a cast iron skillet heavy enough to break someone's skull. But we can't get in there either."

I couldn't believe Mom would say something like that. Breaking skulls. But I could get that skillet for her.

"I can go." I whispered it real quiet, but they all turned to stare at me, even Bree on top of the bookcase, and Jon, who stood holding it steady.

Mom gave me a death stare, but Erik leaned my way. "What do you mean?"

I pointed to the gap between the wall and the ceiling. The wall facing my bedroom. "I can fit through there."

"No, you can't." Mom's voice went louder than a whisper, and everybody shushed her.

Erik and Drake eyeballed the gap, then inspected me like they were measuring.

"No. He's a child. It's too dangerous." Mom stood, arms crossed, her voice still too loud. "What if he gets caught? They'd hurt him." She turned white and shaky again. "He can't fit through such a small gap. And if he does get through, how would we get him back?"

Erik put a hand on her shoulder, but she jerked away. "The rest of us are too big. Chris is the only one."

"No. I won't let him go." Mom reached for me, but I stepped to the side. Her arm hung there in the air, like it belonged to one of those puppets on strings, and when she dropped it, she scrunched her eyes closed and leaned hard against the wardrobe. My stomach lurched bad, but I could do it, I knew I could. I wanted to do it.

Kenzie grabbed hold of Erik. "Don't let him. We can find another way. When I mentioned the supplies in the cupboard, I never meant—"

"We'll be careful. It's too good a chance to pass up."

She looked almost as upset as Mom and wiped one eye with the back of her hand. But everyone else was on my side. Suggestions flew from all directions, coming so fast I didn't know who said what.

"We could use the bedsheet like a rope."

"This canvas bag could hold things."

"Is there anything else in there he should search for?"

Their voices sounded fake like in old video games, not like real voices at all.

Bree shushed them, then leaned down from her perch. "Sonny found the key to the storage shed padlock on the key rack. He says he's going to check it out. That would leave Tremaine here on his own."

Erik waved the others off the bed, set the stuff from pockets on the nightstand, and pulled off the top sheet. He tied knots in it and made it into a rope with a loop at one end. Drake cleared stuff off the top of Mom's dresser, and he and Kenzie backed it up to the nailed-shut door into my room. It made a thump when they set it down.

"Quiet," Jon whispered. He waved me over. "Are you sure about this? It's risky."

"I'm sure." Or at least, that's what I told myself. My stomach did flips like it did when I jumped off the cliff into Sunset Cove. Mom glared at me something fierce, so maybe I shouldn't try. But I'd seen the way Sonny twisted her arm and the way her face looked when she had to open the gun safe. "I can do it."

Bree had her eye to the crack, whispering info to Jon, who passed it on. "Sonny's getting ready to leave."

"Drake, you lift him," Jon said. "You're the strongest."

Drake grunted and gave a nod like he was happy to be doing something. He climbed on top of the dresser and knelt there. Erik bent closer to me with his face at my level. "Get the things from the supply cupboard. Don't go in the kitchen. Tremaine is still in the living room. He could see you."

"But that's where the skillet and knives—"

"No. Don't get caught. That's an order."

I nodded. That meant I heard him. Not that I'd do what he told me. Skagit was the one who always obeyed.

I took my tennis shoes off, and Erik boosted me onto the dresser with Drake. Jon was still holding the bookcase for Bree, but he gave me a thumbs up. "You can do this, Chris."

I couldn't stand straight, but with my knees bent, I could peer through the gap enough to see my bed on the far side of my bedroom. The space between the wall and ceiling looked smaller now that I was right up close. Too small. What if I got stuck, or got through and couldn't get back?

Before I could tell anyone I'd changed my mind, Erik whispered, "Now."

Drake squeezed my shoulder. "Be careful not to kick the wall. Don't worry. I'll help."

The next minute, he hoisted me so I lay flat in his arms, stomach down like Superman flying. He was stronger than I expected, but his face tightened up and his arms trembled. Unlike Superman, I needed to fly backward, and Drake aimed my legs at the gap. My feet went through easy. My knees. My hips. Just that fast, I was hanging, my legs dangling against the wall in my bedroom and the rest of me in Mom's room. The top of the wall dug hard into my stomach, making me squirm.

Drake held me under my arms, and I had hold of his shoulders. His breath smelled like something rotten, but I couldn't turn away. Mom was crying. Kenzie had her arm around her. The others all stared at me, looking scared and hopeful and worried all at once.

"Okay?" Drake asked.

"Yeah."

He pushed me through. My stomach. My chest. The weight of my body dragged me down into my bedroom, and Drake hung on hard to slow me. The back of my head hit the ceiling, and I turned it sideways to let it slide through.

And it jammed there. My chin made it, but the fat round part of my skull was too big, my ears smashed so tight I thought they'd bury themselves in my brain. I was wedged there like in those online videos of kids getting their heads stuck in the bars of a fence, but in real life there wasn't anything funny about it. Drake still had hold of my arms, but he eased his grip, not trying to slow things anymore. Nothing changed. I was stuck.

Then he let loose with one hand, put his palm on the top of my head, and pushed.

My ears felt like they were being ripped all the way off, and my cheek caught on something sharp, but all of a sudden, my head popped through. I dropped a few feet, my arm just about jerked out of place, kept from falling only by Drake's hand on my wrist. His arm dragged forward through the gap. I grunted even though I was trying to be quiet.

I looked down. My feet dangled only a foot or so above the spare bed. "Let go," I whispered. Drake turned me loose.

I landed easy, but the bed squeaked, and I froze. Drake's arm pulled back into the other room.

Silence. Then footsteps in the living room.

"Ryan? You okay?" Tremaine's voice. No answer. Then footsteps came again, followed by the creak of the living room chair. Tremaine, sitting there with his gun.

I tried to swallow but couldn't. I reached out to touch Skagit, but he wasn't there.

Drake's hand reappeared holding a cloth bag. It landed on the bed beside me.

Hurry. I slipped off the bed. Went to the medical supply cupboard and eased the tall doors open. Scissors. Tape. Casting material. Kenzie had asked for scalpel blades, so I looked for something like a knife, but I finally found a small cardboard box filled with blades in foil wrappers. The other things in there didn't seem very helpful, but blood oozed down my cheek, so I grabbed some gauze, antibiotic ointment, and a box of Band-Aids.

My bag had plenty more room. I closed the cupboard doors. Double-checked their latch. Scooped up my book from beside my bed. Tiptoed to the kitchen door.

A hissing sound came from the gap I'd climbed through. Drake must be watching. I ignored him.

If Tremaine was sitting in the chair where Sonny had left it, he could only see the end of the kitchen where the table was. That meant he could see the counter with the cutting board and the knife block. But he couldn't see anything to the right of the sink—the freezer, the refrigerator, some of the cupboards.

And he couldn't see the drainboard, which held Mom's defrosting spaghetti casserole and the long sharp knife she'd used that morning to slice bread for toast.

I could see the knife lying there. I could reach it in three steps. Then only three steps back to safety. I could do it.

I put one foot across the threshold. I didn't make a single noise, I know I didn't, but a grunt came from the living room, then footsteps came closer. I pulled back my foot and flattened myself hard against the wall.

Tremaine came all the way into the kitchen. Opened a cupboard, closed it, and ran water. I heard him drink. A kind of glug, glug, glug like the sound one of the big ugly monsters in my video game makes. A monster with long, sharp teeth. A monster that eats people.

My chest hurt, and I couldn't breathe. If he stepped into this bedroom, he'd find me for sure. Grab me. Maybe even shoot me. Mom would cry more. Skagit wouldn't know what to do without me.

Drake had pushed the knotted sheet through, and it hung white against the wall, only a few feet away. But I couldn't dash toward it with Tremaine so close.

The front door opened. Tremaine put his glass in the sink with a clink, and I could hear his footsteps headed back toward the living room. "Any luck?"

"The shed has some tools, lots of useless camp stuff like baseballs and art supplies, and a rack of canoes, but nothing that gets us out of here. We can't exactly paddle to Canada."

Sonny kept talking, but I was too busy to listen. I hustled onto the bed in two seconds flat, put my foot in the loop at the bottom of the sheet, and jerked on one of the knots. Drake pulled me straight up, hauling the sheet until he could reach through, grab the bag, and drag it over. Then he got hold of both of my wrists and pulled. Going through headfirst was no easier than going through backward, my head just about cracking open when he dragged me over the edge, then the rest of me tumbled over.

Mom caught me and gave me a huge hug, squeezing so tight I couldn't pull in any air. Erik patted my shoulder. "Great job, Chris." He whispered in my ear. "You may have saved us."

Maybe. But I wished I could have grabbed that knife.

"You've cut your cheek." Kenzie fussed, using a tissue to wipe off the blood, then she put on some antibiotic ointment and a Band-Aid from the stuff I'd taken. Her hands shook like something had scared her, and she didn't look me in the eye. "Make sure to keep this clean."

Before I could ask what was wrong, Bree swung off the bookcase. "Sonny's getting food and water. He's coming in."

She and Jon slipped books back in place, Drake carried the dresser to where it belonged, and Erik stuffed the pile of pocket things into my bag of goodies and slid it under the bed. Kenzie hid the sheet-rope in the wardrobe and spread the comforter on the bed.

Jon gave me a tight hug and whispered, "Well done."

Mom wiped her eyes and pulled me close beside her.

By the time Sonny nudged the door open with his foot, there was no sign we'd done anything at all.

Chapter Ten

Kenzie

Sonny pushed the door open a few inches but stepped back at once, too far away for anyone to reach him even if he hadn't held a gun. "Nurse! Come check your patient."

I couldn't help it. I cowered. I heard a few sighs of relief as the others realized they weren't in the crosshairs, but Jon tensed, and Leah leaned my way and whispered, "It'll be okay." Chris hid his bandaged cheek.

I hadn't recovered from Chris's foray over the wall, sweating through every moment, imagining a dozen horrific outcomes, and I had no energy for sparring with Sonny again. In my mind, I launched into a movie-worthy leap, grabbed the gun, and saved us all. But in this world, I kept my eyes on the floor, hunched my body into the smallest possible shape, and took cautious steps into the living room, my legs wobbling like my bones had turned to rubber.

Sonny told Erik to close the door behind me. It snicked shut, confining me with the three men: Sonny and Tremaine with guns pointed my way, and Ryan immobile on the couch. I repressed a shiver and wiped moist palms on my jeans. Bree had probably returned to her spy-post, but knowing she watched and listened didn't help.

"He's been moaning. He opened his eyes once but that's it." Tremaine stood by Ryan, shifting from one foot to the other. "What's wrong with him?"

I walked to the couch and knelt, the back of my neck prickling. It took so little effort to fire a gun. The movement of a single finger. Such a small contraction of a few tiny muscles. Doctors and nurses worked in war zones every day, risking their safety to help others. But reminding myself of the bravery of others did nothing to slow my own heart. Two guns. Pointed my way. They had a heavy presence even when I couldn't see them.

I revisited my examination checklist. Ryan's face was pale, but not worse. Pupils still dilated. Pulse strong. My stethoscope lay tangled in the bandage material Leah had fetched hours before, and I used it to listen to his chest. I should have done this earlier, a sign of how muddled my thinking had been, so I took my time now.

His heart beat steadily. Lungs sounded a little raspy. He moaned and shifted when I pressed the bell low on his chest, potentially a sign of cracked ribs.

"Ryan! Ryan, can you hear me?" I used a sharp tone, and his eyes fluttered open. Unfocused. They closed again after only a few seconds. I called again but got no response.

It had been years since my rotation through a head-trauma unit in nursing school, and I struggled to recall details. I wanted radiographs, CT results, lab work. I wanted facts, not uncertainty, expert guidance, not my own flawed judgment. I needed Betsy to back me up, but she was the one who had banished me here.

My life and the lives of the others could depend on keeping Ryan alive, but waves of uncertainty kept me off-balance. "He's not as deeply unconscious as before, but at this point, he doesn't know what's going on. Even when he wakes again, he'll probably be confused. Without a CT scan, there's no way to know how much brain damage there is or whether it will heal."

Tremaine gasped. Hadn't he realized his brother's head injury could be serious? I stood, twisting the tubes of my stethoscope in my hands. "He's not getting worse, but he'd be far better off in a hospital." That got the reaction I expected. None at all. I was tempted to exaggerate the seriousness of Ryan's condition to force them to seek outside help, but the truth was bad enough and they did nothing. Lying wasn't going to improve anything.

I met Tremaine's eyes. "This will take time, and he needs basic support. He's going to need to urinate at some point. If you don't want him to soil himself, we should get his pants off and put some padding underneath him."

Tremaine stepped back, appalled, and I lost patience. "If he were in a hospital, he'd be in intensive care. He'd have a urinary catheter and would be on IV fluids. Since you're not willing to call for help, at least lend a hand."

I didn't wait for a response. I pulled off Ryan's shoes and undid the button and zipper of his jeans. "Come here and pull."

After a moment, he stuffed his gun into the waistband of his pants and helped me tug off his brother's jeans and boxers. I tossed the grimy cloth aside. Sonny sat, watchful but unwilling to lift a hand.

"Good. Now, I need something waterproof. Maybe there's a garbage bag in the kitchen? And grab a few towels."

This time, Tremaine jumped to get what I needed. I liked being in charge for a moment. Between the two of us, we got Ryan repositioned on his side with a thick layer of towels around his hips and a garbage bag protecting the couch. Tremaine ducked into Chris's room and returned with a blanket he tucked over his brother's bare legs.

"That should hold things for a while." I picked up the stethoscope and other supplies and put them on the end table, hoping to find the pair of scissors I'd used earlier. But they were gone. When I looked up, Sonny sneered and patted his shirt pocket. The handles of the scissors poked out of the top.

Tremaine touched my elbow. "Thank you."

I turned, surprised at the sincerity in his voice. Sonny frowned, but Tremaine seemed not to notice.

"Watch him overnight. Talk to him if he seems to be waking. His brain is trying to sort itself out, but that's a slow process."

Drake had given me a hard time about setting the fracture, but even without Sonny's threats, I wouldn't be able to live with myself if I ignored Ryan's injuries. Guilt about Tim already weighted every waking moment, and I couldn't carry more. Now I could see another possible advantage. Maybe helping Ryan would provide an opportunity to get through to Tremaine.

"Okay, nurse-lady, you're done here." Sonny's tone remained as obnoxious as ever. He stood and waved me back toward our prison. "Take that bowl and pitcher with you."

Leah's large wooden bread bowl stood on the floor beside the door, and I picked it up. It held a plastic jar of peanut butter, a loaf of her unsliced bread, and a handful of paper towels. The plastic pitcher was full of water. No utensils. No metal or glass. Nothing useful as a weapon.

A long length of clothesline lay on the floor, tied at one end to the heavy couch behind me. I stepped over it, opened the door, and stepped through.

"That's it until morning." Sonny sneered when he said it. "I'm tying your door shut, so don't try anything. We'll be right here."

Erik closed the door after I entered the room. The doorknob rattled as Sonny secured his clothesline lock. I surveyed the room, people jammed into every square foot of the small space. As relieved as I felt to leave those men, I couldn't help recoiling at being confined once again.

"Everything okay?" Jon asked.

"I guess. Ryan's still unconscious, but I've done what I can."

Drake snorted but kept his mouth shut, which was just as well since I itched to give him a piece of my mind. I set the food and water on the dresser. "Sounds like we're on our own for the rest of the night. I guess this is dinner."

Not very appealing, but Chris tore off a few chunks of bread and used them to scoop out some peanut butter. The smell roiled my stomach, but he wolfed it down. In a bizarre parody of domesticity, the rest of the group got busy. Leah rigged a blanket across one corner of the room to provide a degree of privacy for the bucket latrine. Jon inspected the door hinges to see if he could pry out the pins, but even with good tools, they would have been hard to extract. Erik spread the things Chris had retrieved on the bed. Drake sorted through it all, and I settled in to watch.

The scissors? Blunt-ended for cutting bandages, so no good as a weapon.

The scalpel blades? No handles, so hard to grasp. Just as likely to cut the hand that held it as the intended target.

The casting tape, however, had potential. Drake found a plastic bag in the wardrobe and used it to protect his hands from the sticky, quick-setting stuff. It couldn't grip a scalpel blade well enough to serve as a handle, but Drake wrapped the tape to create a sharp point. The tape came in bright colors, looking better suited for a kid's craft project than a weapon. The sort of thing Tim would have loved.

Any weekend I wasn't working, I had spent with Paige and Tim. I'd relocated to Seattle to be closer, and my time with them was the highlight of each week. Hanging out at their backyard pool on sunny days. Playing indoors when the weather closed in. Blanket forts and Candyland transitioned to intricate Lego constructions and endless games of Uno as Tim got older. But art proved to be his real talent. Give that boy markers and paints, construction paper and glue, and magic resulted.

My fridge had been covered with Tim's paintings, a joyous riot of color, but after he died, they ripped me open every time I saw them. I'd taken them down, wrapped them with care, and hidden them in the bottom of my sweater drawer.

Watching Drake create his fluorescent blue and green constructions gave me chills. Tim would have loved to play with tape like this, but whatever he made wouldn't have been as deadly as what Drake produced. In an hour of work, he crafted a half-dozen miniature ice picks, fat enough for a good grip and small enough to fit in a pocket.

Erik hefted one. "Lightweight, but sharp. I think it could inflict some damage if you aimed for the neck, an eye, or a kidney."

"Wait a minute." Leah tested one of the picks with her thumb and flinched when it drew a drop of blood. "What's the plan here? These men have *guns*. Real guns with real bullets. If you start poking at them with child-sized knives, they won't react well." She tossed the pick back with the others. "We shouldn't risk it. We need to figure out how to find a boat and get rid of them that way."

If I had the chance, could I attack someone with one of these homemade weapons? I could stab a hypothetical person, a dark evil shape coming at me in the night. I could hurt him in a frenzied moment to defend myself. But could I stab Tremaine, who thanked me and worried about his kid brother? Could I even hurt Sonny, who had aimed at the ceiling when he could have easily killed one of us?

I didn't have an answer, but I would have one of Drake's creations in my pocket the next time I got called out. Even if I never used it, knowing I had it there would make me feel less helpless. Which was perhaps a danger in and of itself.

"We need to think this through." Jon twisted one of the picks in his hands, its bright color flashing. He was breathing fast, and sweat rolled down his face. None of us were comfortable locked in here like this, but he seemed more stressed by our confinement than I would have expected. He looked to Erik. "If we decide we're going to use these things, we need to pick the right moment because we'll only get one chance. Once they see we have one, they'll search us for the others."

Erik agreed, and Drake gave a grudging nod. As I'd suspected, the fiberglass didn't have the strength to remove nails, so Drake took one of the bandage scissors and began a patient scratch, scratch, scratch at the window. He had no chance of success, but at least it kept him occupied.

Bree climbed down from her listening post—the bookcase braced now by an end table so it wouldn't wobble—and rejoined us. "They've gone into the kitchen. I can't hear anything."

Jon tugged the door to the living room. It didn't budge. "Learn anything helpful?"

Bree gave Drake a wary glance. "Sonny found the notes about the treasure and the island map. He seemed excited."

"What? No way." Drake abandoned the window, took one of the small stabbing picks, and resumed his restless pacing, pushing people aside to claim room for a few strides at a time. "They're trying to get away from the cops, right? Escape to Canada? They don't want to hang around here to search. They can't take the treasure."

"Shit, man, they're only here because of you." Erik sounded pissed, but whispering softened some of the sting. "How much do you owe them?"

Drake took another lap, then faced Erik. "Thirty."

"Thirty *thousand*?" Whispering didn't hide Erik's astonishment. "Have you lost your mind? Of course, they're going to take the cache if they can find it."

"You don't understand." Drake's voice rose, edging toward panic. "I need the rest of my share. Sonny's not the only—"

"Shut up in there!" Sonny's shout came fast.

We all froze. Bree tried to calm Drake, but he was too wound up to listen. He stabbed the air with his tiny homemade weapon, a loose cannon that could get us all killed.

I forced myself to eat, tearing off my share of bread and scooping out some peanut butter. Maybe retrieving the casting tape had been a mistake, creating the illusion we had options without giving us a real chance.

My stomach grumbled, the food not settling. To make matters worse, the delicious scent of tomato sauce and basil wafted through the ceiling gap, followed a half-hour later by the pungent smell of marijuana smoke. Sonny and Tremaine had found Leah's defrosted casserole and Erik's stash.

I sat on the floor, huddled into the corner formed by the dresser and the wall, and closed my eyes. I wasn't here in a crowd. I was alone, back in my apartment in Seattle, with instant hot water, a convenient bathroom, and Thai takeout delivered on command to my door. I'd sleep in my own bed, grab a latte on my way to work in the morning, chat with the other nurses before tackling my first patient. Tim would live, not die. My sister and I would still be best friends, and I would no longer hate myself. Everything would be peaceful and calm.

I tried to wrap myself in my fantasy, but the sound of the wind battering the cottage windows pulled me back to the island. When I opened my eyes, I was still trapped in a tiny room, hungry and tired, and every breath trembled with fear.

Chapter Eleven

Jon - Monday

We cut off the lights at midnight after convincing Chris to stop reading, but I'm not sure how much rest anyone managed. The moon gave enough light to see by. Leah's eyes never left Chris until he fell into a restless sleep, then she stared at the ceiling, wiping her eyes as tears trickled silently down her cheeks. She and Bree huddled on the narrow bed with Chris between them, and the rest of us curled up on bits of floor, trying to ignore our rumbling stomachs. Kenzie had fallen asleep propped against the wall, and we let her be.

My normal bedtime routine consisted of a walk, a final email check, and a half hour of reading, all in blessed solitude. The tight press of bodies in such a small space made me desperate for fresh air and stars overhead, and my heart raced as if urging me to run. I wasn't sure I'd be able to sleep locked in on a hard, gritty floor, smelling everyone's stinky feet, but after a few hours of tossing and turning, exhaustion knocked me out.

I awoke at first light when somebody's elbow jabbed my ribs. My back ached, and I would have paid big bucks for a toothbrush and a hot cup of coffee. The others came grumbling to life, but our captors remained silent. Bree climbed the bookcase and reported Tremaine asleep in the living room chair, gun on his lap. I climbed on top of the dresser and peered over the wall into Chris's room, where Sonny lay on Chris's bed, his gun only inches from his hand.

Erik seized the chance for a group conference, and we huddled together by the bed to whisper. We'd finished the bread, but we passed the peanut butter jar around, scraping it clean with our fingers. The water pitcher made the rounds as well, but it, too, was almost empty. When I offered it to Chris, he put it to his lips but didn't swallow, then handed it to his mother and urged her to finish the rest.

"I've been thinking." Erik used his I'm-in-charge voice, and we let him get away with it. "If Sonny plans to try to find the treasure, maybe we can use the search to our advantage." Drake's eyes narrowed, and he opened his mouth, but Erik held up a hand. "Don't start. It's not like we're giving money away. We don't even know where it is. I'm saying the search might give us a chance to get out of this damn room. We know this island, and they don't."

"Anything that gets us outdoors is an improvement." I couldn't wait to get out. The walls had closed in even more during the night, leaving me desperate for open space. My head pounded in caffeine withdrawal and my back twinged every time I moved. The stench of urine from the open latrine bucket burned my throat and made me nauseous. We'd tossed a blanket over it to cut the smell, but it hadn't helped.

"What we really need," Leah said, "is food and water." Dark circles rimmed her eyes, and her voice dragged. "If we get those basics, I'm happy if they just leave us alone. We can wait them out."

"Agreed." Bree sounded sincere, but she kept an eye on Drake.

"No way. We have to be proactive." Drake pounded a fist against his thigh. "We need to turn the tables and capture them. If we can tackle Sonny and get the sat phone, we can call for help."

"Is he keeping it with him all the time?" Erik asked.

"When I checked a few minutes ago, it was on the floor beside him," I said. "I imagine he'll put it back in his pocket when he gets up."

"Okay," Erik said. "Plan A. If we get the opportunity to tackle Sonny and get the phone safely, we jump him. I don't think we'll get much chance here in the house with both of them on guard. Our chances improve if we can get Sonny outside by himself."

Bree jerked to attention. "Are you nuts?"

"Have you forgotten he's armed?" Leah chimed in.

The whispered argument heated up, not helped by the fact that we were all exhausted. Eventually, everyone except Leah approved the idea. High risk, high reward. But how likely were we to catch Sonny unawares? He'd been vigilant so far.

"What about a simple escape?" Leah gestured toward the window. "Drake's got two nails worked loose, and a third is almost free. Only six more to go. By tomorrow, we should be able to open the window. Then it's just a matter of getting the storm glass off."

"What does that get us?" Drake dismissed the idea with a wave of his hand. "We still can't call for help or get off the island." He'd been the one working at the nails, but it seemed more like a way to burn off nervous energy than an escape route he believed in.

"We couldn't leave the island," I said, "but we could hide. I'd be happy to get out of gun range." Far better to forage for food and shelter than endure more hours under constant threat. "We'd only need to hold out until Thursday."

"Okay." Erik acted like he was checking off accomplishments on a list. "Plan B is we escape together once we can get through the window without raising the alarm." He looked around the group. "But what're the ground rules here? If Sonny wants to search for Allman's cache, he may only let a few of us out to help. If some of us get the chance to run, do we take it? Or does that put everyone else at risk?"

"Of course, it does." Leah snapped. "It makes violence more likely. If you can get your hands on the phone, that's one thing. But if some people simply take off, others will pay. We need to stick together." Her hand gripped Chris's shoulder hard.

She was probably right. But from the expressions Drake, Erik, and Bree had, I wasn't sure she had unanimous support. If I got the chance, would I disappear into the neighboring woods? I couldn't abandon Leah and Chris, but if they were with me ...

The doorknob rattled, and we scrambled to spread out, making sure to hide anything that would get us in trouble. Drake stood at the window to block any view of the shredded wood around the nail heads.

Sonny kicked the door open. He remained in the living room, well out of reach. "Come take care of Ryan." He waved Kenzie out with his gun.

She picked up the empty water pitcher, but Sonny looked beyond her. "Who knows about this treasure stuff?"

Erik and Leah exchanged glances, and Leah shook her head. Erik stepped forward. "I do." To my surprise, he pointed to me. "And Jon knows this island best."

Sonny frowned, his hand tightening on his gun, but then he waved us forward. "Okay. The three of you. Come on."

Erik stepped forward. I detoured to the blanketed corner and grabbed the latrine bucket. I was tempted to throw its stinky contents in Sonny's face, but as soon as he saw what I carried, he winced and backed out of splashing range

"Put that damn thing outside." He aimed, not at me, but at Kenzie, and I obeyed, stepping out the front door only far enough to dump the bucket. This was the problem with the idea of dashing for the trees. It would imperil the others.

Sonny had Erik and me sit on the floor while Kenzie and Tremaine worked on Ryan, who had awakened. He sat with Kenzie's help and took sips of water without choking, but he looked around the room with a dazed, unfocused expression.

She checked his eyes, lungs, and pulse.

"Ryan, can you lift your left arm?"

Nothing.

"Can you turn your head and look at me?"

He did so.

"Are you in pain?"

He stared.

"Do you know where you are?"

"Nineteen." The single word came out slurred.

She continued with more questions, using simple words and a patient voice. Sometimes he answered sensibly, but much of the time, what he said was garbled. Tremaine stood close at her shoulder, gun at his side, flinching each time his brother gave a wrong reply.

She checked the wrap that restrained the broken arm. "Ryan, you're doing great. You've been unconscious for a day, and it's normal to feel confused. Your brother is right here to take care of you."

Sonny supervised all this closely, but once she tackled the cleanup tasks, he sat in his favorite chair and focused on Erik and me. A silver cigarette lighter sat at his elbow beside a plate with remnants of toast and egg. My mouth watered, and my stomach rumbled.

"I've been reading about this gold and jewels shit." He tapped Leah's copy of Allman's journal entry. "You're going to find it for me."

Yeah, right. I let Erik take that one.

He cleared his throat and leaned forward. "Anyone who finds this cache will be set for life. It's worth millions."

"You know where it is? That's what Drake claims."

"We're confident it won't take long to find."

Erik launched into a convoluted explanation that greatly over-stated the case. He detailed the history of the Baytree Community, emphasized how accurate Allman's records were, and explained that we knew the island intimately. Even though Allman had hid-den the cache in the thirties, we were convinced no one else had found it.

I struggled to keep my face unreadable in the presence of so much bullshit.

Erik paused. "Don't you agree, Jon? With a little effort, we can find Allman's treasure."

I faked some enthusiasm with a pasted-on smile. "Absolutely. If you pull out the island map, I can show you possible locations."

Sonny leaned back in his chair. The ideal response from him would've been a passionate belief like Drake's, but instead he pursed his lips and stared first at Erik, then at me. "The description in this journal is vague. If it's so easy to find, why haven't you already dug it up?"

"Because we had other responsibilities to take care of first." Erik should have considered an acting career. He sounded confident and fully rational. "And it took time for us to do more research. We wouldn't have all shown up here if we weren't confident."

I nodded along, trying to act like somebody who'd done plenty of research.

Sonny flipped back and forth through the pages, pausing to read individual sections.

Kenzie walked into the kitchen, Tremaine at her heels, and returned with clean towels and something in a bowl that she

spoon-fed to Ryan. She spoke to Tremaine, giving detailed instructions on food and water and bedsore prevention. Sonny
didn't pay any attention. Either he trusted Tremaine to guard
Kenzie on his own, or he viewed her as a minimal threat. Either
way, his inattention was good news. Maybe Kenzie would get a
chance to pocket more supplies.

Sonny spread the island map on the floor in front of me. "Show
me the most likely locations."

My jaw clenched so hard, my molars creaked. This island belonged to me. Not legally, of course, but it was the closest thing
I had to a home. I'd alternated between fear and anger ever since
Sonny first pulled his gun, but seeing the map in his hand, hearing
the possessive tone in his voice, knowing he didn't care at all for this
island except for what he could steal, triggered a more fundamental
fury. He'd already threatened Leah and Chris. Now he threatened
my sanctuary.

I cleared my throat. Forced a calm attitude. "The entry says
Allman buried the cache on a promontory, which could refer to
any high piece of land that juts toward the water." I scanned the
map, reviewing the options. "Since this island has a number of
coves and inlets, there are more than a dozen possibilities ..." I
tapped various places on the map. "But if it were me, I would focus
on these." I pointed to three specific spots on the western shore.

They were the most remote choices, far from the central road
and accessible only on foot or by boat. If Sonny wanted us to do
the digging, we'd have more opportunities to catch him off guard
if we were hiking the narrow island trails. Or, if he was willing to

pull canoes out of storage, that, too, could work to our advantage. Canoes wouldn't get Sonny and his crew to Canada, but I could paddle the three miles west to Vendovi Island without breaking a sweat.

"I agree," Erik said. "Particularly this spot beside Sunset Cove, which is near Allman's homestead. Near the garden where he first discovered the chest. It's ideal."

I met his eyes. Ideal, yes, but not for hiding treasure. It was the ideal spot for Plan A. The cliff that edged this cove dropped straight down to the sound, rocky and treacherous, off-limits to campers. The perfect spot for a nasty fall and a chance to seize the sat phone.

Sonny had no idea what the terrain was like. All he had to go by was a two-dimensional map and a pleasant-sounding name, so he expressed no concern. "Okay. I'll call the marina as soon as it opens. If we can't get the camp boat today, I'd rather look for the cache than sit here doing nothing. You two can lead me to Sunset Cove."

I folded the map, careful to hide the sudden hope that buoyed me. This could work. Erik and I weren't as reckless as Drake. We would bide our time, find the right moment, and attack. By tonight, we could have the Coast Guard here, and this whole mess would be over. Anything was better than staying locked inside for the whole day.

"Sonny," Tremaine stepped closer. "Kenzie wants to fix a batch of sandwiches. And we're running out of towels. She says there's a washing machine in the shed where the pottery stuff is."

I took note of his use of her name, another good sign, but Sonny frowned. "The *nurse* can fix sandwiches if you watch her every minute. No knives. Nothing missing from the kitchen when she's done. I saw the washer out there. Go ahead and let the *nurse* start a load." He sneered at Kenzie each time he avoided her name.

She turned and faced him. "In addition to food and water, the latrine bucket needs to be cleaned and disinfected. And unless you want an even smellier mess on your hands, you need to give people daily access to real toilets."

Sonny's face twisted as though he already smelled an outhouse. "Dammit. You people are more trouble than you're worth."

"I've set your friend's arm. I'm doing everything I can to help him. Erik and Jon told you where you might find millions of dollars in gold and gems. It won't kill you to treat us with a little common decency."

She'd gone too far. Not just her barbed words, but her blunt tone and the way she stared Sonny down. His hand clenched his ever-present gun, and his eyes narrowed. I tensed, wondering whether we'd reached the moment when everything would explode.

A mix of anger and frustration flitted across his face. Then, with a visible effort, he rebalanced. "I've already told you to watch your mouth, nurse-lady. Tremaine, guard her while she fixes food and starts laundry. Then escort her to the bathroom. When you get back, take the others one at a time."

Tremaine wrinkled his nose. "Yeah, okay."

"Remind each of them. If they try to run, you'll shoot. And if I hear you fire, I'll shoot someone here."

"Okay."

We'd heard the same threats before, but getting out of the cottage, even for a few minutes, would be better than stagnation. And Tremaine seemed reachable in ways Sonny wasn't. We could ask questions on the way to the bathhouse and keep forging a connection. If Tremaine learned more names and got to know us better, maybe he'd be less likely to pull the trigger.

He nudged Kenzie toward the kitchen, and Sonny turned back to Erik and me. "We'll head out once the toilet tours are done."

Erik looked a little too eager, and Sonny frowned. "Don't get your hopes up. I'll have the map. You can't get me lost, and I won't give you the chance to jump me." He tipped his head to one side. "In fact, I think I'll take along an extra insurance policy. That kid. I'll keep him right beside me every minute. If you don't dig hard enough, or if you try the least little thing to step out of line, it's the kid who'll get it, not you."

Erik looked stricken, and I'm sure I must have looked the same. Sonny laughed like a poker player who'd just slapped an unexpected ace on the table. Except we weren't playing for poker chips. We were playing for our lives.

We had arranged the perfect opportunity to neutralize him, but we couldn't act without endangering Chris. And I sure as hell wasn't taking that risk.

Chapter Twelve

Chris

Erik, Jon, and Kenzie stayed in the living room a long time, and we only had Bree's whispered reports from the top of the bookcase to know what was happening. Ryan woke up, which made Drake grumble, saying now we had to fight three of them. Sonny talked about the treasure and the map, which made Drake say lots of bad words.

I held my book, pretending to read, but I'd already read it twice and Mom's books were too boring. We pulled the curtains to cover the scraping on the window and hid everything else because we didn't know when Sonny would open the door again. Mom sat on the bed, staring at nothing.

Bree swung off the bookcase with a quiet warning, and a minute later, the door opened. Erik and Jon came in with a platter of sandwiches and more water. Jon set the sandwiches on the dresser. "Tremaine's taken Kenzie to an actual toilet, and when they get back, the rest of us will go, one at a time."

"Thank goodness." Mom almost smiled.

"Sonny wants to search for the treasure?" Of course, that was Drake's big worry.

Jon nodded but didn't look at anyone. "Erik and I will lead him to Sunset Cove."

I wasn't supposed to go to Sunset Cove. Too dangerous, Mom claimed, with the steep cliff on one side and the cove filled with jagged rocks. But for years, I'd gone there anyway to sit and look out over the sound. In summer, I had a hard time finding places that weren't crawling with campers. At the cove, I could be on my own.

But one day last summer, I found a bunch of older campers there, and Skagit and I hid in the bushes to watch. Signs said the cove was off-limits. Mom said kids would get sent home if caught there, but these boys waded in the cove's shallows, searching for sea urchins. They found a deep hole in the water, fifteen feet wide and more than ten feet deep, edged on all sides by large boulders.

Kevin, the biggest boy, shouted to the others. "I bet we can jump off the top of the cliff and land here in this deep part."

The rest of the boys shook their heads. "No way," one said. "I dare you to try."

Kevin looked scared, but I could tell he wouldn't back down. He scrambled his way to the top of the cliff and stood at the edge a long time. Then he backed away, gave a run and a jump, screamed like crazy, and landed right in the middle of the deep part. Everyone cheered, and I had to hold tight to Skagit to keep him from barking.

One boy after another made the leap, screaming the whole way down, then disappearing into the water for long seconds before resurfacing. They laughed and high-fived each other after they reached shore, bouncing on their toes, shivering with cold but excited to try again.

I waited until they'd gone, told Skagit to stay by the water, and climbed to the cliff top alone. I could see footprints leading to the rock where the boys had taken off for their jumps, the deep hole a dark-blue target a little way out from the base of the cliff. Those rocks looked sharp, and I almost chickened out. It was a long way down.

If I landed wrong and got hurt, it would be hard to get home. Plus, Mom would skin me alive if she knew I'd even thought about doing it. I stood on that rock a long time, trying to stop my twisting stomach. But the other boys had done it and they were okay, so ....

I took a good ten steps back. Ran hard. Leaped way out. I couldn't even scream on the way down, my chest clamped too tight to breathe, and when I hit the icy water, any air left inside me whooshed out all at once. I went deep, my feet touched bottom, then I came to the surface slowly, drifting upward because I was too stunned to swim. When I got back to air, I gasped and coughed, then made it to the low side of the cove where Skagit waited.

I'd done it. For real. There was nobody to high-five, so I hugged Skagit instead.

Over the summer, I made dozens of jumps, my insides churning just as bad every time. Mom never found out. Erik and Jon had picked a good place to take down Sonny. There were plenty of spots there where they could turn on him and try to get hold of the satellite phone.

But neither of them seemed very excited.

"What's wrong?" Mom got up from the bed and came closer. "What's happened?"

Erik lifted his hand, but he knew better than to touch her. "He's agreed to take Jon and me. We'll get him there, and we'll do the digging. But he says he's taking Chris as insurance for our good behavior."

"No." Mom stepped back fast like she'd been splashed with boiling water. She reached out for me, and her fingernails dug in hard enough to leave marks on my arm. "He can't take him. Chris won't go." She said it serious, but I could tell she was ready to cry.

"We won't take any chances." Jon patted me on the shoulder. "We won't do anything that could get Chris hurt." He kept his eyes on Mom, but she glared right back.

She let go and stood square in front of me to block him.

I gave her a hug. "It's okay. I'll do what Sonny says. Don't worry." I didn't mind going. Maybe I'd see Skagit to let him know I was okay.

Drake rocked back on his heels, arms crossed, a sneer on his face. "So, your big Plan A falls apart already. A perfect opportunity, and you're going to behave like scared little sheep." He dug in his pockets, pulled out the pointed picks he'd made, and slammed them on the dresser by the food. "No sense making these things unless you're willing to use them." He went to the window and got back to work, scraping the wood in sharp jabs with the blunt bandage scissors.

Erik and Jon talked to Mom, trying to calm her, and I looked at the sandwiches like I was trying to decide which one to take. Nobody noticed when I took a blue fiberglass pick and put it in my pocket. Then I ducked low and pulled the cloth bag out from under the bed.

"What do you need?" Erik frowned at me.

"My lucky shell."

He nodded a go-ahead.

I took care nobody saw, and I dug around in the bag. Found my shell. Found the two dog biscuits. And I slipped two of the wrapped scalpel blades into my pocket. Then I ate half a sandwich, stuffed the other half into one of Mom's socks from her dresser, and put it in my pocket too. That's one of the good things about being a kid. If you're quiet, people forget you're there.

Kenzie came back, and Tremaine took Bree to the bathhouse. Then Drake. Mom wouldn't go, just sat on the bed rocking. Then Sonny opened the door, holding a long length of clothesline. He told Erik, Jon, and me to come.

"You can't have Chris. Take me instead." Mom took a step forward, looking pissed off and ready to attack.

Sonny snorted. "Forget it. Come on, kid. Now." He waved the gun.

I gave Mom another hug, but she was crying and didn't hug back.

"Remember," Sonny said. "I won't hesitate to shoot."

Erik and Jon both took it serious, and I guess I believed Sonny too. We went.

Tremaine tied the door to Mom's room shut and stood outside the cottage with his gun to watch us. I tested the air as soon as we stepped out. No rain coming. It sure felt good to be outdoors in the sun where things smelled better. It would be easy to run. Head straight for the woods. But I didn't think I'd make it before one of them shot me.

We went to the bathhouse first, me looking everywhere for Skagit with no luck. We went in one at a time with Sonny guarding. Nothing there I could steal, and I didn't need to go. When I came out, Sonny grabbed hold of my arm. "Stand still."

He made Erik tie one end of the clothesline tight around my waist with the knot hard against my back. He made a loop in the other end of the rope and slipped it over his wrist like a leash.

"You two are going to lead." He pointed to Erik and Jon. "The kid comes next, with plenty of space between you and him, and I follow with my gun aimed at the kid. With him tied like this, he can't run, and you will stay on the path and do what I say. Are we clear?"

They both nodded.

What did it feel like to get shot? I'd killed plenty in my video games, taken shots at cartoon creatures that spurted fake blood and ended up torn to bits. I'd seen lots of dead things for real—fish washed on shore, a vole Skagit caught and laid at my feet, baby birds that fell out of their nests. But none of that was like getting shot myself. I figured I didn't want to find out.

We stopped at the storage shed for a pair of shovels and a metal detector. Sonny unlocked the padlock on the door, then relocked it after. Jon led. I knew two ways to get to Sunset Cove, one on a main trail, the other on a rocky washed-out path we all avoided. He took the bad route, setting a fast pace, maybe hoping Sonny would fall or twist his ankle. But he stayed right behind me, not even breathing hard enough for me to hear.

About ten minutes along, I noticed the bushes to the left side of the trail rustling. Skagit followed us through the underbrush, invisible except for the branches that shook as he passed. I gave him the hand signal to stay back, careful Sonny wouldn't see, but he must've noticed me looking that direction.

"What is it?" He stopped. The clothesline jerked me backward.

Jon returned to stand beside Erik. "What?"

"Over there. Something in the bushes. It's following us."

Jon looked. "I don't see anything. Probably a squirrel hoping for a handout."

I kept my face still. Jon was right to pick an animal that size, but he knew as well as I did there were no squirrels on Salish. An occasional deer would swim over from the mainland, but we didn't have any wild animals the size of Skagit. I waited, hoping Sonny didn't know that.

He grunted and shrugged. "Okay. Get going."

We started hiking again. Jon threw in a few twists and turns along the way, so it took us twice as long to get there, but the detours didn't help. Each time I peered back at Sonny, he walked steady and alert with his gun way too ready.

We came out on shore on the south side of Sunset Cove, where trees grew right to the water's edge. There was no beach here, just a jumble of boulders in the shallow water, a good place for crabs and mussels. The rocks went all the way around the cove's edge, but the land rose from where we stood, steep in some places, flattening out at the top of the cliff on the other side of the cove.

Erik pointed. "That's the headland we showed you on the map."

Sonny took a few steps and shaded his eyes. I pulled Mom's sock out of my pocket, flipped it inside-out and tossed the smushed turkey sandwich and the two dog biscuits behind me so they landed out of sight behind a log. Sonny looked my way, but by then I was just standing there, doing nothing. At least Skagit wouldn't starve.

Sonny waved us all forward. "Let's go."

The way to the top was a steep scramble, no real path leading up. Jon slung the metal detector on his back, and Erik used the shovels like walking sticks. I used both hands to hoist myself onto the tallest boulders, slowed only when the clothesline leash jerked me back, the rope scraping my stomach through my shirt. All three of us had on tennis shoes and made good time, but Sonny had trouble. One hand clutched the gun, and his city shoes had slick soles. He huffed and panted behind me, swearing under his breath each time he stumbled.

I managed to pitch a baseball-sized rock behind me as though it got kicked loose by accident, hoping to hit him, but it rattled downhill without him noticing. I'd heard the others describing tackling Sonny as part of Plan A, and this was a good place to do it, but he still had a leash that kept me close, and he still had his gun. The middle of my back felt tight and hot, like a target had been pinned there.

We reached the top at last, one of my favorite spots because of the view. Calm blue water stretched west all the way to Vendovi Island, with Sinclair Island visible beyond it on clear days like this one. Back the way we came, I could see across the tops of trees to the boat dock at the southern tip of Salish.

Erik and Jon stopped to look around, too, but Sonny had no interest in the scenery. "Okay, we're here. Finally. Where's this treasure supposed to be?"

Erik gestured around us. "All of this qualifies as a promontory. The box isn't supposed to be buried very deep." That eliminated half the area right off because of the large boulders scattered everywhere. A few saplings grew in the spaces between. "We should be strategic about this. Why don't we begin at the north end of the clearing and work our way south?"

"Whatever." The steep climb seemed to have tired Sonny. "Get started."

He nudged me toward a small madrona sapling and tied the end of my leash to the trunk. "Sit here."

I sat cross-legged in a small patch of shade and practiced being invisible. He sat on a nearby boulder where he could watch all three of us. Jon walked slow laps with the metal detector, and Erik dug where he pointed. He only dug holes a foot or two deep because when he dug farther, he hit solid rock.

Sonny didn't relax his guard. A few times on the climb he'd teetered off balance, and Jon or Erik could have thrown a rock or tossed one of their shovels at his head. But they couldn't do it because of me. When we were done here and went back down that steep stretch, heading home, it would be more of the same. They couldn't steal the satellite phone. They couldn't call for help. Nothing would change. Mom and the others would still be locked in. All because they protected me.

The smooth, flat rock I used to jump from sat only four or five steps away.

Every time I fidgeted, Sonny stared at me. I couldn't reach behind my back to undo the lumpy knot in the rope. I couldn't loosen the tie around the tree. I slid my hand into my side pocket, moving slow. So slow, not even an eagle would notice. I got hold of one of the scalpel blades with two fingers. Pulled it out. Rested my hands low in my lap.

I tried to tear the thick foil wrapper. No luck. I finally figured out it opened the way a Band-Aid does, two layers of flat foil that pulled apart at one end. I got hold of the edges and jerked. The blade flipped out and dropped to the ground, disappearing into the space in the middle of my crossed legs.

Jon's shovel clanged hard against a rock, and Sonny turned. I snatched the blade out of the dirt, and by the time he looked my way, both of my hands rested on my waist, nice and innocent. I grabbed the clothesline in my left hand. Held the blade in my right.

Sonny must have cut this piece of rope from Mom's washday line because it had a plastic coating with thick fiber in the middle. I made the cut a little at a time. It took a while, but the blade was sharp, and in three or four tries, I cut all the way through, only slicing my finger once. I held the cut rope ends in place so it looked like nothing had changed. I waited for my chance. And waited. And waited. For the first time ever before a jump, my stomach wasn't tumbling in somersaults.

I came close to giving up, then three terns swooped low overhead, flying toward the water and squawking loud the way they do. Erik and Jon looked up. Sonny looked up too.

I jumped onto my feet faster than a finger snap, running quick, pushing hard each time a foot hit the ground. One step. Two steps. Nobody saw. Three steps, and Jon yelled. Four steps, and Sonny yelled.

My fifth step hit my launch pad in exactly the right spot, and I leaped as far up and out as I could, my arms swinging forward to gain a few extra inches so I wouldn't land on the rocks below. The first shot came at the top of my jump. It whooshed past my face, then gravity grabbed hold, and I fell. Everyone shouted. The next shot came less than a second later, the scalding burn in my arm hitting first, then the sound catching up, loud in my ears and echoing off the face of the cliff.

The next instant, I hit icy water, not slipping in straight like I should have but going in crooked, my hip and shoulder slamming the surface hard. Then down I went, the water closing over my head, the bitter cold stunning my muscles, my body falling on and on and on until at last I hit bottom a dozen feet later. My hands grabbed at the gravel floor. Before I gathered enough sense to push off toward the surface, the current snatched at my clothes, tumbled me over, and dragged me along the bottom. I fought, but the current was stronger, grabbing hold like it was alive, bouncing me from one rock to the next and pulling me farther and farther away from shore.

I'd managed to get away from Sonny, but I couldn't escape the tide.

Chapter Thirteen

Jon

Chris ran, the rope that had tied him to the tree left curled on the ground, and I froze. Disbelief, fear, anger. It took several seconds to force myself forward. I must have yelled, and I'm sure I raced toward the brink with the wild hope of grabbing him before he went over the edge. But Sonny was faster.

His face twisted in fury, and he fired twice without an instant's hesitation, even though a ten-year-old child was his target. After Chris disappeared, he pivoted fast to aim at Erik and me. I skittered to a halt at the edge of the cliff. Erik slid to a stop, his wild lunge toward Sonny broken off mid-stride.

I leaned over the edge, scanning the rocks that lined the cove for a mangled body, but saw nothing. The water lapped gently along the base of the headland. "Chris!" Nothing moved.

"Get back here. Get back now." The ice in Sonny's voice made the words crackle.

Hot anger propelled me toward him. Not to obey, but to get my hands around his throat and squeeze. My arms stretched forward, and my fingers twitched in anticipation, but Erik grabbed my shoulder and hauled me back. Sonny lifted his revolver, ready to fire again.

I shrugged Erik off and forced myself to freeze while my body screamed for action. Even if both bullets had missed, how could Chris survive such a fall? "You bastard. He's just a kid."

"Could you see anything?" Erik's breath came fast and hard, and his voice rasped in a barely controlled panic.

I choked back tears. Shook my head. "We need to go look. He could be hurt. We need to find him."

Sonny tensed. "No. You've got digging to do."

I took two steps closer, fists clenched. "We're going to search for Chris, and we're doing it now."

The end of the gun's barrel yawned huge in front of me, and Sonny's hand tightened on the grip. A blood vessel pulsed high on his cheek, and his upper lip twitched once.

"Jon. Come on. Let's not have any more bloodshed." Erik tugged on my sleeve, but I ignored him.

I didn't break eye contact with Sonny, every muscle tense, waiting for the impact of a bullet. If his face showed a final decision to fire, I'd jump first. I'd end up dead, but maybe I could throw him off balance so Erik could take the gun. In that moment, death seemed a better option than returning home to face Leah.

Maybe Sonny saw my determination. Maybe he realized he was outnumbered. Maybe some tiny part of him was human. Whatever the reason, he frowned and gestured to the path down the cliff.

"You first. Then you." He pointed the gun at Erik. "I've proven I mean business. Don't try anything."

We didn't even retrieve the gear. I retraced our steps, jumping from one rock to the next at a breakneck pace. Erik followed more slowly, and the gap between us widened. This steep descent was the best chance we had of tripping Sonny and getting his gun, but the possibility didn't occur to me until later. All I could think about was Chris. Battered against a rock. Shot dead before he landed. Injured but alive, desperately needing help.

I ran faster, calling his name the whole way. Called until my voice gave out, pausing every few moments to listen for a response. Nothing.

I reached the water's edge and waded in, skirting boulders and stumbling for footing on the rocky bottom. Sonny made Erik stop on land, holding him hostage while I searched. I worked my way around the cove until I reached the spot below where Chris had jumped. No body at the base of the cliff or impaled on the razor-sharp rocks. The tide pulled out, the drag on my feet and legs strong and insistent. If he was unconscious—or dead—when he landed, he could have been swept away long before I arrived.

I pushed into deeper water, a few yards out from the base of the cliff, and gasped when the bottom disappeared beneath me. One minute, I stood knee deep, and the next, I was treading water. Over time, freaky tides had carved a deep hollow in the uneven bottom close to shore. The strongest current tugged at me down deep, sucking water out through a narrow gap between two boulders.

If Chris had landed here, his body would have been carried right out.

I returned to the shallows and explored the full extent of the cove, my feet and legs numb with cold, my fingers blue, my teeth chattering.

"Enough! He's gone." Sonny sounded serious. Erik sat on a log, and Sonny stood behind him, out of reach, gun at the ready. He waved me back.

I made a final inspection of the cove. Still nothing. By the time I worked my way back to them, I was stumbling, chilled to the marrow, and violently shivering. I dropped onto the log beside Erik, but Sonny shook his head. "Let's go. Back to the cottage. We can come back tomorrow to finish looking for the cache."

I wasn't going to stand just because he told me to, and I wasn't going to dig on command. No more. But Erik stood and tugged me to my feet. "Come on, man. You'll feel better if you walk."

Nothing was going to make things any better, but I took a few awkward steps. On autopilot, I headed toward the most direct path, but Erik steered me onto the circuitous route we had followed to get there. My brain struggled to think, as numb as my feet. My god, Chris was gone.

Sonny followed, careful to keep us in sight without getting close enough to let us tackle him. My wet shoes grew heavy with clinging mud, but the sun dried my clothing and sensation seeped back into my legs. We passed a large, twisted madrona tree, its bark deep red and peeling, the trunk half dead from a lightning strike.

The last time I'd been in this part of the island was the previous summer when I taught the Orcas how to use their compasses. This tree had been the starting point of the course I'd
designed, and we'd hiked here for my lecture. Chris, too young
for camp, had squatted at the fringes of the group with Skagit
beside him, listening while I explained.

The day had been overcast and chilly, and the wind pierced
summer clothing with ease. The boys joked and wrestled each
other, more interested in that evening's talent show than in how
to navigate in the wild. Anything involving numbers caused
their eyes to glaze, but Chris hung on every word.

When I finished, I broke the group into four teams of three
and gave each team a copy of the game directions. "There are
six compass headings listed here. Follow the first heading for a
quarter mile, and you'll find a tree with a red flag. There's a
colored marker hanging from the tree. Mark your paper with it."

That caught some interest.

"Then, from the first tree, follow the second heading for a
quarter mile, and, again, look for a red flag and use the second
colored marker. The sixth marker is back at our tipis. Any team
that gets all six colors in the right order gets double dessert
tonight."

Extra sugar. That brought cheers.

"What if we get lost?" The question came from Freddy, the
camper who tended to get lost on the path from tipi to bathhouse. I'd been careful to put him on a team with a camper who
was a veteran Boy Scout.

"If you get lost, head due east, and you'll hit the road. But if you take that route back, you won't get your marks."

The campers asked more questions, but in the end, everyone appeared to understand. Maybe I even detected some degree of enthusiasm. I sent the groups out at five-minute intervals, laughing and jostling each other as they held compasses at eye level and attempted to walk a straight line.

After the last group hiked out of sight, I gathered my gear. I would take down the flags and markers as I went, while keeping an eye open for any team that got too confused.

"Can I do it?"

I'd forgotten Chris, who still sat to one side. He sounded hesitant, as if he expected an automatic *no*. "Sure. Want to use my compass? I'll come along and help if you need it."

His entire face lit up, but more than that, his entire body expanded. He held my compass as if it were fragile, checked for the first coordinate on the list, and took a sighting. Then, he headed off at full speed with Skagit beside him. I hustled to follow.

Unlike the teams of older boys, who'd left the clearing cautiously, zigzagging as they tried to stay on course, Chris had sighted on the farthest point he could see, and he forged through the undergrowth in an almost perfect line. I'd made the red flags enormous, knowing the campers wouldn't hit their target dead center, but Chris took the most direct route. By the time I retrieved the flag, he'd marked his paper and taken off again.

I walked beside him the last few minutes. "Have you ever heard of orienteering?" He shook his head. "Instead of being given coordinates on an island you know well, you'd be somewhere unfamiliar, often in a park or national forest. You get a topographic map with a series of places marked on it, and it's up to you to figure out how to get from one spot to the next. It's a race, based on the total time it takes you."

"A race? Like with trophies?"

"Yep. And prizes. There are canoe orienteering races too."

He grinned. "I could do that. Could you teach me the map part?"

"Of course. I hope to teach the whole group. I'll be sure to include you when we do it."

He was the only camper who returned with all six colors on his sheet, and I hadn't helped him at all. He ate not two but three huge servings of ice cream that night, and he deserved every bite. Most adults wouldn't have been able to do it, and he was only nine. Every other team had quit before reaching the fourth station, trudging home along the road in defeat. The following week, they howled in protest when I proposed a more advanced competition, and I gave up the idea.

Chris's face crumpled when I told him. "We'll find time to do it when it's just the two of us, I promise." But the summer had passed, and I hadn't found the time. The memory left a sour taste in my mouth. I'd never get my chance now.

"Why?" Erik and I were walking side by side on a wider stretch of the path, and I whispered my question. "Why did he jump?"

Erik shook his head and shrugged. "Did you see the rope? The knot hadn't been untied. I kicked dirt over one of those scalpel blade wrappers. Don't think Sonny noticed."

"No talking!" Sonny yelled from behind, and I dropped back, letting Erik take the lead.

Chris had sliced through the rope. Then, instead of ducking back into the scrub trees behind him, he'd taken the chance of running across open ground to propel himself off the cliff edge. It made no sense, and the illogic of it bugged me. Sonny thought of Chris as just a kid, a vulnerable hostage. But I'd known the boy almost his whole life, and he was no fool. He knew this island in ways even I didn't.

I looked to the side of the path, watching for movement that might indicate Skagit still followed. Nothing. But Chris wasn't with us, and that might explain Skagit's absence.

I hadn't puzzled my way to any answers by the time we arrived at the meadow. My steps slowed, as did Erik's. Leah had counted on us to protect her son. How could we tell her he was gone?

I wanted to protect Leah. I wanted to save her. Instead, I was delivering a lethal blow. She would never recover from this. Nobody could. I'd promised to keep Chris safe. I'd failed.

Pain lanced through me as if I were the one who'd been shot.

Drake stood at the front window, looking out, and the stricken expression on his face as he saw us approach twisted my insides. Erik opened the front door. We stepped inside. Kenzie was kneeling by the couch, spoon-feeding Ryan with Tremaine standing guard. She turned at our entrance, her face relaxing when she saw us. Then Sonny closed the door behind us.

She stared at the door, waiting, then looked to me. I couldn't meet her eyes, but she must have seen the truth on my face. "No. Oh my god. No. No, please." The pottery bowl slipped from her hand, hit the floor with a crash, and shattered. Big gobs of oatmeal splattered against the couch.

She stood and stumbled toward me, then stopped, her chest heaving. Tremaine stared at Sonny, stunned, his gun hanging at his side. "What happened?"

"The goddamn kid killed himself, that's what happened. He ran. I fired."

Tremaine flinched, his face paling. "Sonny. No. My god, no. How could you?"

"What the hell did you expect? Don't look at me like that. I missed. I didn't kill him. He killed himself."

Throughout the past horrifying twenty-four hours, Sonny had been ruthless but calm. Now, his voice dripped fury. His hands shook like an old man's. His claim that his shots had missed Chris had no substance. None of us knew for sure.

He waved his gun at Kenzie, Erik, and me. "Go on. Get inside. I'm not dealing with you lot any longer today."

Erik stepped past me and fumbled at the knot that tied the bedroom door closed. The rope dropped to the floor, the same clothesline that had held Chris leashed to Sonny. I blinked tears away, but it made no difference.

"Come on." I took Kenzie's arm and eased her forward to follow Erik. My final survey of the living room showed Sonny, tense and angry, Tremaine, immobile, looking ill, and Ryan, slumped on the couch with unfocused eyes.

The door closed behind us. Drake leaned against the window, his face in his hands. Bree dropped from the bookcase, tears streaming down her cheeks. Leah stood at the wardrobe, frozen. The others must not have said anything because she stared blankly at the door long after it closed, then seized Erik's arm in a grip so fierce he winced. "Where. Is. My. Son?" Each word forced its way out as if fighting uphill.

Erik was shaking. "He jumped off the top of the cliff. Sonny shot at him. Jon searched, but ..."

She recoiled as if every blunt word landed as a physical blow. "No." A whisper, not a scream. She gasped for air and folded forward, her body crumpling to the floor. A deep guttural moan filled the room, the howl of a gravely injured animal.

Kenzie and Bree rushed toward her. Erik whispered details to Drake. I slid to the floor and pressed my head to my knees. I wanted to smash my way out of the room. I wanted to seize Sonny by the throat. I wanted to turn back time, protect Chris, protect Leah, protect all of us.

Instead, a cold fist closed so viciously around my heart, I could hardly believe it was still beating. My head pounded, my hands shook, my muscles refused to budge. All I could see was Chris in his final moment, his body silhouetted against the sky as he leaped, alive and vibrant and full of intention. Chris, with what looked like a smile on his face. Chris, as he appeared before the deafening blast of gunfire hit, before he fell, before he plunged out of sight.

Chapter Fourteen

Kenzie

Grief lurked always in my core, waiting to pounce, but as I sat on the bed, holding Leah, it clawed its way out of hiding, ripping and shredding its way to the surface, tearing off scar tissue and reopening old wounds. I cried for Chris, for Tim, for the terror and hopelessness of the past thirty hours. For the brutal pain Leah endured now and for the merciless guilt and loss she would carry in the future. I cried for all of us, but my tears changed nothing.

Leah's sobs slowed as exhaustion took over. "I can't believe he's gone. I want to believe he's still out there, but I know that cove—the cliff, the drop. Those rocks. How could he survive? How? My god, I can't even go out and search for him."

That triggered another bout of crying. I rubbed her back and made meaningless sounds. What else could I do? Nothing. She seemed barely aware of my existence.

After a time, she shook her head, and words flooded out. "I thought we were safe here. We could live apart from the world. I got lonely at times, but here I could raise a son who wouldn't be as afraid as I was. Afraid to leave my apartment, afraid to walk down the street, afraid of every man who glanced my way. People always wonder how I can live here unprotected. They have it backward. Alone here, we stayed safe."

Leah, afraid? Since Sonny arrived, we'd all been scared, but fear didn't seem to be part of her core makeup. After a moment, she continued, staring at the floor as if talking more to herself than to me. "I told Chris I came to the island so I could be a potter full time. I told him I only knew his father for a weekend. None of that's true."

The room grew still around us. Her voice was soft, but in the small space, everyone could hear. I held up a hand to warn her, but she seized it in hers, and her words poured out. "A million years ago, I taught middle school in Seattle and loved it. Pottery was only a hobby. I did craft fairs in the summer, sold on consignment a few places, worked on new projects on weekends. I had a busy life."

She took a deep breath and steadied herself. "I dated a fellow teacher for more than a year and hoped we'd make a life together. Then I caught him cheating. When I broke things off, he went ballistic." Her voice dropped. "Months later, I came home from work, and he was waiting for me." She paused, and her grip on my hand grew so tight, my bones ground together. "I fought, but he beat me and ..." She looked away. "... raped me."

A gasp came from somewhere in the room, and I turned. Jon's eyes had widened and his jaw hung slack, but his stunned expression only lasted a second, replaced at once by the brittle tension of intense anger. He turned aside, but not before I saw tears building.

ISLAND ENDGAME   169

Leah's grip on my hand tightened. "For months, I barely left the apartment. I didn't realize I was pregnant until little flutters woke me. I was too overwhelmed to make a decision, so I did nothing. I had the vague idea I would put the child up for adoption, but when they put my baby in my arms, when I actually saw him ...." She closed her eyes. "Chris came from the worst moment in my life, but he turned into the best thing that ever happened to me. How am I supposed to go on?"

I pulled her into my arms and held on tight as her sobs took over again.

I had wondered whether I'd be able to attack one of these men if the opportunity arose. I had my answer now. Rage built in my stomach, expanding fast to encompass my chest, my throat, my mind. Anger displaced grief, and adrenaline-charged power surged. When I turned Leah loose and looked around the room, I saw my determination reflected in the people around me. Bree cried silently. Erik muttered profanities. Drake twisted one of the wire hangers into a shapeless mass.

Jon's face held no expression, a frozen mask. "We have to stop Sonny. Stop him now."

The discussion that followed contained more frustration, more agitation, and more argument than our previous ones, but nobody had answers. Suggestions grew wilder, schemes of attack and revenge that no one with any sense would consider.

When we'd exhausted our ideas, Drake returned to his window. "If we can get out this way, we can go to the cove. Maybe, with all of us searching, we can find ... we can look ... we can try to ...." He gulped and turned away. "This is all my fault ... I'm so sorry, Leah ... so sorry ..." His voice faded to nothing, but his lips kept moving in a catechism of guilt.

Escape out the window would be too slow and too passive, but it was the best option we had. We settled into a restless silence, broken occasionally by Leah's sobs. The quiet offered no comfort. The passage of time didn't kill my rage.

When Tim died, it was sudden and unexpected, but it was accompanied by a wild flurry of activity. EMTs, trying to resuscitate. Police, investigating a child's death. The body, transferred to the hospital, then to a funeral home. Friends and neighbors descended in a steady stream with hugs and condolences and home-baked casseroles. The fuss and commotion forced a pretense of normalcy.

Leah had none of those distractions.

Jon had been quiet since his return, and he sat now on the floor with a spare pillowcase in his hands. He was shredding the fabric, pulling it apart one thread at a time. A mound of white fluff grew on the floor beside him. I joined him in the corner by the bookcase. "Is there any chance Chris survived?" I kept my voice low.

His expression gave me the answer I dreaded. "I searched the entire cove, thinking he could be caught on one of the rocks along its edge, unconscious but alive." He closed his eyes, his face contorting, but his hands still shredded the cloth. "The tide was going out. The currents in the cove are strong. My best guess is that he was swept out fast, before we got down to search." His jaw tightened. "Nothing's impossible, but I don't want to give Leah false hope."

Anger warmed my insides, and the heat spread outward, insistent. I tried to drown the flame in common sense, to be calm and rational, but I couldn't. It was Chris. It was Tim. My hatred of Sonny burned like acid.

Hours passed. Late afternoon. Sonny and Tremaine had been in the kitchen, so Bree wasn't on lookout when the door to our prison opened. Sonny called. "Nurse. Tend to your patient."

Nothing in his voice suggested one ounce of remorse over shooting Chris, and something in me snapped.

"No." I stepped in front of the others so he could see me.

The room had been quiet, but now no one even breathed.

Sonny lifted his gun. "I said, come tend to your patient. *Now.*"

I forced myself to hold still. "No. I'm not helping anymore. Ryan is stable. You and Tremaine can take care of him." The gun had a magnetic pull, drawing my focus, the light from the window sparkling on the bright, shiny metal. It took grim determination to meet Sonny's eyes, but I locked onto them and stood fast.

His face tightened, his anger close to the surface. He stepped across the threshold and surveyed the room.

The others sat or stood, unmoving, but every face showed anger and resistance. He no longer faced a group too cowed to challenge him.

He frowned and fanned the gun in an arc, aiming at each person in turn. "Don't be stupid. There's no need for anyone else to get hurt."

But then his gaze settled on one spot, and his expression changed, an element of puzzlement creeping in. I twisted. He was staring at the brightly colored cover of Chris's book, which sat on the end table where he'd left it that morning. *The Titan's Curse*, the same one he'd been reading when he and I first chatted about books. He'd brought it back from his room to finish and had been reading it again out of boredom.

Sonny stared at the book for an endless moment. Then he looked up at the gap that led to Chris's bedroom, then back at the book.

I couldn't breathe. Sonny had searched Chris's room soon after he arrived. He'd gone in there again when he had Drake nail the door closed. Both times, the book had probably been sitting out in the open, on the bed or end table. And now it sat here, in a locked room where it didn't belong.

The puzzlement on Sonny's face shifted back into anger. "All of you. Out in the living room. *Now.*" I stood closest, and he lunged forward, seized my arm in a painful twist, and pressed the gun against my head, the cold barrel grating hard against my skull. "Tremaine! They're coming out. Get everyone flat on the floor, face down."

He jerked me to one side to allow the others to pass. I thought for a moment Drake would snap. I pictured him lunging, Sonny firing, my head exploding, and I couldn't suppress a whimper. Time slowed, and—for an endless moment—death felt tempting. But only for a moment. I'd come here to fight for my future, and if that meant fighting Sonny, I'd do it.

Drake and everyone else obeyed and headed into the living room. Sonny dragged me in last and flung me to my knees. "Get down."

We packed together on the floor like livestock waiting for slaughter.

"Tremaine, if anybody tries to get up, shoot them." Sonny stormed back into the bedroom.

Drawers opened and closed. The wardrobe doors slammed. Throughout his search, Sonny kept up an escalating stream of profanity. He must have searched every square inch because endless minutes passed before he returned. "Look at this."

He spoke to Tremaine, but I lifted my head to see. Sonny held the canvas bag he'd found hidden under the bed, and he dumped its contents on the sofa beside Ryan. Sonny had stuffed everything he found into the bag. Bandage scissors, scalpel blades, casting tape wrappers. Hanger wires, bookends, extension cord. Most damning of all, two of the lethal fiberglass ice picks.

"I thought you already searched the room." Tremaine poked at the heap. "How'd they get all this?"

"Sent the kid over the wall. This is how that little shit got his rope off." He pointed to one of the blades. "They've even been whittling through the window frame." Sonny looked us over. "Search them."

He kept his gun on us, and Tremaine stepped from one person to the next, forcing us to roll as he emptied pockets and patted us down. Drake growled. Leah gave Tremaine a deadly look.

He tossed aside insignificant items that had made their way back into our pockets—Leah's hair elastic, my decorated rock, a metal trinket of Jon's. But he found three more ice picks, one in my pocket, one in Drake's, one in Jon's. Erik and Jon both had scalpel blades. Drake had a hard chunk of fiberglass he'd shaped to slide over his hand like brass knuckles. Every discovery prompted more profanity from Sonny, and his voice grew increasingly agitated.

When Tremaine finished, Sonny left him on guard and retrieved a hammer and nails from the kitchen. The sound of violent pounding came from the bedroom, and when he returned, he looked tense but smug. "That fixes things. All of you. Get back in."

One at a time, we scooped up the items we'd been left, got to our feet, and trudged back to our prison. Clothing lay scattered everywhere, drawers hung open, books stood piled in random heaps. He'd taken all the hangers. The window had been nailed shut with an additional dozen nails. He'd taken our tools and weapons. Worse, he'd taken our hope.

Sonny slammed the door behind us. He hadn't ordered me to do anything more for Ryan, and that was probably wise because I seethed, ready to do more harm than good. He also hadn't given us any food or water, and there seemed little upside to pointing out the oversight.

Leah crumpled onto the bed, tucking her knees to her chest in a tight ball. Jon and Erik stood shoulder to shoulder with clenched fists and matching looks of frustration. Drake leaned against the window. Bree scooted up to her listening post.

I sat on the floor with my back against the wall and closed my eyes. We were defenseless, and it was my fault. If I hadn't stood up to Sonny ... if he hadn't come close enough to see ... if I'd realized the risk the book carried and hidden it ....

Guilt, my faithful friend, wrapped its arms around me and held me close.

Chapter Fifteen

Jon - Tuesday

No food, no water, no way out. Tuesday dawned with plenty of sunshine, but we were a depressed and surly group. The room stank of unwashed bodies, stale urine, and desperation, making every breath putrid. Hour after hour, nothing happened. I spent much of my time with my eyes closed, trying to pretend I had unlimited space around me, but the trick didn't work. Every time I opened them, the room looked a little smaller. The hard knot of near-panic that lived in my chest whenever I was trapped in small places burned hot, and I struggled to keep it from bursting into flames.

Leah had retreated into a huddle, rocking in an erratic rhythm and humming in a monotone, unresponsive to any of us. Her exhausted crying of the day before had worried me, but I preferred her gut-wrenching sobs to this zombie-like withdrawal. I tried to imagine the anguish of losing a child but suspected my empathy didn't come close.

I replayed the story she'd told about Chris's birth a thousand times. It explained so much. Her choice to live here on the island. The careful distance she kept from men. The silence she'd maintained about her past. I wanted to take her in my arms, hold her tight, and tell her everything would be okay. But I suspected such reassurance would be unwelcome, and in our current situation, it was a brutal lie.

Desperate to do something, anything, to console her, I pulled Kenzie to the side. "Is there anything we can do to help Leah?"

She shook her head. "We can't fix this." She licked chapped lips. "Food and water wouldn't hurt."

We'd had nothing since the sandwiches the previous morning. Hunger clawed at my insides and a headache threatened. The lack of water would soon be critical. I'd done plenty of backpacking trips with limited food, but without water, weakness hit early and thinking became clouded.

Drake stood by the window, running his thumb over the new nails that gleamed in the sash. He'd kept his hands busy every waking moment since we were captured, scraping at the window or shaping the fiberglass tape. Now, he shifted from one foot to the other, restless.

I joined him. "How are you doing?"

Fatigue made his eyes look dark and haunted. "Not so good. I need a drink, and I don't mean water." He wrapped his arms around himself as if he needed their strength to keep himself from flying apart. "I'm screwed. Even if Sonny gets paid off, I owe others. And Chris ... I never meant ... I didn't ..."

He choked down a dry swallow, his jaw working hard. "Once we get out of here, I'm dead."

Even though Drake hadn't killed Chris, I couldn't dredge up an ounce of sympathy for him. He'd brought this all upon us. "How did you get into such a mess?"

He stared out the window. "At first, I just got over my head with credit cards. You know what the last few years have been like. Too little snow, then so much damn snow, nobody could even drive into the mountains. No skiers, no salary, no fallback plan."

"So, what did you do?"

"Went to Vegas."

Ouch. "I take it things did not go well."

"I needed a decent stake. Borrowed from the wrong people. Lost every penny." He closed his eyes and leaned his head against the cold glass.

I gave his shoulder a squeeze, but it didn't seem to register.

Our conversation had been quiet, but of course everyone had heard. Erik, sitting with his back against the door, twisted his hands together. "Drake, it's my fault you and Bree are here. I convinced you a treasure hunt was worth it. I'm so sorry."

Bree shrugged. "This is Sonny and Tremaine's doing, not yours. The question is, what now?"

We all looked to Erik, but he shook his head, apparently out of schemes.

"Damn it all! Do something!" Drake's fist thumped against the wall, and the silver-framed photo of Chris popped off its nail and crashed to the floor. The frame was a standard eight-by-ten in height and width, but it was attached to a box at least two inches deep. The box sprang open on impact, and a cascade of papers and a small leather-bound book slid across the floor. Leah looked up at the sound and gave a heartbreaking groan. I bent to help.

Leah apparently used the box to store valuable documents. Birth certificates and passports for her and Chris. A will. A healthcare directive. A photograph of a man and woman standing with a young girl who looked like Leah. I shuffled them into a stack and returned them to the frame's compartment.

"What's this?" Drake picked up the book. Cracks marred the leather binding, and the edges of the cover were frayed. He flipped through the yellowed pages, which were filled with tight, old-fashioned handwriting.

Leah roused herself. "That's Allman's journal. The bit about the cache is his last entry. Be careful. It's falling apart."

I reached to put the book away, but Drake shook his head and carried it to the window, flipping pages and reading intently.

Kenzie cleared her throat. "In forty-eight hours, the boat will be delivered, right? Let's assume Sonny and his crew take the boat and leave. You've said the other counselors are supposed to arrive that afternoon?"

Leah sighed and turned away. Erik answered. "The rest of the counselors expect us to meet them in Anacortes at two on Thursday. If we don't show and don't answer calls, they'll come to investigate. But it might take until Friday before they get worried enough."

"Seventy-two hours from now?" Kenzie's face grew solemn. "We can hold out without food that long if we have to, but we'll need water before then."

Sit here, locked up, for three more days? My gut rebelled. Claustrophobic nausea wasn't the only problem. "You're assuming they're willing to let us tell the world where they're headed and what happened to Chris."

More silence settled, this time a silence layered with palpable fear. The only way to keep us all quiet was murder. Sonny, shooting someone in an instant of anger? I'd seen him do it. Sonny, slaughtering six people in cold blood? I wanted to believe such a thing was impossible, but after the countless mass shootings of the past few years, I could easily visualize it. *Seven Dead at Island Summer Camp* would barely make a front-page headline.

Drake crossed the room. Picked up a pencil stub from the dresser and leaned over the small journal, making marks.

"Hey! Stop that. Don't mess it up. It's almost a hundred years old." For the first time in two days, Leah's voice had some strength.

Drake set the pencil down and turned to face us, his expression one of pure delight. "I know where the treasure is. I know where Allman hid it. He wrote the directions in code."

He kept his voice to a whisper, as had become normal, but his statement had the impact of a shout. Leah, Bree, and Kenzie stared at him. I leaned back against the wall. Drake had lost it at last.

Erik scrambled to his feet and reached for the journal, but Drake hung on to it. "Hey, I'm the one who figured it out. Back off, and I'll show you."

The others crowded around, and I joined reluctantly. *This had better be good.*

Drake turned the brittle pages to reach the final entry and held it so we could see. The book was pocket-sized, and each line held only four or five words. "Look at the first letter of each line."

Kenzie was closest. "You've circled the first letter of the first three lines. T-H-E. *The.* But you've also circled the first letters of the next four lines, T-O-O-R. That makes no sense."

Drake grinned. "Read the second word backwards."

"*Root.*" She gasped. "Holy cow. You may have it."

The atmosphere in the room electrified. In that moment, we weren't prisoners grieving the loss of a child, we weren't hopeless and helpless, we were adventurers on the edge of discovery.

Drake ran his finger down the page, then flipped to the next one. "The pattern continues. One word is written forward, the next backward, and the next forward, all the way through, using the first letter of each line. When Leah copied it onto bigger paper to send to Erik, they weren't the first letters of each line anymore."

Leah shook her head, looking dazed. "I never noticed. I was so focused on copying every word exactly as he wrote it, making sure I kept even the misspellings and the punctuation the same. It never occurred to me to look for a pattern on the page."

Bree said, "Wow," then we all started talking at once.

But Kenzie waved her hands. "Quiet! Settle down. Drake, what does it say?"

We all turned to him, and he stood tall, looking like his old self despite his gaunt cheeks and dirty hair. He cleared his throat and took in his rapt audience, then dropped his eyes to the page. He'd only circled the words on the first page, so he read slowly, picking out one word at a time, pausing when it was hard to figure out where the forward word ended and the backward word began. Everyone leaned forward, their balance suspended on the meaning of each and every syllable.

"The root cellar. South wall, third row of stones from the bottom, fifth stone from the left. Dig with care."

We remained silent when he finished. Nothing about a promontory. That text must have been meant to confuse anyone who stumbled on the entry.

"Root cellar?" Bree asked. "I've never heard of a root cellar on the island. And I don't remember seeing it on the map." Drake shrugged, and some of the excitement in the room fizzled away.

But I knew where it was.

"I've been there." Everyone turned to look at me. "It's caved in now, but you can still see its outline. The walls were stone. Probably with a sod and timber roof. It's near Sunset Cove, close to Allman's original homestead."

Erik laughed. "You mean we almost led Sonny to it by accident? Unbelievable."

"I know that place," Leah said. "I thought the stones marked some sort of outbuilding. I didn't realize they'd dug down for a root cellar."

Amazing. We had specific directions. If the cache Allman described was still there, we could find it. A sense of pleased anticipation filled the room until Drake slammed the flat of his hand onto the dresser. "It doesn't matter. Nothing matters. We're never getting out of here. If we tell Sonny what we've figured out, he'll take it all and probably kill us in the bargain. And if we do get out, the treasure might not be there, or it won't be enough. I'm dead either way. It's hopeless." His voice had a frantic edge that had become all too familiar.

We'd all been eager to indulge in a moment of fantasy, kids delighted with a treasure map with a giant X marking the spot. But his tirade flipped a switch. The walls closed in even tighter than before.

"Dammit." Erik's face reddened. "I've had enough." He gestured toward Bree, his movement jerky. "Are they still in the kitchen?"

She popped up to her spy post. "I can see Tremaine at the table. They must have Ryan with them. The couch is empty. Can't hear what they're saying."

"To hell with this." Erik pounded on the door. "Hey there! Hey! We need food and water! Hey there! Sonny!"

"Erik, wait. What's the plan? What do we do if—" Bree dropped to the floor, but he ignored her, pounding steadily. Drake crammed the fragile journal into his back pocket and stepped forward to stand behind Erik.

"Shut up in there!" Sonny yelled from the opposite side of the door.

"Food! Water! You can't leave us like this!"

Leah got off the bed and joined Drake, her face haggard but intense. The three of them stood together, eager and ready to pounce. I exchanged glances with Bree and Kenzie, but they seemed as uncertain as I. Was this merely a demand for food and water or something more?

I held up a hand. "Wait, we need to—"

Erik staggered backward, pushed by a sudden thrust of the door. He fell into Drake, who caught and steadied him. The door bounced off the wall and stopped, half open.

Sonny stood far enough from the threshold to stay out of reach. He held his gun in the same competent way, but his eyes narrowed, and his lips were stretched so thin they were nearly invisible. His entire body pulsed with anger. I instinctually stepped back.

"Stop talking!" It was more of a snarl than a command.

"No!" Drake stepped in front of Erik and pulled the door open the rest of the way. "You can't keep us in here like this."

I glanced into the living room. Tremaine was stepping out of the kitchen, heading our way with a full pitcher of water and a plate piled high with sandwiches. "Drake, wait a minute, we should—"

Too late. Drake raised clenched fists and lunged forward with a guttural scream, his legs churning hard, propelling him straight at Sonny.

His shoulder slammed into Sonny's chest with an audible thud, and they teetered together, lost balance, and fell. Sonny's gun disappeared between them, his hand trapped by Drake's weight. The instant they hit the floor, the muffled bang of a gunshot sounded, and Drake's body gave a galvanic jerk.

Leah screamed. Tremaine dropped the food and water with a crash. He raced across the room, yelling, focused on the two bodies on the floor.

Erik and I jumped forward and rolled Drake over. Kenzie gasped over my shoulder, and I turned away after a single glimpse. Drake's chest had vaporized, replaced by a bloody, mangled mass of shattered bone, shredded muscle, and bloody bits that might have been chunks of lung. His eyes were open and fixed, already glazing over. The air filled with the harsh, metallic smell of raw meat.

Sonny lay unmoving on his back, stunned. Blood saturated his shirt, and pieces of Drake's flesh clung to his skin.

Tremaine bent to shake Sonny's shoulder. "Sonny! Sonny, are you okay?"

The moment froze for an instant. Sonny's gun rested on his belly. Drake's body lay on the far side of him, with Erik on his knees, plucking at Drake's sleeve. Tremaine leaned across the body, his focus still on Sonny. In the bedroom doorway, Bree and Leah clung to each other, staring at the scene.

That left Kenzie and me, standing together with the cottage door behind us. The front door. The unguarded door. The door to freedom.

I couldn't leave the others. I couldn't flee while they were trapped. I couldn't abandon Leah. Or could I?

As prisoners, we'd run out of options, trapped at the mercy of Sonny's every whim. But if I could escape, perhaps I could find a way to save us all. I had supplies in my tipi and maybe others had the same.

Leah would believe the worst of me. Running branded me a coward. But it might be my only chance to save her.

My throat tightened, cutting off air. My stomach clenched, my body went numb. I seized Kenzie's hand, took a giant step back, turned, and ran, dragging her behind me.

Two steps to the door. Grabbed the knob. Hauled the door inward. Kenzie pulled back, saying words I didn't hear. I yanked her forward, raced outside, and headed left toward the shed, hoping to use its bulk to protect us.

Kenzie's hand twisted in my grip, but I had no patience for an argument. "Run, damn you. Run!"

I checked behind us. Tremaine stood in the doorway, lifting his gun, and I jerked Kenzie to the side at the same moment a bullet whizzed past.

The near miss made up her mind. I let go, and we zigzagged across the meadow, stumbling through the thick grass in a race toward the forest.

Tremaine ran after us, shouting and firing until he emptied his magazine, but after that first shot no other bullets came close.

We reached the tree line and kept going, plunging through a mix of ferns and scrub that slowed us only slightly. A hundred yards in, Kenzie stopped, panting hard. "Far enough?"

I checked behind us. No movement. "For now."

She stepped forward, lifted her arm, and delivered a slap that rocked me. "How could you drag me out of there? You bastard! We abandoned them!"

My cheek burned, but the bruise to my ego hurt worse. "You think I wanted to leave them? You think I'll be able to live with myself if this ends up harming Leah or the others? Drake is dead. You saw him. On top of what happened to Chris? This situation is going straight to hell. I just saved you."

"You can't know that. You don't know what Sonny will do now."

"Well, he's sure as hell not going to apologize, hand over his weapons, and turn everyone loose, is he?"

We stood red-faced and glaring at one another, more like mortal enemies than two people on the same team.

I dropped my gaze and tried to calm my tone. "Maybe this is the only way to help. Maybe, out here, we can do something."

Kenzie scrunched her face, looking doubtful, but at least she'd stopped yelling.

"Do you want to go back?"

She flinched. There was quiet for a moment, then she whispered, "No."

"What? I couldn't hear you."

Her head snapped my way. "No." Defiant. Almost obnoxious. But the right answer.

"Okay. We're out. Next step is water, food, and supplies, all of which should be in my tipi unless Sonny has done more scavenging. Come on."

I turned and headed through the trees to skirt the meadow, doing my best to pretend I knew what I was doing. The fresh air energized me with every breath, and the ability to move and make choices gave me hope, but none of that meant success.

After a long moment, the small sounds of Kenzie's uneven steps on the underbrush followed me. I would have been far happier if someone else could take charge, but I was stuck. The lives of everyone else depended on the decisions I made next.

Chapter Sixteen

Kenzie

I stumbled through the woods behind Jon, angry, sad, relieved, and scared. Too confused to pull the snarl of emotions apart. Too confused to make a plan. Too confused to do much more than put one foot in front of the other. Joy at being no longer trapped bubbled deep below the surface, but I kept the lid clamped tight and didn't let it escape. My thoughts tasted sour. Joy had no place here.

Drake, dead. His anxiety, his rage, and his money problems, all snuffed out in an instant. But Bree. Leah. Erik. They were still trapped, now in a worse situation than before. Only a week earlier, I'd been the new kid, the middle-aged outlier who didn't fit, but after all that had happened in the past few days, these people had become my friends. And now Jon and I were traitors, out in the sunshine, free, while the others remained captive.

For years, I'd made split-second decisions without hesitation. A patient in crisis? I knew what to do. I was experienced. I was confident. At times, I was arrogant—I took action while those around me hesitated.

But no more. I'd been wrong with Tim. What if I was wrong now? By running, Jon and I might have put the others at even greater risk, angering Sonny to the snapping point. I choked down guilt with every swallow.

Jon kept a furious pace, this terrain far more familiar to him than to me. Erik had been our leader, and whenever a key question arose, we relied on him. It was unsettling now to follow Jon instead, but I forced my inner turmoil aside and focused on keeping up. I sure as hell couldn't do this on my own.

We traveled an arc, the meadow and cottage on our left, invisible through the trees. The only time he paused was when we reached the road. We stood for a careful look, then ran across. The scramble resumed. We arrived at the Dolphin tipis and waited for long minutes to make sure no one was there.

"Erik's gear should be in the tipi in the center." Jon pointed. "Let's see if Sonny's searches reached this far."

We dashed across the clearing, the momentary exposure sending my heart into overdrive, then ducked inside and found complete chaos. Clothing lay tumbled in random heaps. Erik's duffel sagged open, half empty. His backpack gaped and the contents of his wallet were scattered across his sleeping bag.

Jon flipped through the mess. "Sonny beat us to it. Credit cards and cash are gone. I don't see a flashlight or a knife." He searched further and passed me items that hadn't been worth Sonny's time but were invaluable to us.

An empty water bottle. A six-pack of granola bars. A package of nylon cord. We wolfed down a granola bar apiece, the nuts and sugar dancing on my tongue and leaping straight into my bloodstream, an intense reminder of how desperately empty my stomach was.

Jon stood by the door flap, ready to go. "See anything else?"

I grabbed a long-sleeved shirt—the nights got cool—and he nodded. "Good idea." He crammed Erik's sleeping bag into its stuff-sack and tucked it under his arm. "Let's go."

"Wait. Do you think Sonny will retaliate against the others because we've escaped?"

"You know I can't answer that." He wouldn't meet my eyes. "He's capable of anything, but that would also be true if we'd stayed. I had the chance to run. I took it. Now that we're out here, we have to fight back."

He looked at me, but I wished he hadn't. His eyes held the same sort of worry and guilt that I carried as constant companions.

He straightened. Firmed his jaw. "We can second-guess ourselves later, but right now there's no turning back. Come on."

His admission didn't make me feel any better, but at least I wasn't alone.

We headed through the woods again, toward Jon's tipi in the Orca group. "Do you think Sonny searched your place as well?"

"Only one way to find out. I'm hoping he didn't make it that far."

We repeated our cautious inspection when we arrived. A careful pause at clearing's edge, a mad dash to Jon's tipi. Nothing out of place. A pillow on the bed, and a duffel zipped closed. A paperback mystery, a guide to native birds, and a leather-bound journal rested on a folded towel.

"Thank goodness." I sank onto the bed, feeling safer than at any time since we left the cottage.

But Jon was shaking his head. "Things are missing. My sleeping bag is gone. My daypack." He unzipped the duffel and pulled out several items. "Someone went through my daypack. They put my wallet, pens and pencils, and my spare watch into the duffel, but took the rest with the pack."

"What else was in it?"

"Day-hike stuff. A full water bottle. Some beef jerky, a few chocolate bars, packs of nuts. Knife. Compass. First aid kit. Matches. A lightweight rain poncho."

His voice got more puzzled as he went through the list. He opened the wallet and riffled through cash and credit cards. "Everything's still here."

"Why would Sonny trash Erik's place, then take such care with your stuff?"

Jon shook his head, then he froze, eyes wide. "Oh my god. I don't believe it." His face transformed, a giant grin hijacking his entire face.

He laughed a deep, rolling, gut-shaking laugh, a laugh that went on and on without any sign of stopping. He'd stretched himself too thin. Taken on too much responsibility. Drake's death had been horrific, and such gory violence could push someone over the edge. Jon had snapped. He was hysterical.

I stood and stepped closer, my hands shaking. If Jon lost it, I was sunk. There was no way I could fend for myself on this island, much less do anything to help the others.

He flung his arms wide, swept me into a hug, and lifted me off my feet, laughing nonstop as if he'd forgotten where we were. "Kenzie, don't you get it? Sonny and Tremaine don't need a sleeping bag. They wouldn't tuck my wallet into my duffel and take only supplies for survival."

He dropped his arms, still smiling. "It's Chris. It has to be. He's alive. He's well enough to have crossed the island. And he's thinking clearly enough to come here for supplies."

The words couldn't penetrate. "How is that possible? How could he have survived the fall you described?"

"He must have landed in the one deep spot in the cove. The little devil must have known it was there. Then the tide swept him out before we could spot him."

That first day when I arrived, Chris had seemed at home in the water. He knew the details of this island the way I knew every inch of my apartment. Jon must be right. Chris was alive.

I dropped to my knees, my heart so high in my chest, I couldn't breathe. Tears poured down my face as if I'd saved them for a lifetime, building a reserve for exactly this moment.

Chris was alive. He and Skagit were somewhere out there, safe. He would read more books. Explore more trails. Leah would be whole again. The joy I'd kept under wraps erupted, sweeping me away. But not for long.

Tim was still dead. He would never swim or hike or play. So unfair. So utterly, totally, completely unfair. I blinked back tears, happiness turning into acid in the space of a microsecond.

Jon lowered himself beside me, his arm around my shoulders. "Kenzie, it's okay. Chris can't have been badly hurt or he wouldn't have made it this far. We're safe. We'll find him. We'll help the others. It's okay. Please don't cry."

"No. Not Chris. Tim." I gasped the words.

His arm tightened around me. "Who's Tim?"

I shook my head, but the words built inside with so much pressure, so much insistence, I couldn't keep them in. My truth rose to the surface.

"My nephew. Chris's age. Smart. Always smiling." His face floated in front of me, so real, I wanted to touch it. "My sister's neighbor had a pool. We went over for a cookout. Tim was a good swimmer. So were the other kids. All the adults hung out around the pool. We stayed right there. We were watching, all of us, but ... at the critical moment, none of us."

The razor-sharp memory sliced deep. "When I saw him floating, face down, not moving, I jumped in, pulled him out, began CPR."

I twisted to face Jon. It was suddenly important that he understood. "I was so careful. I did everything right. Every. Single. Step. I didn't stop, not for a second. Made the EMTs take over when they arrived, although by then ... by then ..." The words trailed off to nothing.

Jon rubbed my back. "Drowning is tricky. You know the statistics. Sometimes CPR doesn't work, even when you do everything right."

I couldn't let him believe I was innocent. "They did an autopsy. He didn't drown. One of the kids admitted later that he saw Tim slip when he jumped into the pool. He hit his head on the edge. It broke his neck."

"Oh no."

He still didn't get it. "Don't you see? What if he was alive when I pulled him from the water? I didn't support his neck. His head flopped all over when I dragged him out. What if it's my fault? What if I killed him? I can't even face my sister, my only family. She claims she doesn't blame me, and she keeps reaching out, but I've lost her too."

Jon held me, murmuring kind words that I didn't want to hear and couldn't believe. In this moment of relative safety, the tight ball of despair that hampered my every move unraveled and wrapped around me. I cried until I was empty. At last, I straightened, wiped my face on the hem of my filthy shirt, and stood, determined to start fresh.

"I took this job to forget. But then Chris was here. So like Tim. And then Ryan, with his neck injury. Now Drake, so much blood, his chest torn open like a gory prop from a horror movie." I took a shaky breath. "I'm okay now." I wasn't okay. "I'm fine." I wasn't remotely fine.

It took everything I had to keep from flying apart. But we had to keep going. I couldn't collapse now.

"Kenzie, you can't blame yourself for—"

"Stop. I said I was fine." I sounded nasty, but I didn't care. "What do we do now?"

I was hungry, thirsty, exhausted. But I stood straight and stuck out my chin, and Jon had the grace to ignore my blotchy face and trembling legs.

"We can't stay here. If Sonny decides to search for us, he'll get this far eventually. There's a small spring not too far away. It's not on an established path, and there's no way he'll find it. We can get water there and use it as a base camp. Figure out our next steps."

He stopped and gauged my reaction. Seemed to find my faked confidence believable. "Chris knows that spring. Maybe we'll find some sign of him there." He pulled two sweatshirts out of his duffel bag, grabbed a pad of paper and a pen, and looked around for anything else that might be helpful.

"Good. Let's go." I led the way out of the tipi and charged across the clearing without worrying about safety, doing my best to look competent and efficient, not a sniveling mess. Of course, once I hit the trees, I had to stop. I had no clue which way to go. I let Jon pass, then stumbled behind him.

They say it helps to talk. Like draining an abscess, it lets the putrefied rot escape.

They're wrong. Confession had hacked my heart into tiny, sharp-edged fragments. With every step I took into the island forest, the jagged edges grated against each other, sending jolts of pain through my chest. Instead of trekking through trees, hiding from a killer, all I wanted to do was curl into a tight little ball, make my mind an eternal blank, and disappear.

Instead of blanking out, images of Chris appeared. Alive, but he might be hurt. Alone and on the run. He had to be scared. Jon had said we might find signs of him at the spring.

My uneven steps smoothed out, and I lifted my head, searching the woods in front of us. We were going to fight Sonny and save the others. But first, we needed to find Chris.

Chapter Seventeen

Chris – Earlier That Morning

I tiptoed into the bathhouse before it got light to refill Jon's water bottle, then Skagit and I hid in the thick bushes beside the big metal storage building, hoping Sonny would go out to search for treasure again. If he left Tremaine on his own, I could maybe duck in the front door and untie the rope on the bedroom door before he caught me. A stupid plan, but it was all I could think of. I sure didn't want to get caught again, so I waited.

Waiting was boring. Not even a book to read. I'd used all of Jon's bandages on my arm where Sonny's bullet got me, but I wasn't as good at wrapping as Mom, and blood dripped onto the leaves. It worried Skagit, who kept licking my hand, and he didn't believe me when I told him I was okay. Maybe I could search some of the other tipis later and find another first aid kit. If Mom escaped, she could fix it.

All morning I lay there, watching. I had to make Skagit stay still, too, which he didn't like one bit. I ate some of Jon's jerky and fed some to Skagit. Sonny and Tremaine used the bathroom one at a time, not giving me enough of a chance to do anything. Nobody else came out.

Then, a gunshot. Not as loud as I would have thought, but loud enough that Skagit jumped to his feet, and I had to hang on to his collar. Should I run into the house? Run away? I couldn't decide, then the front door of the cottage banged open, and Jon came tearing out, dragging Kenzie with him, running like crazy.

I would have shouted, but Tremaine ran out next, shooting his gun over and over, really loud this time, making me think about when Sonny shot at me. Jon and Kenzie dodged back and forth like in a movie. Tremaine kept running and shooting until he ran out of bullets.

Jon and Kenzie disappeared into the woods, and Tremaine came back, kicking at the ground and saying things I couldn't hear.

Sonny stood in the doorway. He kept rubbing his hands down his jeans, and the front of his shirt was bright red. It looked like thick, gooey, red paint, but my stomach lurched like it knew something worse.

Sonny looked beyond Tremaine. "Did you get them?"

"Maybe winged the guy."

He was just acting tough. He missed, every time.

"Good."

"What about the others?"

"Locked up."

"Sonny, what are we going to do? Those two are bound to make trouble. We need to get out of here."

Sonny examined Tremaine like he'd never seen him before. His eyes got real small and angry, eyes I wouldn't want staring at me, then he shrugged. "We can't leave until we find them."

"Then what? Lock them up again?"

Sonny frowned with tight lips. "Two dead now, including the kid."

He meant me. Hearing him say I was dead made my skin itch.

He looked at the ground. "We can't leave witnesses." He said it slow.

Tremaine frowned like he didn't get it, but then he took a fast step away from Sonny, shaking his head hard. "All of them? I don't know, that's not what—"

Sonny grabbed him by the arm and pulled out his gun. "Too late. You're either with me or not. Decide now." He pressed the muzzle against Tremaine's side.

I was busy trying to recover from *two dead* and trying to sort out what Sonny meant about *no witnesses*. The answers I came up with made me hang onto Skagit with both hands. He was talking about Mom. The others too.

Could Mom already be dead? Something in my chest broke into pieces, and it got hard to breathe. I blinked hard and forced myself to focus on the two men.

Sonny was leaning forward, digging the muzzle in deeper. Tremaine still had his gun, but he'd used all his bullets and hadn't had time to reload. His eyes got big like an owl's and his suntan disappeared. I couldn't see him shaking, but I'd bet anything he was. "Okay, Sonny, okay. I'm with you. All the way. You know I am."

For a minute, Sonny didn't react, then he lowered the gun to his side. "Okay."

Tremaine stepped farther away. "Now? You're doing it now?"

"No. There's no way those two runaways can get off this island without a boat. Best way to catch them is to keep the others as bait. Those two are probably out there right now, trying to cook up a plan. We'll catch them, then we'll take care of all of them at once."

Tremaine looked sort of green, like when I eat too much watermelon on a hot day, but worse. A lot worse.

"Go lock the storage building. We don't want them getting a canoe." Sonny waved Tremaine off and went into the cottage.

I grabbed Skagit and tucked him close, snuggling deeper into the low branches. Tremaine walked right past us. Locked the padlock. Took the key. Slipped it into the back pocket of his jeans and never noticed us at all.

Up close like that, I could see the sweat on his face even though the day was cool. He walked part way back to the cottage. Stopped. Stood a time with his head down and shoulders drooping. Then he straightened and went inside. I guess he decided he was with Sonny for sure. Or maybe he remembered his brother was in there.

I wasn't sure what to do. I wanted to go after Jon. But that first gunshot got fired indoors. What if it was Mom who got hurt? My arm ached bad. The blood dripped more. But I had to wait.

After not too much longer, the door opened again. Sonny and Tremaine came out with something heavy, wrapped in the bright blue Star Wars comforter from my bed. Sonny had taken off his messed-up shirt and now wore one of Mom's old sweatshirts stretched tight across his chest with the sleeves too short.

At first, I thought they were moving Ryan, but a small brown book dropped to the ground and a hand slipped out from the blanket. The hand didn't move, and red stuff dripped off the fingers. Not gooey paint. Blood. I tried not to throw up, tried to stare hard at the hand.

Was it Mom? Could it be her?

I tried to picture what her hand looked like, but all of a sudden, I couldn't remember anything about her. This hand looked bigger. One of the men. Maybe. Or maybe not. All the blood made it hard to tell.

Sonny and Tremaine lugged the body into the pottery shed. Closed the door when they came out. Headed back into the cottage. The way Tremaine was gagging, I wasn't the only one trying not to barf. Sonny bent and grabbed the book that had dropped from the body. The old journal. The one that talked about the treasure. Mom had kept it hidden where Sonny couldn't find it, but there it was in his hands. Did the book mean for sure the body was Mom?

I had to know. Had to know for sure.

I grabbed Jon's daypack, belly-crawled back out of the bushes, and worked my way to the back of the storage building, Skagit tight beside me the whole way. Then I ran for the trees, keeping the building behind me. If I couldn't see the cottage, they couldn't see me. Reached the forest, ran along the edge of the meadow the whole way around, then crossed again to the back of the pottery shed. Told Skagit to stay.

This was the part where they might see me, when I ducked around the shed and opened the door. I took a deep breath. Moved fast. Opened the door the tiniest crack and squeezed through, shutting it behind me, the hinges squeaking way too loud.

Nobody yelled. Nobody came running across the yard.

No light inside, just pitch-black darkness. I rooted in Jon's pack for his flashlight. Clicked it on. The lump in the comforter lay on the floor between Mom's wheel and her kiln, leaning against the washing machine. Blood had soaked through the top of the comforter, turning it brown. The room smelled like raw hamburgers on camp cookout days, and I never wanted to eat a burger again.

I reached for one edge of the comforter, trying to pretend it didn't matter who I found beneath, but when I saw Drake's hair, his ear, the top of his strong shoulder, I dropped the cloth and had to lean against the shed's wall. It mattered. It mattered a lot. *Not Mom. Not Mom. Not Mom.* The rough-edged relief that rushed through me hurt as much as the fear had.

The next minute, guilt hit. I couldn't be happy about Drake being dead. I'd known him every summer I could remember. I liked his big, loud laugh. The way he could chug a whole can of beer in one, long swallow. One year, he let me join his group when he taught them canoe strokes. And now he was lying here dead and I was by myself and my legs wouldn't stop shaking.

I wanted out. I wanted to be somewhere else. I wanted some-body with superpowers to show up and make things okay.

Nobody showed up.

Sonny shot Drake. His comment about *no witnesses* made sense now. He planned to kill everyone. Mom. Jon, Erik, Bree, and Ken-zie. Me, too, if he caught me. Maybe even Skagit.

No way. It couldn't happen. I told my legs to stop shaking. Pushed off from the wall. Worked some too-little spit down my too-dry throat. The air in the shed got real cold, and I bit down hard to keep my teeth from chattering. My breath came fast even though I was standing still, and I had to force myself to think.

I hadn't heard any more shots from inside, and I'd heard Sonny say he'd keep Mom, Bree, and Erik as bait. I hated to leave Mom there, but now I knew things Jon didn't. I needed to find him and Kenzie so we could plan.

Where would they go? Jon's tipi, for sure, like I did. After that, lots of possibilities, but I'd check the spring first. Best place for water away from camp, and he always told me, if you're lost, find water first.

I put the flashlight away, sneaked out through the door and ran behind the shed. The sun hit me square, and I hugged Skagit for a long time, the two of us crouched low against the building. At last, some of the cold went away. Everything stayed quiet. I made it to the woods, pulled out Jon's compass, and headed out. I'd pick up Jon's sleeping bag from where I'd stashed it behind the big bear-shaped rock, then I'd head to the spring.

I heard Jon and Kenzie's quiet voices before I reached the small clearing that edged Jamison Marsh. The Baytree people had long ago made a pond here in this low spot, building an earth dam and piping water in this direction from a few small springs, but they'd ended up with a salty marsh, not a freshwater pond.

The most reliable spring was up ahead in the clearing. Well, Jon called it a spring. Mom said it was only a seep. Not much water, but it emptied into a rock-lined basin, and what collected there wasn't salty at all.

I planned to approach quietly, wanting to see how close I could get before calling out to them, but I forgot to tell Skagit. As soon as he heard voices, he raced to Jon, tail beating the air, bouncing on his toes and looking for a head scratch.

Jon jumped to his feet with a shout and spotted me. He charged into the trees and pulled me into a hug so tight I could hardly breathe. It made my arm hurt, too, but I didn't say anything. Being held, getting led into the clearing, seeing Kenzie so excited—all of it made me feel so relieved. It's not like I needed them. I'd been doing fine on my own. But three could be better than one if we were going to save Mom, and now that I was with Jon and Kenzie, my shivers stopped.

"Chris, I can't believe it. We thought you were dead." Jon kept going on and on, patting me on the back like he wasn't sure I was real. Kenzie grinned like crazy but then zeroed in on my arm, which had gotten gross with dried blood during the walk.

"Sit," she said. "Let me take a look." She frowned at the soaked-through bandage, but after she poked around a bit, she squeezed my hand and gave me sort of a smile. "The bullet missed the bone. Bored a hole right through your bicep. You landed in salt water after it happened?"

"Yes." That awkward landing. The icy water. I went deep, couldn't twist myself around to push off the bottom, and the current swept me out fast. By the time I surfaced, lungs so empty they hurt, I was out beyond the edges of the cove. I swam to shore as far from the trail as I could. Hid behind rocks.

I heard Jon calling, but he was far away, and I knew better than to answer. There was no way I wanted Sonny to know where I was. My arm didn't hurt at first, it was so cold. But after a while, it started bleeding. Scary. I took my T-shirt off and used it to get it stopped. Then Skagit found me, and having him there made things better.

"The salt water did a good job of flushing it out. I don't see any infection." Kenzie picked up a shirt that looked like Erik's and asked Jon to hand her his knife from the pack I'd carried. She cut long strips from the bottom of the shirt, put thick pads of folded cloth where the bullet went in and where it came out, then used strips of the cloth to tie them in place. She did a much better job than I'd done. But I only had one arm to work with.

"Why did you jump? I thought for sure you'd gotten hung up on those rocks." Jon's voice got tight and weird, the way it had sounded when he was looking for me in the water.

"I'd jumped there before. There's one spot deep enough."

"What? That cove is off-limits!"

I shrugged. Too late to get in trouble for it now. "I knew I could do it. And without me in the way, I thought you and Erik could take Sonny down. I heard you calling. I'm sorry I couldn't answer."

After I pulled myself out of the water I tried to follow them home, but I had to sit for a time and let the sun warm me, my arm hurting for real by then. It took me the rest of the day to get to Jon's tipi and get supplies. Skagit and I slept in the woods before going on watch that morning. I'd camped out lots of times, but that was the first time I'd been scared. My arm hurt bad, and every noise sounded like Sonny sneaking closer. Skagit curled tight against me in Jon's sleeping bag, but even that didn't help.

Maybe tonight would be better, with Jon and Kenzie here.

"Chris, something happened this morning." Jon sounded like he didn't want to say it.

"I know. I was watching. They carried Drake out to the shed." Too much blood. The white skin of Drake's forehead. I had trouble swallowing. "I went in and saw him. And I heard Sonny and Tremaine talking." I told them what they'd said. Jon and Kenzie both leaned forward, listening to every word. "I didn't hear any more shots. I don't think they—" I couldn't say it. Couldn't say *killed Mom* yet. What if I was wrong?

Jon knew. He gave me a hug, careful this time not to touch my bad arm. "Sonny made it clear he wanted hostages, so that means he won't hurt anyone." He and Kenzie traded a look, and I could tell they were thinking *won't hurt anyone YET.* Jon's forehead wrinkled, then he frowned a sad sort of frown. "They'll be waiting for us. No question about it."

Kenzie picked at the ragged edge of the shirt she'd shredded. "Should we stay here in the forest? Keep out of their way? Once the boat gets dropped off, we can go for help. That's only two days away."

"Tempting. But we can't count on Sonny staying logical. Leah was right when she predicted that, once things got violent, it would change the balance. Who knows what else could go wrong in the next two days? We need a plan, and we need to make it good. We'll only get one chance."

We sat a few minutes, nobody talking but everyone acting like they wanted someone else to speak. Jon stood and stretched. "First things first. Let's work on dinner. We'll think better with food on board."

I pulled out the rest of Jon's nuts and chocolate. Kenzie had some granola bars. Jon took off his tennis shoes, emptied his pockets, and waded into the marsh with his knife. He came back with a big armful of cattails. "We can't build a fire. Sonny might notice smoke. But cattails are good raw."

"You've got to be kidding." Kenzie shut her mouth tight.

He peeled off the muddy outer leaves of each stalk, working down to the clean white middle. He rinsed it, then cut lengths like Mom cuts celery and passed them around. "Go ahead. Try it."

I munched on a piece, and, okay, it could have been worse. "It'd be better with ranch dressing. Or maybe peanut butter."

Kenzie rolled her eyes, but she ate plenty. With the cattails and the other food, my stomach ended up full for the first time in days.

"We've got water here," Jon said. "And we won't starve. There are plenty of edible greens around, plus some of the salmonberries are ripe. We can collect mussels and eat them raw." Kenzie wrinkled her nose, but Jon didn't notice. "Hopefully, we won't have to live off the land for long. We need to focus on a plan to help the others."

He'd left a few things from his pockets sitting out like he didn't want them, so I took two rubber bands and the silver half-scissors that was too small to do much with but was still kind of pretty. It was getting dark, and I could barely see their faces. A cold wind picked up off the sound, and Skagit and I snuggled deep into Jon's sleeping bag. I tried to pay attention to what Jon and Kenzie were saying—*communication, front window, storage shed, canoes, generator*—but my eyes wouldn't stay open.

"There are things we could use in the storage building, but I don't know how we'd break into it without making a lot of noise. It's designed to hold off burglars when no one's on-island, so the doors are heavy metal, and the padlock is solid. Leah usually keeps the key in the kitchen, but we can't count on it still being there. If we can't find it, we're sunk."

There was something I knew about that key, but I couldn't remember. Skagit woke and rolled over, snuggling close. I wished Mom was here. I wished I was back in my own bed and she was there, too, and we were safe. My arm hurt. My stomach didn't feel too great. I pulled the sleeping bag tighter around me, but when I closed my eyes, I saw Drake wrapped in my bloody comforter, his skin white and waxy and fake.

It took a long, long time before I could sleep.

Chapter Eighteen

Jon - Wednesday

I set the alarm on my watch for three a.m., but I woke fifteen minutes early to the gravelly hoots of a pair of great horned owls. Every muscle screamed at me, cold and stiff and aching. Kenzie and I used Erik's zipped-open sleeping bag as a blanket, but the chill from the ground hadn't been dulled much by the heaps of leaves and moss we'd piled beneath us. I stood and tucked the bag around Kenzie. She slept on, her head resting on her bent arm.

We'd spent hours trying to decide on the best plan—one that wouldn't get everyone killed—but too many unknowns remained.

I clicked my flashlight on and paced the clearing, swinging my arms in giant circles to warm myself. My whole life, I was the guy who lived alone. Worked alone, thrived alone. I stayed a contractor because that way I was responsible for only my assigned task. No employees to manage. No shareholders to keep happy. I claimed my miniscule piece of turf, put up a fence, and didn't stray off it.

But the minute I grabbed Kenzie and ran for the door, I took this whole mess on as mine, with no one else leading the way. Lives depended on me. On me. *On me.* The thought made me stumble, and my stomach executed an Olympic-class flip.

I can do this. I have to do this. I have no choice. Maybe if I kept repeating those words, I'd convince myself. Leah was in danger. I couldn't let her down.

Chris, zipped into my mummy bag, slept the deep sleep of an exhausted ten-year-old. Skagit, curled beside him, watched me circle, glaring as if he didn't trust my intentions. Chris worried me. It was a miracle he was alive, and we needed to keep him that way. Kenzie wanted to exclude him from any rescue plan, but if we told him to hide, he'd probably dash off on his own and get himself hurt or recaptured. There were ways he could help. We just needed to be careful.

And then there was Kenzie. Her story about her nephew's death explained a lot. The way she'd reacted when Chris went over the wall to forage for supplies, turning white and shaking as if her own child were at risk. Her desperate grief when she learned of his disappearance. Guilt. Once it got hold, it didn't turn loose.

When I was ten, I stole an Aquaman comic book from a kid at boarding school whose mom sent him each new issue the day it came out. Once I had it in my hands, I couldn't even turn the pages, and I spent the rest of the school year avoiding that boy. After all these years, I still cringed every time I thought of it. Guilt over the loss of a child? How could you recover from that?

My watch chimed the hour, and I gave Chris a nudge. He woke in stages, protesting, then sitting and rubbing his eyes. "It's still dark." Skagit yawned and did a down-dog stretch, then trotted into the trees to do his business.

"Yeah, it's early. We need to get to the cottage before sunrise. We have to check out the situation before we settle on a plan."

He climbed out of his bag to stretch. I shook Kenzie out of her sound sleep, and she woke fast, looking startled, then frightened, then calming once she saw both Chris and me there. "Time to go?" She tossed the sleeping bag aside and stood.

"It will get light before five. Eat something. Drink. Then we'll head out."

She stuffed both sleeping bags into their sacks and ran her fingers through her hair. She must have been as chilled and stiff as I was, but she didn't complain.

I munched on more of the cattail hearts, choking down the tough fibers, and filled both water bottles from the spring while they finished the last two granola bars. "Chris, it's going to take all three of us to rescue your mom and the others."

He nodded.

"Your part will be important. But if this is going to work, you have to do exactly what Kenzie and I tell you. Even when you don't like what we say. Can you agree to that?"

"But Jon, I can—"

"No. If you won't agree, you can't help at all."

Chris stood as tall as his ten-year-old body would let him. "How are you going to stop me? Tie me to a tree?"

"Don't tempt me." I selected my sternest I'm-in-charge-and-you're-not voice. "Chris, I mean it."

He made a face, acting defiant, so I pulled out bigger ammunition. "You saw what happened to Drake. We don't want the same thing to happen to anyone else."

Kenzie glared at me. Chris looked away, his shoulders drooping.

"Sorry to remind you, kiddo, but this is serious. We need to be like a commando unit, working together. You get what I'm saying?"

He kicked at a loose stone but finally met my eyes. "Yeah. Okay." He gave a giant sigh.

"Good."

"I remembered something. When I watched yesterday, Tremaine locked the storage shed and put the key in his pocket."

"Good to know." Kenzie gave him a quick hug. "If we're going to do this, let's get going."

"You've got the notepad?" I asked.

She lifted it. Step one. Communication with the others. We needed to understand their situation before we could decide what to do. I grabbed my packed daypack, turned, and led the way toward the cottage, careful to aim the flashlight at the ground. Along the way, I hunted for a suitable weapon and finally found a solid madrona branch, about the size of a baseball bat but with a jagged edge at one end. I shook off bits of dried dirt and hefted its bulk. It would do.

Kenzie and I had debated whether Sonny and Tremaine would stand guard all night. If one of them stayed hidden outdoors, gun at the ready, then we took a big risk by approaching. But why would they bother? With the cottage locked tight, we couldn't easily break in, and if we were foolish enough to try, they had the means to defend themselves.

They probably had full stomachs and were sound asleep inside, resting to prepare for whatever they planned next. At the edge of the meadow, we paused for long minutes, watching for movement. The waxing quarter moon provided enough light to make out the outlines of the camp buildings. Enough light to see a human being if he was careless enough to move.

Nothing.

Flashlight off, we dashed across the open space between the meadow's edge and the metal storage building.

Silence.

I leaned close to whisper to Chris. "We're going to go around the building. You and Skagit hide in the bushes like you did yesterday." He frowned but didn't protest. "You're on watch. If you see anything move or see a light that's not ours, whistle like you do when you call Skagit. Got it?"

A long hesitation. Then, a nod.

We shifted around the building. If anyone was watching from the front of the cottage, they could see us. But nobody shouted. I gave Chris's shoulder a squeeze, and he and Skagit melted away, rustling the bushes as they settled themselves at ground level.

I put my mouth near Kenzie's ear. "Ready?"

An immediate nod. I handed her the flashlight, and we ran. Across the road. Across the front yard. I flattened myself against the wall beside the front door, clutching my stick, ready to attack if Sonny or Tremaine appeared. The stick had gotten smaller since

I first chose it, now but a feeble weapon against a man with a gun. My heart whammed double-time. My breath jerked in and out of my lungs as if I'd run for miles. I stood poised, a predator awaiting his prey, but I didn't have any teeth.

Kenzie stood at the front bedroom window, the one Sonny had doubly nailed shut. I could see the white of her face but couldn't make out her expression. All remained quiet, and I gave her a go-ahead wave.

She switched on the flashlight, a sudden burst in the dark, and shined it in through the window, aiming for the gap between the curtains. She turned it off. On. Off. On. Off. If Erik, Bree, or Leah were awake, they should see it.

Nothing happened.

Kenzie left the light on, still aimed inside, and tapped twice on the glass storm window.

In the night's silence, it sounded deafening. I'd been on adrenaline-overdrive since we reached the meadow, but that buzz was nothing compared to the tension now stressing my every muscle. Sonny would come to the door. He'd have his gun. When he did, I had to stop him. If I failed, Kenzie and Chris would pay the price. I gasped for oxygen.

Nothing happened.

Kenzie raised her hand, ready to tap again, but the curtains jerked open, and a face appeared, a white blur. I couldn't tell who it was. Kenzie raised a hand in greeting. The face disappeared, replaced in seconds by three faces, crowded together, peering out.

A surge of relief eased some of the painful tension that had hijacked my entire body. Three faces. Erik, Bree, and Leah, alive.

Kenzie lifted the spiral notebook and aimed the flashlight at the first page, holding it close to the glass. We'd written our messages the night before, and I knew what each page said. This first one read *Bree, stand watch, and let us know if someone is coming.*

One face disappeared. Kenzie flipped to the next page.

Have you been hurt?

Two heads, shaking no. Sonny might be planning vengeance, but he hadn't acted yet.

Next page. *Food? Water?*

Two heads shook no again. Damn. Kenzie and I now had unlimited water plus the food we'd scraped together, and it had made a huge difference, clarifying our thinking and giving us enough energy to act. The three inside had to be getting weak by now.

Is Ryan strong enough to be a threat?

Both heads shook no. One face disappeared, but Kenzie turned the page.

Do Tremaine and Sonny use the bathhouse toilet?

A nod. Then the second face reappeared, pressing something against the window. It looked like a book. Kenzie peered at it a moment, then waved it away.

Next page. *We'll try to act when one of them is in the bathhouse.*

Two nods.

Sonny plans to kill us all. Be careful.

This time, the nods came slower.

And now, the final page. Kenzie had argued we should put this first, but I'd insisted it had to go at the end. Once they read it, they wouldn't think clearly. Kenzie held that last page even closer to the glass with the light aimed straight at it. Both of her hands shook so hard, I was surprised anyone could read what we'd written.

Chris is alive. Arm injured, but not major. He's with us.

Both faces jerked back, then collapsed together in an obvious hug. Kenzie gave them a smile, turned off her light, and gestured me over. I waved at Leah and Erik at the window, wishing I could do more, grabbed Kenzie's hand, and raced for the storage building.

"Chris!" I whispered as soon as I was close enough.

He and Skagit materialized as if by magic.

The sky had brightened in the east, vague streaks of pale yellow tinged with pink materializing over the treetops. "Wave to your mom. She's at the window."

He gave her a huge full-armed wave. I wasn't sure she could see him from such a distance in the dim light, but the delight on his face lifted my spirits.

I led Chris and Kenzie behind the building, out of sight.

"What happened? Is Mom okay? What are we doing now?" Chris's idea of a whisper would wake a hibernating bear, and I made shushing noises.

Kenzie gave him a hug. "Your mom is fine. When I showed her the message that said you were okay, she was so happy she couldn't stand it."

Chris blinked fast and gulped faster but tried to hide it.

I turned to Kenzie. "Bathhouse attack still our best bet?"

"Yes."

"Okay. Chris, here's your job. We're going to go hide in the bathhouse. You and Skagit are going to wait here, hidden in these bushes. You can't be seen, but you can see anyone who goes into the men's bathroom. We think either Sonny or Tremaine will come to the bathhouse eventually. If one goes in and doesn't come back out, we hope the other one will come to see what happened. If both go in—Sonny and Tremaine, both of them, all the way inside—then you run into the cottage, untie the rope on the bedroom door, and yell to let your mom know it's open. I don't think Ryan will be a problem but be careful."

His eyes lit up. "You're going to fight them when they're pissing?" He sounded appalled and excited at the same time, as if it wasn't fair play but he liked the idea anyway.

"We need the element of surprise."

Kenzie tapped his shoulder. "Don't wait for your mom to come out. Untie the rope, let them know, then run back here into the trees. Got it?"

"I can do it."

"But only go if both Sonny and Tremaine are all the way inside the bathhouse. Otherwise, you wait here. If things don't seem right, you head for the trees." He probably hated the repetition, but I needed to pound the message in.

This plan would let Chris feel part of things but hopefully keep him hidden and out of danger. And in the unlikely event that both Tremaine and Sonny did come to the bathhouse at the same time, then Kenzie and I would be in trouble, and Chris might be the only hope left for the others. "If Kenzie and I get hurt, even if you're convinced you can help, you stay away from Sonny and Tremaine." And their guns.

"Yeah. I get it. Stay hidden. Go to the cottage when they're both gone, then run."

I clapped him on the back and handed over a full water bottle, the last of the jerky, and a handful of cattail hearts. "We're counting on you."

"I won't let you down."

I didn't like the gleam in his eye, but I'd done what I could.

The sky had grown brighter. I could see all the way to the beach now. "Okay, Kenzie, let's go."

She leaned forward and kissed Chris gently on the forehead.

He pulled back, startled, but she took off running. We raced behind the Lodge, behind the bathhouse, then looped around it and ducked into the door to the men's side.

No shouts. No pounding feet. No gunshots.

Instantaneous relief.

Kenzie leaned against the wall inside the door. "Could you see their answers to the questions we'd written?"

"Yes. Good news except for the lack of food and water. Someone held up a book?"

"That was Erik. He wrote a note on the inside cover of a paperback. Sonny has Allman's journal, and he saw the notations Drake made. He figured out the clue. He's demanding the others take him to the root cellar, but they keep insisting they don't know where it is. Thank goodness it's not marked on the map."

I tried to figure out a way to use the treasure's location to our advantage but couldn't come up with anything. We wanted to defeat Sonny, not negotiate with him. "Did they write anything else?"

"Ryan can walk with help. Tremaine brought him to the bathhouse last night. Sonny stood on the front porch of the cottage with his gun, guarding while they came down here."

"Good. I still think our idea of attacking here is our best bet."

"I guess." She gave a determined nod but wouldn't look at me.

We'd gone around and around this the night before. It would be suicide to try to force our way into the cottage and equally risky to attack on open ground. Kenzie wanted to set a trap of some sort in the forest, but how could we lure Sonny or Tremaine there? It wasn't practical, and I'd argued her out of it.

That left us here. Bad, because there was only one way in or out of the bathhouse, it was a small space, and anyone stepping out the door could be seen at once from the cottage. But good, because the stalls provided places to hide, and it was unlikely Sonny and Tremaine would leave the cottage unguarded and come together. With surprise on our side, we could hopefully handle one at a time.

They had guns. I had a stick.

I hoped those sentences wouldn't end up engraved on my tombstone.

Chapter Nineteen

Kenzie

J on and I hid together in the bathroom, waiting to attack another human. Two other humans. I'd spent decades caring for people, yet here I was, planning an attack instead. My hands shook so hard I had to stuff them into my pockets to keep them still. My meager breakfast didn't want to stay down. Being threatened and imprisoned had been frightening. Losing Chris had been worse, and seeing Drake dead and mangled was too horrible for words. But waiting and wondering what would happen next was a whole new level of torture.

The men's bathroom was a mirror image of the women's next door, a cinderblock rectangle with a rough concrete floor and faded green paint. A counter with a row of sinks lined the wall facing the cottage, and a long band of windows ran above them, just beneath the roof. Four toilet stalls and four urinals lined the opposite wall, and benches stood in a line between them and the sinks. The far end of the room contained a common shower, separated from the rest of the space by a shoulder-high cinder block wall with peeling paint and flaking mortar.

Jon checked out the space. "When we see someone coming, I'll hide in the last stall, crouching on the toilet seat. You hide behind the wall in the shower area."

His plan put him closer to our quarry, but he'd have to get through a swinging door to attack. I'd have an easier path but farther to go. He hefted the thick branch he'd brought with him, but against men with guns, I would have preferred a stun gun. Or a crowbar. Or maybe an army.

He hid his pack behind the shower wall. I checked out my hiding place, found a chunk of loose mortar, and pried it out to create a peephole I could use if I bent low. "This will work."

Jon grunted, tense and distracted.

I climbed onto the counter by the sinks and stood at the edge of the window where I couldn't be seen, taking first watch. Chris should be tucked into the shadows behind the storage shed, but he'd hidden himself too well for me to spot him. Tim had always been good at hiding too. I could never find him when we played hide-and-seek. "What do we do if they use the women's side instead?"

Jon recoiled for a second, then shook his head. "They won't. It's automatic." He paused. "They expect us to try something. They'd be safer if they avoid toilets entirely and use the great outdoors instead, but I don't think they're wired that way."

He was probably right. "We're not planning on killing them, are we? You brought the rope we got from Erik's tipi?"

Jon let the silence build for an endless moment. "We're not planning on killing anyone. But, Kenzie, this isn't a game."

"You mean, someone might die, despite our best intentions."

He turned away.

I stared out the window, seeing nothing, my stomach a hard, tight knot. I was no stranger to death. I'd lost patients before. I'd seen horrific injuries, although nothing as horrible as Drake's chest wound. This was different. It wouldn't be an accident or a reflexive choice made in an instant of anger. This would be cold and calculating and intentional.

We were making the right choice, the only choice, to fight instead of hide. Leah, Erik, and Bree depended on our success. I just wished I could find peace with our decision.

The sun rose higher. Clouds drifted in. The air grew heavy and damp, threatening rain. When I tired of my post at the window, I traded with Jon and sat on the gritty floor while he took over. When he grew restless, we traded back. We drank water. Ate another few cattail hearts, which tasted worse every time I choked one down.

The view out the window changed little. An occasional bird landed on the meadow, pecked around, and flew on. A gust of wind sent the tall grasses rattling.

I played songs in my head, made a list of twenty places I wanted to travel to, tried and failed to avoid memories of Tim. My tension should have eased in the boredom, but instead, every barren moment passed like the tick of a countdown clock, bringing me one step closer to calamity.

We talked very little, but at one point, Jon stirred. "Why did you become a nurse?"

I'd asked myself that question a lot lately. "My mother was diagnosed with cancer when I was in high school. Paige was only in third grade, and Dad couldn't cope. I ended up managing Mom's treatment. Driving her in for chemo, organizing her pills, trying to find foods that she'd eat. I quizzed the doctors and fought for explanations. I was the one holding her hand at the end."

"Losing your mom like that must have been terribly hard."

"Yes." I dropped for a moment into those weeks of anguish, the sleepless nights, the steady sense of foreboding. By the time the end arrived, Mom embraced it as a blessing, but I was a wreck for months. "All that year, I was reading drug inserts and trying to understand what was going on, and I discovered I liked the science of it all. I liked knowing I'd helped her. It seemed natural to learn more in college and inevitable to end up in a hospital job. Until ..."

I paused, gritted my teeth for a moment, and forced out the rest. "Until Tim, I loved nursing. The things everyone complains about—long hours, weird schedules, the COVID nightmare—none of it bothered me much when I knew I was helping people. Saving them even."

He looked thoughtful. Said nothing. I'd shared my worst with him when I told him about Tim. Did he believe that mistake erased the good I'd done before? I couldn't tell what he thought, but even worse, I wasn't sure what I believed. If I put good and bad on a balance scale, which way would it tip? It wasn't a question I wanted to face.

"Why did you become a software engineer?"

He snapped back from wherever his thoughts had taken him. "I'm good at it, it pays well, and I can make my own schedule and come here in the summers." He stared out the window. "But really? I think I set up my work life this way because it lets me hide in my little room and avoid other people. Don't get me wrong. I'm no hermit. I have friends to call when I'm in the mood for dinner or a drink. But if I die today, no one will grieve too much. They'll meet at a bar, hoist a glass, and tell a few stories. They'll be a little shaken because death hit someone their own age and nobody likes to believe they could be next. But that's it. My death will be no one's tragedy. Nobody's life will have a hole in it when I'm gone."

It wasn't his air of sadness that hit me. It was his calm. He'd analyzed his situation and reached this conclusion. He'd been far too successful at building a box for himself. I searched for the right words, but he spoke before I found them.

"You need to make up with your sister. You said you lost her when you lost your nephew. But she's still there, isn't she? You said she keeps reaching out. She'd grieve if you died. She'd notice the hole you'd leave behind. If we get out of all this, you have to call her."

Paige had left so many tearful voice mails, I'd quit listening. So many texts, I'd quit reading. Delete, delete, delete. Yes, she still reached out. And, yes, all this talk of death made me think of her.

But she hadn't reached out a single time since I deleted that first text when I arrived on the island. Maybe she'd given up on me. I'd told her countless times to leave me alone, so if she finally listened, that was a good thing, wasn't it? That's what I wanted, right?

But I, too, could die today, and the knowledge twisted my insides. Dead without reconciling with Paige. Dead and leaving a hole behind. I blinked fast and swallowed salt.

Jon watched me, waiting for a response, but what right did he have to tell me what to do? Acting like he had all the answers.

Heat raced to my face, and words surged out without passing through my brain. "Call her? Tell her what's in my heart? The way you'd tell Leah you're in love with her?"

He stared at me, his mouth hanging open. It took him a moment to find his voice. "How do you know that?"

"The way you look at her. The way your face lights up when she walks into the room. How upset you seemed when she told us why she'd come here to the island. If you're trying to hide how you feel, you're not doing a very good job."

"Do you think she knows?"

"She's not an idiot."

His head jerked back, and a dazed look appeared in his eyes. "I thought I'd kept it from her. Why didn't she say something? Maybe she just isn't interested."

"That's not the vibe I'm getting. And don't blame her for silence when you haven't said anything either. Come on, man, one of you has to make a move."

That took a few moments to soak in. His lips softened, and his face relaxed—stunned, amazed, and delighted all at once. He looked years younger. As if I'd conjured riches out of thin air or explained all of life's mysteries in a single magnificent sentence.

He straightened his spine. Threw back his shoulders and tightened his jaw. "That's it then. If we get out of this alive, I'm telling her." He gave me a barbed look. "And you're calling your sister. Promise. It's a pact."

He kept his eyes glued on mine.

No. I wouldn't do it. I couldn't. No way. The chasm that existed between Paige and me was vast, and bridging it would be far too painful. But I didn't have energy to argue. What the hell, Jon and I weren't likely to live past today. I wouldn't have to pay up. "Yeah. Okay. I'll do it."

He believed me. He let the subject drop.

But the promise rattled in my head like a loose wheel on a hospital gurney. The gentle kiss I'd placed on Chris's forehead mirrored the way I'd always said goodnight to Tim. More than that, it mirrored the gesture I'd used to say goodnight to Paige as a child.

As soon as I could read, Mom happily delegated Paige's bedtime story to me. We'd snuggle side by side under the covers and I'd read aloud whatever books she chose. _The Hungry Caterpillar_ and _Where the Wild Things Are_. _Go, Dog, Go_ and the Berenstain Bears' books. The Box Car children, _Encyclopedia Brown_, and _Ramona the Pest_. Long after she could read herself, I read on, through Mom's illness and after her death, all the way until I left for college.

"Good night, Mackenzie," she'd say before I scooted out of her bed. The kiss I placed on her forehead was my promise that the night would hold no fears.

I wanted such a guarantee right then, as I waited in that cold, bleak bathhouse for a battle I'd rather not face. I wanted Paige to protect me the way I'd protected her. But I no longer had the right to ask anything of my kid sister.

It was a bit after noon, and I stood on watch, when the door to the cottage opened. "Something's happening."

Jon scrambled onto the other end of the counter and leaned toward the window.

Tremaine stepped out, gun in hand, and looked around the meadow in all directions. He startled when a blackbird flew past, but after survey of the meadow, he stepped back inside and led his brother out.

Bandages still strapped Ryan's broken arm to his chest, but he could walk. He leaned heavily against Tremaine and took slow careful steps. Several times, his toe caught, causing him to stumble. Tremaine kept the gun in his right hand and looped his left arm around Ryan's waist. A towel hung over his shoulder.

Sonny stepped out of the cottage and stood a few feet in front of the door, gun ready. Head never still, he scanned the meadow from left to right and back again. He called out something I couldn't hear, and Tremaine froze, tugging Ryan to stop him. After a moment, Sonny waved them on, and their slow progress resumed.

Jon jumped off the counter and gestured me toward him. "This is it. I'll focus on Tremaine. You tackle Ryan. Don't move until I do."

I nodded, my throat too dry to ask the countless questions that now occurred to me. Jon disappeared into the toilet stall, and the door swung partway closed behind him. I ducked into the shower and crouched beside my peephole.

"Almost there, buddy. You'll feel better when we get you cleaned up." Tremaine's voice sounded close, kind and patient. Gravel crunched under uneven footsteps. The door squeaked open.

Ryan stepped in first. Tremaine followed, using his brother as a shield. He held his gun ready, stopping inside the door to look in all directions. He bent to peer under the toilet stall doors.

I held my breath. A break in the clouds sent a shaft of sunlight through the windows, highlighting dusty scuff marks on the countertop where Jon and I had stood for so long. I tore my eyes away, as if staring at the prints would draw his attention to them.

The longer Tremaine stood there, the more he relaxed. Ryan took a few halting steps toward the bench closest to the door, and he followed, helping him sit. "Give me a minute." He squeezed his brother's shoulder, walked to the first stall, and slammed the door all the way open, his gun aimed. He repeated the process at the second stall. The third.

I rolled forward on my toes, braced to jump as soon as he discovered Jon. We had counted on just such a search, and we'd reached the crucial moment. As soon as Tremaine pushed that last door, I would yell, hopefully distracting him for a critical split-second so

Jon could leap. I drew in air, waiting for the right instant. Tremaine lifted his hand. Stepped toward the final door. His fingers neared its surface.

Ryan coughed a series of harsh, wet rattles, sounding like his lungs held more liquid than air. He shifted his broken arm in its wrap and groaned. Tremaine pivoted to his brother. "You okay?" He stepped toward the bench, waited until Ryan's coughing subsided, then set down the towel. "Hang on a minute. Let me finish checking things out."

I tensed again, ready.

But instead of returning to the last stall where Jon waited, Tremaine stepped toward the shower.

I doused a fiery flare of panic and crouched at the ready, a runner poised on a starting block. As soon as Tremaine's foot stepped across the threshold, I lunged forward and grabbed his arm, wrenching it sideways while shoving my shoulder into his chest. It caught him off guard, and he stumbled back, arms flailing. He tried to yell, but what came out was a gurgle. I drove hard, pushing him backward. We fell together on the floor, and the gun skittered across the concrete and stopped beneath the sinks.

Ryan stood, looking confused, and Jon raced out of hiding, madrona branch at the ready. He scooped up the gun and stepped back to keep everyone covered. "Don't move. It's over."

I'd landed on top of Tremaine, breaking my fall, but he'd hit the concrete floor hard and gotten the breath knocked out of him. A mix of adrenaline and raw fear left me shaking, and it took several tries to get to my feet. I stepped close to Ryan and took his arm, flinching at the stench of urine and body odor that hovered in a cloud around him. "It's okay. Sit."

He sat at once, childlike in his obedience, a puzzled expression crinkling his brow.

Tremaine lifted his hands and slowly sat up. "Don't hurt me. Please. I didn't shoot anybody. Honest. This is all on Sonny."

Jon didn't react. "Kenzie, check and see what Sonny's doing."

We'd been away from the window for only a few short minutes, but I envisioned him standing right outside, ready to attack. I climbed onto the counter. "He's still outside the cottage. Doesn't seem worried. We didn't make much noise." I tried to find Chris again, but he remained hidden. I turned back to the others but stayed on the counter to keep an eye on the situation.

Jon frowned at Tremaine. "What will he do when you two don't come out?"

Tremaine licked his lips and glanced at his brother. "Hey, I just want out of this."

"Okay. Then answer. What will Sonny do next?"

"Nothing. He won't risk himself to help us. I guarantee it." He gave Jon a pleading look. "He's crazy. He's totally lost it. Talking about killing people. Dumping bodies in the sound."

"Is he going to start shooting people now?"

Tremaine dropped his hands in his lap and shrugged. "He wants to get you two first."

I took a deep breath, light with relief.

But Tremaine kept going. "He's not telling me everything. Just says he has a plan."

I didn't like the sound of that, and from the tension that etched Jon's face, he didn't like it either.

Ryan coughed, another series of wet, wracking gasps, and Tremaine's focus shifted to his brother. "He coughed like that all night. Is he okay?"

I checked outside. Sonny hadn't moved, so I slipped off the counter and stepped to Ryan. His skin had a dull greenish-gray tinge. When I rested my palm on his forehead, heat boiled off him in high-intensity waves. He sat quietly, uninterested in anything around him. I bent closer and held my ear next to his chest. Even without a stethoscope, I could hear rattles and rales with every breath. "He's got pneumonia. He needs a hospital."

Tremaine had seemed unfeeling when he spoke about dumping bodies, but this news had an impact. His face clouded, and he searched my expression. "You'll get him to a doctor, won't you? Even if I'm locked up? He didn't hurt anyone."

I wasn't in the mood to reassure him, but Ryan hadn't been an aggressor. "If we survive this, I'll do what I can."

Tremaine's face relaxed, and he gave me a small nod. He looked at Jon. "Now what?"

"Now, you two are going to spend some quality time here on your own."

I checked to make sure Sonny still waited, unworried, then I retrieved Jon's backpack from the shower and grabbed the rope we'd taken from Erik's tipi. I helped Ryan to his feet and led him to the far end of the shower area. Once he sat, I tied his feet together and tied his good hand to his knee. He leaned back against the wall and closed his eyes, his chest struggling for every breath.

Back in the main room, I tied Tremaine's hands behind him, careful not to block Jon's gun while I worked. "Come on," I said. He got awkwardly to his feet, and I nudged him into the shower with Jon close behind. "Sit." When I finished, Tremaine lay on his side with a short length of rope connecting his bound feet to his hands.

"Check his pockets." Jon gestured toward Tremaine. "Chris said he has the padlock key to the storage shed."

"What?" Tremaine's jaw dropped. "The kid's alive?"

We ignored him. I found the key in the second pocket I checked and handed it to Jon.

"Hey, what about water? And food?" Now that he was im-mobilized, Tremaine seemed to realize how helpless he was. His eyes were the size of dinner plates, and his voice shrilled in panic.

Jon snorted. "You're kidding, right? After the way you've treated us? If things go well, you won't be here long. Sit tight, don't make any noise, and you'll be fine." He pulled a sock out of his pack, stuffed it in Tremaine's mouth, and used a short length of rope to tie it in place. It looked like a clean sock, but it would have been more fitting if it was well-used.

He pulled out a second sock for Ryan, but I shook my head. "He doesn't know what's going on, and he can barely breathe. Leave him."

Jon frowned but put the gag away. We left them trapped there in the shower and checked on Sonny. Still watchful but unconcerned.

"You okay?" Jon took my arm, his face creased with worry, acting like he expected me to collapse at any moment.

I caught sight of myself in the mirror. My unwashed hair hung in tangled knots. My face looked tense and colorless except for dark circles below sunken eyes. I needed food, sleep, and a shower. I needed to be somewhere safe.

I straightened. Tried to channel the toughness of somebody who actually had their act together. "I'm okay."

He gave my arm a gentle squeeze, then climbed onto the counter. "You're straight on the plan?"

"Yeah." But I didn't think I could face Sonny so soon after tackling Tremaine. This needed to be over. It needed to be over *now*.

Jon must have sensed my lack of enthusiasm. "If Sonny comes into the bathhouse, we follow the same plan again, but I'll have this gun. Got it?"

I forced a nod. Tremaine was an amateur. Besting Sonny wouldn't be so easy. But if we kept him occupied long enough, it would give Chris the chance to race for the cottage and help the others.

"If Sonny tries to go back inside the cottage, I'll run out, yelling, and lure him toward the trees. I'll get close enough so he'll notice, but I'll stay out of gun range. Tremaine's gun will help, but I'm not a good shot. Once I get Sonny's attention and lead him away, you sneak out, stay behind the buildings, and head for the cottage to help free the others."

We'd been over this a million times. Jon acted like he was reviewing things for my benefit, but I could tell he was trying to convince himself that we had a chance of success.

"We'll be okay. This is almost over." I hoped I sounded convincing. I didn't believe a word.

I climbed onto the counter at the end opposite him. I'd rather watch than wait blind on the floor.

Five minutes passed. Sonny checked his watch.

Ten minutes. "Tremaine! Everything okay?" Irritation dripped from Sonny's words.

"He sounds pissed." I kept my voice low.

Jon's lips tightened, but he said nothing. It looked like he was barely breathing.

Sonny took three steps away from the cottage. Called again. Scanned the woods. Took three steps back. He checked his watch. Glanced at the cottage. Then he walked toward us, slowly. Looking left and right. Probably wondering if one of us lay in wait. But he kept coming.

"Tremaine guessed wrong." Jon spoke quietly. "He's coming to check on them."

Sonny had walked within firing range. Now he came closer.

He stopped. Glared at the silent bathhouse. Opened his mouth as if to shout. Closed it. Took another step closer.

At that moment, a small shaggy shape burst onto the roadway behind him. Skagit, barking and growling, trying to act tough.

Chris tumbled out of the bushes beside the storage building and raced toward him, calling his name.

I froze, horrified but unable to look away. Jon jumped off the counter and ran for the door.

Sonny whirled at the first bark, his gun raised and ready, then his arm sagged for an instant. The boy he'd believed dead stood only a few feet in front of him.

His surprise didn't last long. The gun snapped up. Chris scooped Skagit into his arms and stood there, facing Sonny only a few feet away.

At the same instant, Jon raced out of the bathhouse, the door slamming hard behind him. "Sonny! Hey, Sonny! Over here!" He fired Tremaine's gun into the air, not daring to aim at Sonny with Chris so close.

Sonny spun toward Jon, giving Chris his chance to run, but as soon as he took his first step, Sonny seized him by the arm and jerked him to a halt. Skagit tumbled to the ground with a yelp and tore off into the underbrush. With a quick pivot, Sonny aimed at Jon's running figure, and I leaped off the counter.

I grabbed Jon's backpack, pushed open the door, and ran for the trees. I heard two shots fired in quick succession, the sounds coming from where Sonny stood. A pain-filled yell echoed from down the beach, and my heart plummeted.

It was Jon's voice. He'd been hit. And Chris had been captured once again.

Chapter Twenty

Chris

I promised Jon I would hide, wait, and watch. I promised I wouldn't run to the cottage until both Sonny and Tremaine went inside the bathhouse. But I didn't promise I'd stay where he put me, behind the storage shed, where I couldn't see the cottage door.

Skagit and I wiggled around the building after Jon and Kenzie disappeared inside, and we hid in the same bushes we'd used the day before. From there I could see the front window and watch for Mom, but it was so far away I couldn't see inside. I pretended she was there, keeping an eye on me, and that made the day not so cold.

We waited. It was boring. Skagit slept for a while, then he wanted to play. I fed him the last of the jerky, but even food didn't keep him happy. Every time he wiggled, wanting to run, I had to hold onto him and whisper *Stay*.

He kept fidgeting, and hanging on made my arm hurt. We waited and waited but nothing happened.

Finally, long after a lunchtime with no lunch, Tremaine and Ryan came out. Tremaine was jumpy, looking everywhere while Ryan wobbled, hanging onto his brother. Sonny came out, waving his gun and acting mean. Tremaine and Ryan went into the bathhouse. Still, nothing happened. Skagit tried to bark at Sonny, so I had to hold his mouth closed. I couldn't hear anything from the bathhouse. Did silence mean Jon and Kenzie had won? Or maybe something had gone horribly wrong.

Skagit licked my hand, but that didn't help.

Sonny stood there. Not bored. Waiting and watching.

He called to Tremaine. Then he walked down the road with his gun out. Close to us now. Hunting.

Skagit fidgeted again, and I held onto him hard to keep him safe. Maybe too hard because all at once he jerked away, twisting so fast I couldn't keep my grip. He ran onto the road, growling and barking at Sonny, more like a killer pit bull than a pissed-off ball of fluff.

I went after him. I had to. Grabbed him up fast. When I held him to my chest, he didn't fight me, pressing close like he knew he'd blown it. Sonny stood with his mouth hanging open and his eyes big and round.

"What the hell?" He sounded surprised and maybe a little scared, not angry, but he pointed his gun at me and Skagit.

My arm hurt worse than ever, and my stomach got heavy. I couldn't make my feet run.

The door to the bathhouse banged open so loud, I jumped. Jon ran out yelling and shooting into the air, and finally my legs could move again. I took one step, but Sonny grabbed my bad arm, and

I yelped. Skagit ran off, and I didn't blame him one bit because I would have run, too, if I could have.

Sonny whipped around and fired straight at Jon. He missed. Then he planted his feet solid and aimed more careful. He fired again, and this time Jon yelled and fell on the beach. Fell hard enough to hurt. What if he was dead? But then he got up again, limping toward the steps and boardwalk, holding onto the top of his leg with both hands, not running so fast now.

"Damn it." Sonny shot two more times and swore like the campers did sometimes. He didn't hit Jon again.

He jerked my arm. "You little brat. You're supposed to be dead. You're nothing but trouble, but maybe now your mother will behave herself. Come on." He dragged me down the hill toward the bathhouse.

I'd gotten away at the cove, then stayed hidden. It was almost like I had magic powers from one of my video games. But now here I was, trapped again. Mom would be mad at me for sure. Skagit poked his head out of some bushes, and I waved him back. He'd be safer on his own. Sonny looked angrier than I'd ever seen anybody before. I didn't want him turning that anger at Skagit.

He stopped a few yards from the bathhouse door. "Come on out nurse-lady. Your friend has a gun, so I know you've done something to Tremaine and Ryan in there. I got a solid hit on your friend. He's off in the trees somewhere, bleeding out. So, give up. I've got the kid, and my gun's buried in his back. If you try anything, he's dead. I'll make damn sure of it this time."

Nobody answered and nobody came out. Kenzie for sure would have run for it when Jon tried a distraction. But Sonny stood there, waiting, getting madder, mumbling to himself and squeezing my arm so hard I thought the bone might break. It took a long time before he walked the rest of the way and shoved me through the door ahead of him.

Nobody was there, of course. He slammed open the toilet stall doors one at a time, keeping a tight hold on me every step and acting gruff and kind of embarrassed that he'd been yelling to an empty room. He dragged me toward the shower area and stopped in the doorway.

They looked pretty funny, Tremaine and Ryan tied up the way they were, but I was too scared to laugh. Ryan stared at us like he didn't know what was going on, but Tremaine grunted through his gag and tried to rock himself onto his knees. He couldn't make it, just fell back onto his side, staring at Sonny with giant-sized eyes.

"You stupid assholes. You let yourself be taken by a fool and a girl? I don't know what made me put up with either one of you." Sonny stepped closer to Tremaine like he planned to bend down to untie him. Tremaine thought so, too, because he relaxed and lay back. "I've got the kid now, and his mom is going to cough up the location of the treasure. I might as well tidy up, since the two of you are so neatly wrapped for me."

Before I could sort out what he meant, Sonny shifted his gun away from my back and pulled the trigger. The noise exploded in my ears and bounced off the walls, and a small round hole appeared in the middle of Tremaine's forehead. Hardly any blood at all in front, but plenty on the floor behind him, and the smoke in the air smelled like rotten eggs. Tremaine's eyes were wide open, more surprised than scared.

My stomach knew he was dead, and sour-tasting stuff lurched high into my throat. My muscles knew it, too, and they seized up to hold me locked in place. My bladder must have known it, and a wet warmth spread down my legs. But even though I said the words to myself and knew they were true, I couldn't quite believe what I saw. This was nothing like death in my video games.

The gun moved again, and this time I closed my eyes and turned away. It fired. More noise. More smoke and smell. I didn't want to look, but my eyes did anyway. The hole in Ryan's forehead matched the one in Tremaine's.

Sonny dragged me out of the bathhouse. Back up the hill, my legs not working too good. Into the cottage. I forgot to check for Skagit. Forgot to check for Kenzie. I ended up tied to a chair in the kitchen, my hands behind me, but I wasn't sure how it happened. The kitchen smelled like toast and coffee, but instead of making me hungry, I had to try hard not to puke.

Sonny undid the rope lock on the bedroom door and called in. "You three, stand back. Don't try anything. I've got the kid out here." He nudged the door open with his foot. "Okay, Mom, come say hello to your dead son."

He let her out, then slammed the door again, locking Erik and Bree in. Mom came running, kneeling beside me and hugging my neck. Crying a little, but not sad and not scared and not angry I'd let myself get caught.

"Mom. He shot them. He shot both of them." I didn't want to cry, but my nose stuffed up and my cheeks got wet anyway. I was shaking so hard, the chair rattled.

Her head whipped back fast. "Jon? He shot Jon?" Horrified. Like she couldn't imagine something so terrible. "Kenzie too?"

"No. Yes." My brain wouldn't work right. The words hid away, hard to find. "I mean, yes, he shot Jon, but he could still run. He shot Tremaine and Ryan. In the head. Both of them."

Sonny stood right there in the doorway to the living room, but he didn't say a thing. Mom stared at me like it wasn't me she saw. She got to her feet real slow and faced Sonny, standing between me and him but backed up so her leg touched mine like she didn't want to leave me all the way. "What now?" She sounded very tired.

"Now, we're going to talk. Because now you know I play for keeps. I have your kid, and you're going to lead me to this fricking treasure."

The sat phone rang, loud and out of place in the middle of so much that wasn't normal. He pulled out the phone, and Mom sank onto a kitchen chair beside me, resting her hand on my arm.

"Yeah?" He answered gruff, then listened. "Thank you. Yes, I sure appreciate it." His voice had gotten sicky sweet. "Three o'clock? Yes, I can be there then."

I checked the wall clock. Two-fifteen.

Sonny listened more. "I don't think that's necessary. I'm authorized to ...." He frowned. "Yes. I see ... Of course ... It's not an issue. She'll be there to sign ...We'll meet you at the pier in forty-five minutes."

He disconnected. Stared at Mom. "That was the marina. They've finished repairs early, and they'll deliver the boat at three. I told them yesterday they could charge extra if they got it here ahead of schedule, and since you signed the original estimate, they need you to sign off on the bonus or they won't hand over the keys."

"I won't sign." She said it real fast, like speed would make him go along.

He lifted the gun. Aimed it at me. "Yeah, you will."

Mom's fingernails dug deep into my skin. "You're right. Of course, I will. I'll sign."

"Damn right." He stepped into the living room, grabbed two lengths of clothesline like the ones on my wrists, and tied Mom to her chair.

"It's too tight."

"Don't whine. It won't be for long." He tucked the gun into the waistband of his pants, went into my bedroom and came back with sheets, pillows, blankets, and a bunch of T-shirts and jeans from my dresser. He piled them all in a heap against the locked door to Mom's bedroom. Next, he came back to the kitchen and rummaged through the freezer. He stacked up a bunch of casseroles, checking the labels. Carried them and our last bag of apples and a few sacks of canned goods—soup and corn and tuna—out the front door. Filled two empty gallon jugs with water and took them out too. He stepped out back with one of Mom's good chopping knives, came back with a short length of hose he must have cut off from the long one we used in the garden. He locked the back door and double-checked it.

I looked at Mom, but she didn't seem to know what he was up to either.

Sonny grabbed the empty mop bucket and dropped the piece of hose inside. He walked around in the living room for a few minutes. I heard noises like moving furniture, then he was standing in front of us again. "Now then. We're going to go outside together. Nice and easy. Don't forget I have this gun."

He came beside me and untied the knot that attached one hand to the chair, but he left the rope tied around my wrist, the free end dangling. He stepped back out of reach. "Untie your other hand. No. Don't get smart. Untie it from the chair but leave it on your wrist."

I did it.

"Now untie your mom. Same way."

I did that too.

"Into the living room. Both of you. Pick up the pillows from the couch. The blanket. The afghan from the chair." He held the bucket with the hose in his hand.

We did what he said. He'd tied three ropes to hold the bedroom door shut, stretched across the pile of cloth he'd heaped against it and anchored to groups of furniture. We had to step over them, our arms full of stuff.

"Outside. Pile all that crap under the bedroom window."

I did it, but Mom hesitated. She seemed even more worried now, but I still didn't get it.

"Go on. Do it."

She did.

He marched us to the van. Held the gun in one hand and tied us to the back seat, careful every minute, never giving us a chance to do anything.

Next, he picked up the hose and bucket and stood where I couldn't see him, back where you put in the gas. I didn't know what he was doing back there, but Mom must have figured it out. "Stop! No! Don't do it!" She yelled loud, but the words bounced inside the closed-up car. "Erik! Bree! Break the window! Get out!"

They couldn't hear. No way. Not with us locked inside the van. And they couldn't see enough from their window.

Then Sonny lugged the bucket into the house. A minute later, he came out fast, and thick black smoke chased after him.

Chapter Twenty-One

Jon

I jolted back to consciousness with a scream locked in my throat and pain in my leg shooting up my back, detonating electric sparks in my brain. Somebody moaned in horrid distress—maybe me?—and I grabbed for the gun I'd held in my hand when blackness closed in. Instead of cold metal, my fingers found cloth and flesh, and I pushed hard at my attacker, trying to stop the agony.

"Hey! It's okay. Let me finish."

I forced my eyes open. Kenzie's face. And Kenzie's hands, doing something unspeakable that hurt like hell, poking around in the gaping wound on my leg. The pain overwhelmed any relief I might have felt at seeing her. "What are you—?" It came out more scream than question.

"Hold still."

Ten more seconds, ten more years of anguish, then she lifted her bloody fingers from my leg, her thumb and forefinger grasping a bullet.

"Got it." She sounded pleased with herself, but all I cared about was the fact that she'd stopped. "You're lucky. It shredded muscle but missed bone and the big blood vessels."

Something nudged my side. When I reached to push it away, it licked my hand. Skagit. I gave him a pat and looked around. "Where's Chris?"

Kenzie avoided my eyes, picked up a rolled strip of cloth, and began bandaging the wound.

"Stop that. Where's Chris?"

She didn't stop, just stared fixedly at her task. "Sonny grabbed him."

The three words punched me in the gut, a triple blow far more painful than my leg. "Shit. I thought I could distract him so Chris could get away."

She tied off the bandage, her jaw clenched so hard, her teeth grated. "Chris tried. Sonny was too fast. He grabbed him before he shot you."

"Is Chris okay? Did he get hurt?"

Kenzie turned three shades whiter. "He's okay. At least, he was okay half an hour ago. Sonny dragged Chris into the bathhouse, and a few minutes later, I heard gunshots. Two. Close together." She blinked hard. "Jon, I nearly died in the minutes before Sonny hauled Chris out and I knew for sure he hadn't shot him. He looked terrified and walked with staggering steps, but he didn't seem injured. Once they went into the cottage, I ducked inside the bathhouse to look." She gulped. "I needed to see what he'd done."

I reached out and squeezed her hand. There was nothing she could have done to help.

"Tremaine and Ryan were still tied up like we'd left them. Both shot in the head, execution style. Tremaine still had the gag in place. He couldn't even beg for mercy. We'd made them helpless. And Chris must have seen Sonny kill them."

A wave of nausea swept through my chest and left me retching. My head spun and my leg throbbed. "Why would he do such a thing?"

A deep shudder shook her entire body, and I hung on tighter to her hand, trying to stay grounded. She closed her eyes. "Do you think Sonny always planned to get rid of them? Or, when he saw them tied up, did something just snap?"

I kept picturing Tremaine, wide-eyed and frightened. Gagged and unable to talk after I'd refused his simple request for food and water. And Ryan, coughing and struggling for every breath, confused and no risk to anyone. How could Sonny step into that shower, see those two helpless men, and feel nothing but the urge to kill?

And now he had Chris again.

I wiped sweat off my face. Tried to shift my leg into a more comfortable position. I had a vague recollection of staggering down the beach and along the boardwalk after I was shot, then diving into the trees to hide in a hollow. I'd been careful in the last stretch not to leave a blood trail. "How did you find me?"

"Skagit deserves full credit. After I checked on ... After I left the bathhouse, I ran in this direction. I called but couldn't find any sign of you. Skagit came running. He ducked off the path and led me straight to you."

"Did Sonny see you?"

"I don't know. Maybe, if he looked out the window at the right moment. But if so, he didn't react."

If he was dealing with Chris, he may have had his hands full. *Dealing with Chris.* I pushed the sickening thought away. There wasn't much doubt Sonny had lost all control. Drake's massive debt was old news. Now, Sonny's fixation on finding Allman's cache consumed him. I tried to speak, but dismay clogged my throat, and I coughed instead. Kenzie handed me a water bottle. I drank, trying to kick my brain in gear. "We counted on the idea Sonny wouldn't hurt the others until he caught us."

"He has to leave the cottage if he wants to search for us. And he has to leave tomorrow to get the boat when it arrives at the dock. He must know that the minute he clears out, we'll go in and rescue the others. We have plenty of witnesses to what he's done. So, what do you think he'll do next?"

"I don't know." I tried to put myself in Sonny's shoes, but the murders of Tremaine and Ryan blocked my thinking. We out-numbered him now, and we had Tremaine's gun, but that might only make him more desperate. "Where's the gun?"

Kenzie handed it over, holding it by the end of the barrel with as few fingers as she could manage. I fumbled for the release, disen-gaged the magazine, and counted the cartridges, including the one in the chamber. "Four left." My gaze fell on the bloody bullet she had set aside on a rock. "Give me that, please."

She handed it over. I rubbed it against my jeans to get rid of the blood and set it next to the others. "Sonny's is a lot bigger." The little I knew about bullet calibers came from television cop shows, but I knew you had to have the right sized bullet for your gun. "That means he can't use the box of bullets he found in Leah's lockbox to replace the ones he's fired. They'll only fit this gun that we took from Tremaine. So, the question is, how much ammunition did he bring with him?"

She thought for a moment. "I've never seen him carry anything except the gun. He didn't have any sort of pouch or pack with him when he arrived. If he has spare ammunition, it must be in his pocket."

We spent a few minutes trying to remember how many bullets he'd fired. Two at Chris, four at me, two at poor Tremaine and Ryan. But we had no idea how many he had in his gun to start. I didn't like the math. "The bottom line is that he may be low on ammunition, but we can't know for sure."

I reloaded our gun. Four bullets, four shots, one man. But only useful if we could get close enough to use it.

"We've got the key to the storage building," Kenzie said. A belted kingfisher gave its harsh rattling call nearby. She recoiled and twisted her hands together. "Is there anything in there that can help?"

"Maybe. Tools. Canoes and paddles. There might be a few things we could use." I fought my way to my feet and took a few careful steps. Putting weight on my injured leg triggered jagged arcs of pain, stealing my breath. I could walk, barely, but I couldn't run. I would slow Kenzie down. And I'd lose in any kind of fight.

"You should sit still." She tugged at my arm.

"I can't. Those in the cabin are in even more danger now, and that includes Chris." And Leah. I had to save Leah. I'd asked Kenzie why Leah had said nothing if she knew I cared for her, but I knew the answer. She'd been too badly injured to take such a step. I needed to take the lead. But first, she needed to survive. "If we hide, we can't help the others. We have to come up with another plan. And we're running out of time."

"I agree." But then she looked at me as if she expected me to come up with a great idea. As if I weren't muddling through minute by minute and making nonstop mistakes.

The biggest problem with her faith in me? I had no idea what we should do next.

Chapter Twenty-Two

Kenzie

J on and I spent the next few minutes trying to brainstorm a coherent plan to get rid of Sonny and rescue the others. I wanted to be optimistic, but our assets consisted of a man so badly injured he could hardly walk, a small scraggly dog, a gun with four bullets, and me. Every idea we considered sounded crazier than the one before.

"We need to find out what Sonny's doing. His actions dictate our options." Jon fought his way forward a few steps, leaning hard on a madrona branch I pulled from the underbrush. "Let's work our way back to the edge of the meadow."

We took the path through the woods that led past the Heron tipis, then inched our way to the edge of the forest. Every rustle in the undergrowth made me jump. Every bird call made me whip around to confirm its source. I couldn't shake the unsettling feeling that something watched us, the skin between my shoulder blades twitching any time my back was to the forest. I worried something waited for us there. Something hidden. Something bad.

The wind gusted off the sound in powerful bursts, setting the tall grass dancing. Jon struggled through every step. By the time we found a sheltered spot and stopped, he was gasping and soaked with sweat. He collapsed onto a nearby boulder. "Sorry, need to take a break."

I handed him water, and he chugged it. The makeshift bandage I'd applied had already soaked through, and blood oozed down his leg in long ribbons. The wound itself was a tangled mess of badly shredded muscle. The bullet had lodged so close to his femoral artery that I hadn't wanted to leave it there, but the poking around I'd done to extract it hadn't improved things.

He needed sutures. Antibiotics. A proper bandage. But we weren't likely to get any of that in the foreseeable future. I pulled the last remnants of Erik's shirt from the backpack, tore off a final few strips, and used the shirtsleeves to tie a thick cloth pad in place. It would have to do.

We could see the cottage, but we'd stopped too far away to make out details. I forced aside my hunger and an overwhelming desire for sleep. "You stay here with Skagit, and I'll work my way to the potter's shed."

Jon shook his head, picked up his crutch, and started to get up. "I don't want you to go by yourself. I can—" His leg collapsed beneath him, and he dropped onto the boulder with a groan.

"Wait here. Rest. You're not missing anything. I'm going to see what I can learn. Then I'll come back." I got to my feet, trying to act businesslike and confident. My heart knew better and crawled up my throat in protest. "Don't worry. I'll be careful."

"Take the gun." He pulled it out of the pack and held it toward me.

I didn't reach for it. On my ER rotations, I'd seen up close the damage a bullet could do, and now I had Drake's death to haunt me as well. Paige had let Tim have a plastic gun when he begged for it, but I wouldn't let him play with it when I was there. Guns and me? Not a good combo. "I'm more likely to shoot myself than do any damage."

"Come here."

I didn't want to, but my feet stepped toward him anyway.

"This is the safety catch. On. Off." He flipped it back and forth. "When you want to fire, hold it steady in both hands." He demonstrated. "Aim for the body, not the head. It's a bigger target. Don't fire unless you're close enough to hit."

My heart left my chest. The idea of shooting somebody made my skin crawl. Jon had said *aim for the body*, but a body was a living breathing person. I held the gun as if it would detonate on its own, double-checked the safety, then hung on tight to the grip.

Jon rummaged through the pack again. "Here. Take this too." He held out a pocketknife.

I slipped it into my pocket, the smaller lump far more comforting than the heavy weight in my hand. "Thanks." I gave Skagit a pat. "You stay here, boy." I hoped he understood because I couldn't risk him giving me away.

The meadow remained quiet and empty, so I ran to the potter's shed, careful to stay shielded from the cottage windows. No bushes concealed me here. I had to go inside the shed to hide and have a view of the cottage,

Inside the shed with Drake's body.

I hadn't thought to bring a flashlight, so I wouldn't be able to see him, but that did nothing to calm my imagination.

I peered around the corner of the building. Saw no activity. Ducked around front, eased open the door, and slipped inside. I settled onto the floor, leaving the door open a few inches to see out. If Sonny noticed the gap, he'd blame the wind. The foul smell of day-old death permeated the shed, and I could sense Drake's presence only a few feet behind me.

I'm trying to help your friends. I didn't say it out loud, just sent the message out to whatever spirit might be listening. My spine tingled with the creepy feeling that I wasn't alone, and I couldn't repress a shiver.

With Jon in no shape to fight, every movement and every decision I made carried more weight than I could bear. I'd worried that a summer of tipis and teenagers would be more than I could manage. I was the city girl who knew nothing about the outdoors or guns and fighting. I was the screw-up who'd killed her own nephew and lost her sister as a result. I couldn't take on Sonny alone.

But Drake's silent presence pressed hard against me, a grim reminder of how much was at stake. I reached into my pocket for Tim's stone. This time, it provided no comfort.

We shouldn't have put Chris on watch. We shouldn't have trusted a child to stay where he belonged. We shouldn't have left Tremaine and Ryan tied up and alone. We shouldn't ... we shouldn't ... we shouldn't ...

I pounded my fist against my thigh. Waiting was hell. I didn't want to sit there full of regrets, I wanted action. Instead, I put the gun on the ground beside me and braced for a long vigil.

Less than five minutes later, Sonny came out of the cottage, with a set of keys in his hand. He held his gun high and paused for a moment to inspect the field in all directions, but he didn't act worried. He knew he'd hit Jon, and he must have figured I wasn't much of a threat.

I feared he might be right.

The aging van still stood beside the road where Erik had left it after picking up the others the week before. The keys had been hanging on a hook in the kitchen. Sonny stepped to the far side of the van, opened the driver's door, sat, and turned on the engine. It sputtered to life, and he leaned forward, peering at the dashboard.

A minute later, he turned it off. Left the door standing open, went into the cottage, and came back carrying two brown paper grocery bags. He opened the back door on the side of the van facing me and tossed the bags onto the back seat. One tipped, and three cans tumbled onto the ground. He picked them up and pitched them into the van, doing everything one-handed, his gun held ready.

Tremaine's gun sat beside me, demanding action, but I couldn't get close enough to fire without Sonny seeing me first.

He didn't pause. He went back to the cottage and came out carrying two gallon jugs of water, a six-pack of Erik's beer, a bag of apples, and some packages that looked like Leah's casseroles from the freezer. Next came a battery-powered lantern, a blanket, a pillow. All were things he might use to provision the boat, but it wasn't supposed to arrive until the next day. Gathering everything now made no sense.

The curtains fluttered in the front window of the cottage, and I could make out the pale whiteness of a face. At least one of the prisoners had enough strength to stand and keep watch, but if they'd gone yet another day without food and water, they had to have lost ground. Maybe Leah or Erik or Bree could figure out what Sonny was up to, but I wasn't having any luck.

He returned to the cottage, and this time when he emerged he pushed Leah and Chris in front of him. Chris's tense, blotchy face looked like he'd been crying, and I swallowed a hot gulp of anger. Leah wobbled on her feet, her face a pasty gray. They both carried armloads of pillows and piled them below the bedroom window. Sonny made quick efficient work of imprisoning them in the van, then he picked up a bucket that rattled with something in it. He disappeared around the far side of the van. I could see his feet—he was standing still—but I couldn't tell what he was doing.

Leah must have known. She screamed something inside the van, but I couldn't make out the words.

I could run to the van, but I couldn't get in and set either of them free without Sonny shooting me. I could probably make it to the back door of the cottage, but Sonny had been careful to keep it locked. If Jon were with me, maybe he'd have ideas, but I didn't. Whatever Sonny was doing took almost five minutes. Then he dropped what looked like a cut section of garden hose onto the ground, brought the bucket back to the cottage, and disappeared inside.

Every muscle in my body tensed. Something was wrong. Sonny carried the bucket differently this time. He leaned against its weight and held it a little to one side, taking care that his leg didn't bump it. He carried it the way I held a full bucket of mop water when I didn't want to spill it.

Panic threw me off balance. I realized what he had in that bucket.

I swung the shed door open, ready to warn the others, but ducked back for an instant when Sonny came out of the cottage in a hurry. This time, smoke chased him.

No time to waste. I ran straight at him, Tremaine's gun in my hand.

Sonny had his weapon tucked into the small of his back, and his hand jerked toward it, but he didn't grab it. He twisted instead and seized the rim of the bucket with both hands. I was still thirty feet away when he swung it in a giant arc, flinging several gallons of gasoline through the air. The wind caught it and blew it sideways. Thick streams landed on the pile of bedding, the aged cedar siding of the house, the wooden frame of the window. Thinner streams hit the ground, and a narrow band of gasoline led directly from the cottage to the bucket, still clutched in Sonny's hand.

I was five yards away, running with the gun held the proper way, when I sucked in a huge lungful of harsh gas fumes and stumbled, coughing. My eyes streamed, and I struggled to drag in air. Sonny pulled his lighter from his breast pocket, flicked it on, and with a casual jerk of his wrist, threw it.

Time slowed. The lighter, one of those old-fashioned silver ones that held its flame, arced through the air. Bree's face pressed against the bedroom window, eyes wide and mouth open. I dug my heels in, skidding to a stop, scrambling to reverse my momentum. The lighter paused at the peak of its flight, then dropped.

It landed in a powerful whoosh of flame, the gasoline igniting so fast, it looked more like an explosion than a fire. Flames flared on the pillows and danced on a cotton blanket. They raced up the cottage siding, propelled by the wind, crackling and popping. Fire attacked the house, but it also sped along the narrow band of gasoline leading back to the bucket. The bucket Sonny still clutched in his right hand.

The flames leapt from the spilled gasoline on the ground to the rivulet that dripped over the outside of the bucket, then raced upward, feeding on every remaining molecule of gasoline. Sonny screamed, dropped the bucket, and stepped back, jerking his hand to his chest. His face contorted in anguish, his gun forgotten.

My gun was ready. I was the only one who could do this. I fumbled for the safety. Stopped, held the grip in both hands. Aimed straight at Sonny's chest and squeezed the trigger. The noise and recoil threw me backward, but Sonny didn't react. A miss.

I shifted my hands to get a better hold, aimed again, and pulled the trigger. I yelped. My hand had slipped too high on the gun and the slide delivered a painful cut to the skin beside my thumb. But I was the only one who cried out. I'd missed again.

Sonny jumped into the van, no longer a target. He turned on the engine, jerked the wheel, and shot up the road, heading south toward the pier. The last thing I saw was Leah's face, pressed against the van's window. I couldn't waste another precious bullet. I'd blown the one chance I had.

In the strong wind, the fire raced along the cottage's tinder-dry siding, the front bedroom window already engulfed in flames. To get the others out, I had to force my way inside. "Shit, shit, shit." My heart raced, my breath came in gasps, and my whole body shook.

The awning over the front door caught, and sparks rained on my head and shoulders as I burst through the unlocked door. Jon shouted behind me.

The living room furniture had been heaped together in groups. Instead of a single rope tying the bedroom door closed, three ropes now stretched taut to the doorknob, each one anchored to a different pile of heavy objects. The entire room reeked of gasoline, and a mountain of sheets and bed pillows blazed in front of the bedroom door, blocking access and giving off waves of chemical fumes.

I screamed as loud as I could. "Bree! Erik! I'm trying to get in!"

"The door's our only chance. The window's hopeless." Erik's voice came at once, but it sounded weak and shaky.

"The door's blocked! I need to clear it!" I fumbled for Jon's pocketknife. Pried out the main blade. Smoke poured from the mound of bedding and more blew in through the open front door. Every breath triggered a cough from deep inside my lungs. I sawed through the first rope. Thanked Jon for having the presence of mind to give me the knife, then sawed through the second. A crash came from inside the bedroom, followed by a scream that sounded like Bree.

I flinched. "Are you okay?"

"Hurry!"

Erik's urgency made my hand tremble. I sliced through the third rope. "Cover your hand! Open the door!"

The door flew open, and Erik charged out, pushing a broad plank from the bookcase in front of him, using it like a shovel to scoot the burning pile of bedding to one side and clear a path out. As soon as he had an opening, he dropped the plank and ducked back inside the bedroom. He returned with his arm around Bree, her face sheet-white, her right arm bent against her chest at an awkward angle. Her left arm clutched the silver frame that held Leah's documents.

"Come on! Hurry!" I waved them forward. Flames devoured the ceiling near the front door. Fire engulfed the walls on both sides. Erik and Bree were both gaunt and hollow-eyed, and neither moved with enough urgency. All three of us coughed nonstop now, the black smoke thick and choking. "Head for the back door."

I lunged toward the kitchen. Erik dragged Bree, half-carrying her, but a section of the ceiling gave way, sending flaming plywood and smoldering shingles tumbling in a heap in front of the door. A burning two-by-four swung down from above and caught Erik hard on his back, dropping him to his knees. He screamed and slumped forward. Bree staggered, barely staying on her feet.

Splintering sounds came from behind me. The back door flew open, and Jon stood there, clutching a chunk of firewood he'd used as a battering ram. "Hurry! The entire roof has caught!"

The smoke kept thickening, burning my eyes and throat, making it difficult to see. Heat pulsed from all sides, scalding my skin. I pushed Bree into Jon's arms, then turned for Erik.

He had forced the timber off to one side, and with my help, he struggled to his feet. But he was sucking in too much smoke, far too much. Flames danced on the back of his shirt, but he made no effort to put them out. I grabbed a scrap of unburned toweling from the floor and beat at his flaming shirt. "Come on."

He groaned and made no effort to move.

"Erik, come on, you have to help." Blackened skin, already peeling, marked his back. His shirt hung in tatters. I grabbed his arm, and at last, he let me drag him toward the back door. Jon returned and hobbled toward me. He seized Erik around the waist, and between the two of us, we managed to hustle him outside.

Bree sat slumped on the road with Skagit on guard at her side. Jon and I eased Erik, barely conscious, to the ground beside her. At a horrendous crash, I spun to look back at the cottage. The roof caved in, first one section, then another, sending bits of flaming shingle flying through the air. Fire devoured the entire back wall.

My throat shrank as if I were breathing through a soda straw. I couldn't rip my eyes from the destruction. If Jon and I hadn't decided to keep watch .... If I hadn't been close by .... If Sonny hadn't burned himself and, instead, pulled his gun ... it all would have ended differently.

We had injuries to tend to. Water and food to gather. But for an endless moment, I could only stand in one spot and shake.

Chapter Twenty-Three

Chris

Sonny drove the van way faster than Mom or Erik ever did, sliding from one side of the road to the other with only one hand on the steering wheel, swearing like crazy and tossing us around in the back so we jerked hard against our ropes. The burn on his right hand looked gross, black on the edges and red in the middle with skin peeling off. His clothes smelled like gasoline. The way the flame had leaped off the ground to attack him made me like fire a bit more.

"You just killed two people. My friends. Burned them to death." Mom spat the words. "Have you no conscience at all?"

Sonny didn't answer. He set his jaw hard and kept driving, the van creaking and groaning every time it bounced over a hole. I pulled on the knots that kept me tied, but I had zero luck. One hand couldn't reach anywhere near the other. Sonny had been too careful.

When we got to the pier, Sonny slammed on the brakes. The camp boat was chugging toward us, only a quarter mile out, a small skiff towed behind it. Sonny twisted in his seat to give Mom one of his nasty looks.

"Here's how this is going to work. I untie you. Then you and I walk out on the pier together, like two happy coworkers. I keep my burned hand hidden. My hand with the gun in my pocket. You sign the paperwork. You thank the fool who's dropping the boat. You wave good-bye like you haven't a worry in the world. Got it?"

Mom nodded.

"If you do anything, anything at all, to make them suspicious, I will shoot you, I will shoot the boat guy, and I will shoot your son. Do you understand?"

"What prevents you from shooting us both as soon as you have the boat?" Her voice sounded so strange, if I hadn't seen her mouth moving, I wouldn't have known who it was. Her face had an odd whiteness to it and her arms shook, worse even than the time she had bad flu and stayed in bed for a week.

Sonny grimaced and wrapped his burned hand in a rag from the van's floor, cringing when the cloth touched his skin. "You're going to tell me where the root cellar is, so behave yourself, and you'll be okay." He got out of the van, came around and untied one of Mom's wrists. Waited for her to fumble the knot off the other hand. She turned in her seat and reached for my ropes, but Sonny jerked her back. "The kid stays here."

Mom gave a small smile and Sonny noticed. "Oh, I see. The kid usually goes, too, huh? They'll expect to see him. Okay, go ahead and untie him."

She did, and I scooted out beside her.

"Both of you, remember, I'm watching every move."

I rubbed my wrists where the rope had cut in. Gave Mom's hand a squeeze. Sonny was right. Jeff would've wondered if I wasn't with Mom. I always went with her to meet the boat. We walked down to the pier, Mom and me in front and Sonny behind.

Jeff stood at the wheel of the boat, and he slid it into place beside the pier without even a bump. "Good afternoon, good afternoon! How are you all doing this fine day?"

After days of nobody acting normal, it was so strange to hear someone talking like he always did. He killed the engine and tossed me the bow and stern lines just like always. I tied them both to cleats.

"We're fine." Mom didn't sound fine to me, but Jeff didn't appear to notice. "Thanks for getting the boat here so early."

He laughed and rummaged beside him for a clipboard full of papers. "Nothing like a five-hundred-dollar bonus to encourage some overtime. I'm glad the camp is doing so well this summer."

He tucked the clipboard under one arm, picked up a square metal tin, and stepped onto the pier. "Here you go, Chris." He handed me the tin. "Marilyn baked pound cake this morning and thought you might like some."

My stomach rumbled just from hearing the words. "Thanks. That sounds great."

He reached into a pocket of his overalls and pulled out a handful of dog biscuits, then looked around. "Hey, where's Skagit? Gotta feed that pup up. Maybe one day he'll grow into a real dog."

I didn't know what to say, but Mom jumped in. "He's not feeling well today. We left him at home."

For the first time, Jeff looked puzzled. He checked out Mom's greasy hair and dirty clothes. He looked hard at me, then at Sonny, who stood there, silent. I would have never left Skagit alone if he were sick. Jeff knew it. He had three German Shepherds that he treated like babies.

He opened his mouth like he was going to say something, and I froze, worried Sonny would shoot. But then Jeff shrugged and held the clipboard out to Mom. "Just need your signature to authorize the extra charge."

She took the clipboard and pen, and Sonny stepped forward and peered over her shoulder, making sure the only thing she wrote was her name. She passed the pen and clipboard back. "Here you go. Thanks again for the hustle." Her voice cracked at the end.

"Any time. We love the business. Hey, next time you're off-island, be sure to stop by. Marilyn's growing a new variety of tomato this year, and she wants to show you how well it's taking off."

"Tell her I will. For sure. Next time we're over."

"Great." He turned to step back into the camp boat. But he glanced down at the cleat with the bow line, and he caught himself before his foot left the pier. He turned his head to check the cleat with the stern line.

I held my breath, my body stiff and solid like a tree trunk.

Years ago, Jeff taught me the proper way to moor a boat. A neat figure-eight around the cleat, ending with a smooth locking half-hitch. It didn't just look good. It kept the line from slipping or getting kicked off by mistake. But today when he tossed me the lines, I wrapped them around the cleats in big, lumpy circles the way some of the campers did if they knew nothing about boats. No figure-eight. No half-hitch. No proper knot at all.

Don't say anything. Please, please, please, don't say anything. Just know something is wrong and go.

Real slow, Jeff stepped onto the camp boat. Went to the stern. Untied his skiff and pulled it around to the far side. Stepped from the big boat to the little one, and only then turned and looked back at me. Looked hard. Looked straight into my eyes, and I nodded once. "Thanks again for the cake."

He looked at Mom. At Sonny. Lifted his hand in a final wave. "No problem, kid. When it comes to pound cake, I've got your back."

He pushed off. Started his engine. Sped off toward Guemes Island without looking at us again.

Mom's shoulders slumped, her face closed off like she'd shut a door, but she hadn't noticed what I'd done. Me? I could breathe again. Jeff had our back.

"Nice job." Sonny had his gun out in the open again. "See how easy it is when you do what I tell you? Come on. You two need to carry all this stuff to the boat and load it."

Sonny stayed by the van while we went back and forth. Mom and I walked together and took small loads. It was the first chance we had to talk, and I had plenty to say, but Mom jumped in first. "If you get a chance to run, take it." She whispered the words, but it sounded like she meant it.

"I can't—."

"You can. That's an order. Chris, he plans to kill us. If you get the chance, go."

She was trying to send me away the same way I'd sent Skagit. He must have felt abandoned then like I did now. But I got it. We stayed quiet going back to the van, worried Sonny would notice us talking, then grabbed the next load and headed back toward the boat.

"Jon is okay? You're sure the shot only hit his leg?"

"Looked like it. And you saw Kenzie. She looked okay too."

"I hope the two of them were able to help the others."

I decided not to say anything about Jeff. Maybe he just thought I was playing a game. Maybe he wouldn't do anything at all. Mom had too much on her mind without adding another worry. Neither of us talked about the smoke we could see now, rising thick and gray above the trees. A shame there hadn't been enough smoke for Jeff to see when he was here. Our cottage. With Erik and Bree locked in. If I got the chance to run, I would go, like Mom said. But if I got the chance to hurt Sonny, I'd do that instead.

"Okay," he said when we finished loading the boat. "Now, we talk."

I looked at him a little closer. He still talked the same way, still the tough voice, the tough words, but his face looked stretched tight. He'd taken his burned hand out of the cloth wrap. It was bright red and swollen, with giant puffy blisters now, and he took care not to move it or brush it against anything.

Mom and I stood there, waiting.

"I read the clue in the old journal. Now you're going to lead me to the root cellar he mentioned."

I kept still. I didn't know what he meant about the clue in the journal, but Jon had shown me the root cellar a while back. I knew where it was.

Mom said nothing.

"You all claimed you didn't know where it is. I don't believe it. You live here. You know this island. Tell me now, or I shoot your son."

Mom still said nothing for a long, long time, then she licked her lips and grabbed my hand. "It's not too far from the cliff where you went searching with Erik and Jon. We can get there in the boat."

Sonny stared at her, considering, then stepped close to me and jammed the gun hard into my chest. I yelped. I stopped breathing. I think my heart stopped beating.

"Last chance. The truth."

Mom closed her eyes. "That's the truth. There's not a path, but I can lead you there. You can see the tops of all four of the stone walls of the cellar. The roof is caved in now, but the cellar is still there."

"Let's go then. You'll drive the boat."

Mom shook her head and didn't move. "We need water. Something to eat."

"Yeah. Okay. On the boat."

So, we went back down to the pier. Mom, then me, then Sonny with the gun nudging my back. Mom headed straight for the water jug. I headed straight for the cake tin. But Sonny stood still and looked around. "Where are the stairs? The stairs to the kitchen? To the bathroom? The bunks?"

Even though Mom's face had shown only tiredness up until then, she managed to look astonished. "What are you talking about?"

The camp boat had been built to transport people across the sound. Twenty-five feet long, it had two swivel chairs in the bow for Mom and me and six benches behind that could seat more than a dozen campers. The entire boat was open, with only a metal awning to keep off the rain. We used the big space in the stern to pile the campers' gear, running cords from the gunwales if the stack got too tall, and that's where Mom and I had put the supplies we'd carried on board. Mom stood there now, drinking steadily and taking bites from an apple.

Anyone who knew anything about boats would know it had no galley. No head. No sleeping berths.

Sonny glared at the stuff he'd brought. "How am I supposed to heat those casseroles? Where am I supposed to sleep? I didn't even bring a can opener!"

We didn't look at him. But he sounded totally pissed, and inside I was laughing.

Mom handed me the water, and after I drank, I wolfed piece after piece of pound cake, so rich and sugary my stomach jumped with surprise. She ate two pieces, too, and maybe looked a little better.

Sonny didn't eat a thing, and he looked worse. "Enough already. Let's go." He pulled out Mom's satellite phone, slammed it against the side of the boat until the plastic cracked, then tossed it overboard. "They'll figure out I have the boat eventually. No sense letting them track me that way."

No way to phone for help now. I untied the mooring lines. Mom sat in the pilot's seat. Sonny had me sit on the bench behind Mom, and he sat beside me.

Jeff had left the key in the ignition, and the engine started right away. Mom steered us along the western edge of the island. The smoke from our house had gotten thicker and darker, boiling over the end of the island near the camp. But the air smelled like rain, and the scattered clouds had gotten thicker and darker too.

Maybe rain would stop the fire. Erik and Bree had to be okay. Jon and Kenzie would have helped them, wouldn't they? But I'd seen the way those flames zoomed up the side of the house. The way the gasoline lit up and spread like it was alive. Maybe all four of them ended up burned.

I told myself I had enough to be scared of sitting right here beside me, but I couldn't stop worrying. Then I noticed how hard the boat rocked. I set aside all those troubles and paid attention to what Mom was doing. She steered the way she'd always told me not to, zigging and zagging, gunning the engine, then cutting the wheel sharp as if she was in a big hurry and needed to dodge something in her path.

Sonny rocked side to side, looking a bit green like the campers who needed vomit bags. He couldn't hold on with his burned hand, and his other hand was full of his gun. "What are you doing? Stop turning so hard. You need to drive straight."

"Underwater rocks. You don't want me to slam into one, do you? I would think one wrecked boat would be more than enough for you."

We weren't tucked in close to shore. There were no rocks out here that could damage the boat. I watched Mom real close. We'd almost reached Sunset Cove. If she planned to try something, it would be soon.

Her right hand gave a little wave, and I hung on tight to the front edge of the bench. I'm not sure what she did, but the boat skewed hard right, and the stern whipped left, the hull making horrible noises like it couldn't hold itself together. Sonny pitched hard to the side and fell off the bench. Mom cut the engine and spun out of her chair in the same instant, leaping at him, grabbing for the gun. "Jump, Chris, jump! Swim for it!"

But before the words could sink in, before I could do anything but scramble to my feet, it was over. Sonny lay on the deck, but he still held the gun. Mom stood over him, panting.

"If you jump, kid, I shoot your mother."

I sat. What else could I do?

Sonny got up. Mom sagged into her seat and restarted the engine. We slid toward the cove real slow with no zigzags and no rocking. Mom had me climb out on the bow deck to watch for rocks—real ones this time—and she eased close to shore at the edge of the cove. I jumped off with the anchor and carried it into the trees until the line stretched tight. Mom got off and tied the bow line to a sapling. No tricks and no sudden moves.

Sonny stayed alert and watchful. We'd landed on the opposite side of the island from camp, far away from Jon and Kenzie and the others, stuck here with Sonny. Even if Jeff figured out something was wrong, he wouldn't send help here. And with Sonny on guard again, maybe we'd lost our last chance to escape.

Chapter Twenty-Four

Jon

I paced the edge of the road, taking care to avoid dark plumes of smoke that spiraled out from the roaring cottage fire. The smoke didn't have the woodsy smell of a campfire—it stank of chemicals and melted plastic. It carried soot that clung like glue. The wind still gusted, and the cottage burned with frightening intensity. My leg throbbed in sync with every heartbeat and every smoke-rattled cough, but I kept moving, desperation preventing a moment's rest. Sonny had taken Leah and Chris. I could think of nothing else. Every second that passed without action was time wasted. Time we'd never get back.

But before we could act, we had to take care of the wounded. Bree and Erik sat together nearby, with Kenzie doing what she could for their injuries. Erik sat curled in a tight huddle, his back wrapped loosely in strips from an old T-shirt Kenzie retrieved from her tipi. His blistered and peeling skin looked more like jagged knife wounds than burns, and his ravaged lungs rasped with every breath. Every few minutes, his face contorted, and he gasped in pain.

He needed morphine. We couldn't even offer an aspirin. Bree had been able to drink water when I brought it to her, but Erik struggled to swallow, retching at each attempt. We'd managed to save these two, but with Leah and Chris lost, the victory felt hollow.

Kenzie examined Bree's arm and shoulder, her probing fingers making Bree gasp. "The bookcase must have slammed straight into you."

"We tried to pull one of the shelves out, and the whole thing toppled."

"You've got a broken shoulder blade. Probably a cracked collarbone." Kenzie used the pocketknife I'd given her to slice another T-shirt and fashion a sling. "This will help until we get back to civilization."

Bree gave her a tired smile, but starvation and dehydration had taken a serious toll. They were both weak, and their sentences trailed off as if they had a hard time concentrating.

Bree looked up. "Thank you for getting us out. We knew things were getting out of control, but we didn't expect fire. If you hadn't come when you did ..." Her voice faded, and tears trickled down her cheeks.

Kenzie gave her a gentle hug that avoided her bad shoulder. "You would have done the same for us." She stood, took a few steps, and gestured for me to follow. Fatigue lined her face, and it looked like every motion took brutal determination. She stopped far enough away that Bree and Erik couldn't overhear.

"How bad is Erik?"

"Bad enough." She ran her fingers through her hair. "He sucked in more smoke than the rest of us, and he's got second and third-degree burns on his upper back. He's riding an adrenaline shock wave, but the pain's going to swamp him soon. I've done what I can, but he needs more." She glanced toward the cottage. "Do you think I can get into the medical supplies in Chris's room?"

As though in answer, another wall collapsed with a loud whump, sending sparks and ash flying. Clouds massed, growing darker by the minute, but even a sudden deluge would be too late to salvage anything in the cottage.

Kenzie sighed and massaged the back of her neck. "We need to move them under cover and decide what to do next. Bree says the boat's being delivered today."

Today? That explained Sonny's quick exit. "The Puffin tipis are closest. Let's get them settled fast. I want to hear more about the boat."

Erik was shivering, big soul-wracking chills that shook his entire body, but we somehow managed to get him into the tipi and wrapped in Kenzie's sleeping bag. Within minutes, he lost consciousness. The rain began, a light mist that cooled the day but wouldn't kill the fire anytime soon.

Kenzie sat on the ground beside Erik's bed, and Skagit curled beside her with his head on her knee. I eased myself onto the mattress beside Bree and tried to get my leg in a position where it didn't scream. "Bree, tell us what you heard Sonny say about the boat."

"He came back to the cottage with Chris, pulled Leah out, and started asking about Allman's clue. We'd been insisting we didn't know where the root cellar was, but with Chris there as leverage ..."

Leah would have no choice.

Bree gulped some water. "Anyway, the phone rang, and I went up the bookcase to listen. He agreed to meet the boat at the dock at three o'clock. Apparently, Leah had to sign for it—they wouldn't hand it over to him alone. It ticked him off, but he agreed."

I checked my watch. Three-thirty. By now, Sonny had the boat. If he hurt Leah ... If he hurt Chris ... "He's still fixated on finding Allman's treasure?"

"He's obsessed with it. Ever since he found the journal and figured out the code, he's talked about nothing else. He and Tremaine kept arguing about how to share. It makes sense that Sonny got rid of his partners."

Maybe the outcome for Tremaine and Ryan would have been the same even if Kenzie and I hadn't left them helpless, but logic couldn't stop guilt from eating away at my insides. We took away any fighting chance they might have had.

"Leah insisted she'd never seen an old root cellar. Is that true?"

I thought back. "I suspect she knows where it is. Chris definitely knows. I've taken him there."

Kenzie must have read the worry on my face. "They're both tough, Jon. They'll be okay."

"Maybe. But once they lead him to it, they're no longer useful. And we know what that means."

"No, no." She shook her head. "Don't be too sure. He got badly burned. He may need extra help."

I wanted to believe her, but I couldn't. Sonny no longer acted rational. "Leah and Chris will be forced to tell him where the root cellar is, but then they'll have to lead him there. It will take time for them to dig, and they're all wounded or weak. We need to get to Sunset Cove to either help them escape or take Sonny head-on."

"How?" Kenzie asked. "The cove's too far. You can barely walk, and even if we recover the van, there's no road on that part of the island."

"We take a canoe." I said it as if this was the most natural thing in the world, but the statement dropped into stunned silence, as if I'd proposed a flying dragon or a magical transporter. It wouldn't be easy, but it was the only option we had. "We've got the storage shed key." I struggled to my feet. "Bree, you'll stay here. Help Erik. We'll leave you plenty of water and whatever supplies Kenzie has in her duffel. Kenzie, you and I will paddle around the north end of the island. I can't do it alone. If we can flag down a fishing boat with a radio, that's ideal. We can call for help. Otherwise, we'll continue to the cove."

Exhaustion lined Kenzie's face, but by the time she stood, determination had taken over. My plan was half-baked at best, but we had to try.

"Be careful." Bree said. "It's a tough paddle. The currents are tricky, and your leg is a mess. Can you do it?"

They deserved the blunt truth. "I don't know. Kenzie will help. All I need is arm power." I did my best to sound convincing. The leg would be a nightmare, and I could no longer claim much strength.

Bree fought her way to her feet. "The other counselors don't expect us in Anacortes until late tomorrow, but they'll be here by Friday. Erik and I can hold out until then."

A sudden wave of gratitude left me speechless. No one was giving up. "Okay, Kenzie, let's get going."

The rain had tapered off, though the clouds remained heavy. In less than half an hour, we were ready to go. Canoe, extra paddles, life jackets, flashlight, compass, water bottles. I left half the remaining cattail hearts with Bree, and Kenzie and I forced down the rest. We were a feeble-looking crew, worn even by the effort of preparations. Between us, Kenzie and I probably had the muscle power of three-quarters of a normal person.

"Where's the gun?" I asked.

"In the tipi."

"Bring it. Two bullets are better than nothing."

I waited by the canoe for her return, and Skagit bounded along the beach, tail wagging. He leapt into the canoe and stretched out on a life jacket, acting like the expedition had been organized for his benefit.

"No. Come on, Skagit. Get out." The last thing we needed was a dog who would potentially get underfoot at the wrong moment. I hadn't yet forgiven him for causing Chris's recapture.

Skagit ignored me. Kenzie arrived and handed me the gun. I reached for the dog to drag him out, but Kenzie stopped me. "He might serve as a distraction. He usually listens."

"He's not listening now. I told him to leave."

"Well, maybe he knows something we don't."

We had no time to argue. I scooped Skagit out and deposited him on the beach. "Stay. Let's get out of here."

We pushed the canoe out, the frigid water numbing my feet, and climbed in. I took the stern, hoping I'd make my leg more comfortable with extra space in front of me, and Kenzie sat in the bow. She held her paddle at an awkward angle and took short, inefficient strokes, but it was better than nothing.

We maneuvered through the cove's shallows, and I glanced back to shore. Smoke still rose from the smoldering ruins of the cottage. In the meadow, Bree stood outside the tipi watching us leave, looking small and alone. I choked on a tennis-ball sized lump in my throat. Once again, we were abandoning people.

I stopped paddling and let the boat drift to get a feel for the tide. "We'll head north and work our way around the Point, staying close to shore. Keep watch for any sort of boat. Ideally one that might have a radio."

"Does the camp boat have one?"

"No. Leah relied on the satellite phone when she went out on the water."

I took a final look behind and froze. "Shit."

"What?" Kenzie turned. Skagit, his small head barely visible above the water, his legs churning, was closing in fast. "We can't leave him." She tapped the side of the boat. "Here, boy, come on."

He headed straight to her, and she scooped him into the boat, a soggy, shivering mass of fur. He shook himself, spraying both of us with cold water, circled twice, and curled up again in his spot on the life jacket.

I gave up. We'd wasted too much time already. If we took him back to shore, he'd probably follow again. I angled the boat in the right direction and bent to the task. My leg throbbed, and blood trickled from the bandage, leaving pink swirls in the bottom of the boat. My arms trembled with every stroke, but we made headway. Past Nesting Cove and the bluffs with the empty Eagle tipis. Around the Point, where the current shifted against us. Then south, still hugging the shore, watching for landmarks so we wouldn't hit Sunset Cove unexpectedly.

A chilly, misty drizzle resumed, soaking us to the skin and cutting visibility to only a few dozen feet, but we kept going. Skagit curled into a tighter ball, doing his best to shrink into invisibility.

I tried to match my strokes to Kenzie's for more power, but her erratic paddling made that impossible. I settled into my own rhythm. Every stroke pulled a little harder than the one before and each effort sent my leg into painful spasms, but I concentrated on Leah and ordered myself onward. The only sounds were the gentle slaps of paddle blades against water, the rustling of leaves in the gusting breeze, and the occasional distant bark of a sea otter.

We neared Sunset Cove, and Kenzie straightened and stopped paddling. "What's that boat ahead?"

I peered around her. With such poor visibility, it was hard to make out, but the shape looked familiar, and it was tucked into shore at the edge of the cove, the only place where a boat that size could moor without running into rocks. "I think it's the camp boat."

We sat for a moment, listening. No voices. No sound of movement onshore. Dead silence.

"Take it slow," I whispered. Sound carried too well across water.

We eased our way forward in the canoe version of a tiptoe, taking care not to splash or hit our paddles against the side. The camp boat rocked quietly, properly moored to shore with two taut lines. Not Sonny's style. Leah and Chris's work. They'd made it this far. We paddled beside it, and I reached up and grabbed the gunwale railing to steady the canoe. The boat was empty.

We paddled to the other side and stopped when the boarding ladder aligned with Kenzie. "Go ahead. Take the bow line with you."

She lifted Skagit over the railing, stowed her paddle, and scrambled aboard. I followed, awkwardly, my leg stiff and complaining. I tied the canoe's line to a cleat, and we looked around.

No key in the ignition. No satellite phone lying conveniently abandoned. The things Kenzie had seen Sonny carry from the cottage had been tossed about on the stern deck, as if thrown by rough seas. No blood. No bullet holes. No bodies. It was a tragic reflection of our situation and my mood that I viewed the lack of corpses as something to celebrate.

"They must be inland searching for the root cellar." Kenzie peered toward the cliff, but an army could have hidden in the thick mist.

"A safe assumption." I eased myself onto the closest bench and massaged my leg. "I'd hoped to follow them, but to be honest, I don't think I can make it. Our best bet is to hide and try to catch Sonny off guard when they return."

She frowned. "I don't like it. What if he shoots them up there before they come back?"

"It's my biggest fear." Images of Leah, dead, Chris, dead, their bodies sprawled in the forest, their blood dripping into dirt, crowded in. We might be able to capture Sonny if he returned alone, but if his defeat came at the price of their lives, I'd never be able to live with myself.

"We know Sonny will come back to the boat. Hopefully all three of them will. Let's hide the canoe in the trees, hide ourselves here, and wait."

She nodded a reluctant agreement. We'd moved heaven and earth to get here in time. Now we needed patience and all the luck the world could give us. We deserved a win. I just wasn't sure we'd get it.

I limped back to the ladder but was distracted by a loud splash.

"Shit!" Kenzie kept her voice low but didn't hide her aggravation.

I looked past her in time to see a wet, shaggy dog climb out of the water and shake himself off on shore. Skagit circled once with his nose to the ground, then took off at top speed, heading inland, straight toward the location of the collapsed root cellar.

Chapter Twenty-Five

Chris

We left the cove behind us, and with Sonny following, Mom and I took our time climbing to the top of the cliff. The rocks were slick, and the rain made it hard to see far ahead. I kept waiting for Sonny to yell, to tell us to hurry, but he panted behind us without saying a word. He may have wanted to go slow—his hand burned, the gun getting in the way on the steep climb—but he wasn't taking chances. Every time I checked, the gun stayed pointed at our backs.

We reached the top. The rock I'd jumped from stood on my left, but when I looked that way, Mom grabbed my arm and held on. She didn't have to worry. No way would I leave her alone with Sonny.

"Get the shovels and metal detector." Sonny pointed ahead, where I guess Jon and Erik had dropped everything when I jumped. I walked over and grabbed the two shovels. Mom got the metal detector and shook the water off. She clicked it on, and it lit right up.

"Now where's this damn root cellar?"

Mom pointed to the trees. "Allman's homesite is about twenty minutes that way. The root cellar is a little beyond."

"Get moving."

Mom led the way, taking the worst possible route, heading in a curve through thick salmonberry bushes and dense clumps of sword ferns instead of traveling a straight line. I couldn't manage both shovels, so I dropped one. Sonny grunted, but he didn't pick it up. The rain cut back to a thick mist, but I stayed just as cold, just as wet, and just as angry.

We reached the homesite. Moss-covered stone steps and a tumbled-down stone chimney were the only markers. Trees grew thick where the house had once stood. Mom stopped, breathing hard.

"Keep going." Sonny breathed even harder.

"I need a break." She sat on the wet steps with the metal detector on her knees. I sat beside her. I couldn't get any wetter.

Sonny looked around as if expecting to find somewhere dry, didn't find it, and stayed on his feet.

Ever since Mom's plan on the boat hadn't worked, I'd waited for her to try something else, but she looked worn out and beaten. Maybe I needed to come up with the next thing.

The shovel would work if I could get close enough to hit Sonny, but so far, he had kept his distance. My arm still hurt. I didn't want to get shot again. And I sure didn't want to see Mom with a hole in her forehead like Tremaine and Ryan. Thinking about them made my stomach hurt, so I pushed the worry into a closet in my head.

Maybe if we found the cache, it would distract Sonny enough to give me my chance.

"Come on. Let's go."

I could tell Mom wanted to say no, but she saw the look on Sonny's face and didn't say a thing. I stood and helped her up.

We found the old root cellar about five minutes later. It looked like just a dip in the ground, but if you looked closer, you could see stones around the edges, covered in places by dirt and leaves and vines. Jon told me the stones had supported a roof over the dug-out middle, a place for the Baytree community to store crops where they would stay cool and last longer. Now, dirt filled it completely.

If I had come here with the others, looking for treasure, I would have felt pretty excited. But with Sonny in charge, I could only think about how much work it'd be.

He got more alert, acting interested now. "South wall. That's what the clue said."

He pointed north, and we didn't correct him. Mom clicked on the metal detector and walked slowly, moving the detector back and forth in front of her, careful not to miss an inch. It beeped over one spot and Sonny told me to dig. I found a quarter from 1937. Sonny snorted and tossed it aside. I rescued it and put it in my pocket, where it clinked against the half-scissors Jon had carried.

"Keep going. The next side."

The weeds and ferns grew thicker there, and Mom had a harder time. The detector beeped for a bent spoon and again for one of the metal rings like Mom used to seal jars with when she canned tomatoes. Sonny swore and threw it into the trees.

Now we moved to check the south side. Mom straightened and squeezed my arm. "Here goes nothing."

She waved the detector over that corner, and it went nuts right away, beeping and squalling like something huge waited there.

I couldn't help it—I got excited. Maybe the treasure was real, and we'd be the ones to find it. Sonny got excited, too, stepping close behind me and leaning forward. "Now we're getting there. Start digging."

His breathing hit hot against my neck. I gave Mom a look and made sure she saw it, then I lifted the shovel like I planned to dig. Instead, I swung it toward Sonny, the blade heavy and awkward, hard to balance, tipping me back.

I aimed for his head, wanting to smash his face or dig out his eyes, but he threw up his arm and the shovel landed on his hand, the one with the burns he'd been keeping tucked tight against his chest.

He screamed something awful and doubled over. Mom dropped the metal detector and charged him, her arms outstretched, reaching for the gun. But he had more strength and speed. He smashed Mom hard on the shoulder with the gun, and she fell across the tumbled rocks. I swung the shovel back, ready to try again, but he stepped out of reach and pointed the gun at me. "Drop it."

I did.

I was panting like Skagit after a long run. Mom lay on the rocks, struggling to get back on her feet. Sonny made little moaning sounds like a hurt animal, and his burned and smashed hand dripped blood. He stood still for a minute, glaring at me. Then he stopped moaning and seemed to grow taller. He took two long steps and jammed his gun into my stomach, his face red and twisted like when he shot Tremaine.

I couldn't talk. Couldn't swallow. At least he'd shoot me before Mom.

"Don't!" Mom, on her knees, tried to stand. "Shoot him, and you'll have to shoot me too. Without us, you won't ever get that treasure."

His face didn't move. No emotion flickered in his eyes. I wasn't sure he'd even heard. He took two more breaths, his teeth clamped tight. Then he pulled the gun away, lifted his arm, and hit me hard with the back of his hand. It slammed into my cheek and snapped my head around. Hurt like crazy and brought tears to my eyes. But at least it wasn't a bullet.

He stepped back. "If I had two good arms to dig, you'd both be dead. Quit sniveling, kid. You deserved more. Start digging."

Maybe our only chance, and I'd blown it. I helped Mom stand. She gave me a hug and rested a cool hand on my flaming cheek. "I'm sorry. I should've been faster."

"It's okay." She looked so sad, I wanted to cry.

I picked up the shovel, put the tip of the blade in the right spot, and used my foot to force it into the packed soil. My face hurt, and the inside of my cheek oozed blood. The taste made my throat hurt, and my stomach lurched like it wanted to climb out of my body, but I kept digging.

Rocks from the cellar wall lay only inches under the surface, so it took a long time. I dug around each stone and levered it up, and

Mom added it to a pile. Every ten rocks or so, we stopped, and she'd check with the metal detector to make sure we were still on track. It went crazy every time. Sonny paced, talked under his breath, and paced some more, but he never came close enough for me to reach him.

I dug so deep, I had to make the hole bigger to keep it from caving in. I levered up one more rock, stuck the shovel down there, and it clanged off something metal. I looked at Mom. She looked at me. I couldn't tell what she thought, but I shook a little, excited and scared and nervous. We'd found it.

Sonny bounced on the balls of his feet. Sweat poured down his face, even though he hadn't done a bit of work. "Get it out! Get it out!"

Easy to say. Hard to do. I had to clear around the edges, then dig on each side. More rocks got in the way.

Digging. Levering. Carrying. Finally, I eased the treasure out using the shovel. It didn't look anything like a real treasure chest, just a rusty green metal box, the size of three or four big shoeboxes stacked one on the other. On top, a flat metal handle hung off two metal rings. On one end, a weird-looking loop handle might have opened the box somehow, but it had rusted solid.

Sonny danced from one foot to the other, careful to stay out of reach. "Open it! Open it!" He held his burned hand in a fist pressed tight against his chest, so swollen now, it looked like it belonged to a bear, not a human.

I tried to work my fingers into the loop handle on the side, did my best to pry it up, but it stayed frozen solid. "I can't get hold of it."

"Get back. Go sit." He waved me toward Mom, and I sat beside her. He knelt beside the box and looked at it. Set the gun down and glared at us. "Don't try anything. By the time you get to your feet, I'll put a bullet into you."

Tempting, but Mom rested a hand on my leg to say no. We sat too far away, and we'd already seen how fast Sonny could react.

He hefted the box. Yeah, real heavy. I could have told him that.

He tried to pry the handle up.

He hit the box with the heel of his hand.

He stood and kicked it.

He grabbed the shovel and tried to pry the top open, but he got nowhere one-handed.

He needed two hands, a screwdriver, and a mallet. Maybe something more. Maybe dynamite. For sure, we had no way to get the thing open here on this hillside.

Sonny picked up his gun, and he peered into the edge of the hole. "Nothing else here."

I could have told him that too.

"Get the metal detector. Check again."

Mom used my shoulder to stand. She clicked on the detector and went over the whole area again. Zero beeps except over the large metal box.

Sonny frowned. I could guess what he was thinking, and I didn't like it one bit. If he didn't have to keep the gun pointed at us, he'd have a free hand to carry the box down the hill. He could shoot us here and be done with it. Leave our bodies to rot among the trees.

Mom tensed, and I could see inside her head too. She was thinking if she jumped toward him and made him shoot her, maybe I could run away.

My mouth dried out. I couldn't let her do that, but I didn't know how to stop her. My face where Sonny'd hit me pulsed. My chest hurt like a huge person sat on it. But I gathered myself to leap at Sonny.

Then I froze. Behind Sonny, a furry face peered at me from under a bush. I grabbed Mom's arm, my *no* as strong as the one she'd given me earlier. *Don't try anything.*

I gave a *stay back* wave to Skagit. He must have followed our trail from the cove. And that meant somebody had brought him here.

"I guess we'd better get going." I said it like we'd assembled for a picnic, and we needed to pack up before dark. I stood and stepped to the box, not looking at Sonny. "Mom, should we take turns? Or is there some way we can both carry this? It's pretty heavy for one person." I grabbed the box by the handle and heaved on it with a groan without lifting it from the ground. I should maybe be an actor one day.

Mom looked puzzled but joined me. We hefted the box, her on one end and me on the other. Only then did I look in Sonny's direction.

Maybe he wouldn't have shot us even if I hadn't put on the show, but I think the idea of lugging such a troublesome box through a trailless tangle by himself convinced him to let us carry it to the boat. "Get on with it."

We walked in front of him, heading downhill, making a lot of noise, pushing through the undergrowth. I whispered to Mom, "Skagit's here."

For a moment, she gave me a look like *so what?* Then it clicked. She threw her shoulders back. Looked into the forest instead of staring only at the ground. We weren't alone. For the first time since we got on the boat, we had a chance that someone could save us.

Unfortunately, that someone stayed hidden instead of helping with the stupid box. Sometimes I carried it, wrapping both arms around the middle and holding it to my chest, trying not to tip over from its weight. Sometimes Mom took it, both hands on the handle on top, with it bumping against her legs at every step. Sometimes we shared it, which made a lighter load but kept us tripping and stumbling. My arm hurt every step of the way, and blood oozed from under the bandage Kenzie had used.

Sonny stayed back, out of reach and on guard, but he didn't look good. His face turned bright red. He sweated. His breathing came out hard and rough. Once, he tripped over a root and swung his injured hand, trying to get his balance. The burned part hit a branch, and the noise he made would have been a scream if he'd let it come out.

My arms must have stretched out at least two extra inches from lugging that idiot box. But my complaints were probably nothing compared to his horrible burn. If I got a chance to hit him again, I would aim at his hand.

Most of our route went downhill. We avoided the steep rocky way we'd come up, taking a longer loop that wasn't so tricky. Madrona blossoms clustered thick here, but their sweet smell, which usually made me think happy things, only made me ill. I spotted moving branches and heard small rustles, letting me know Skagit followed, but he stayed hidden.

We came out at last on the edge of the cove, but nothing had changed. The camp boat bobbed on its mooring lines where we'd left it. We picked our way along the edge of the water, dodging roots and boulders. Maybe I was wrong. Maybe Skagit had come by himself. I'd seen movies like that—dogs lost in a strange place who magically find their owners somewhere they'd never been. Maybe Mom and me really were on our own with nobody around to help.

I dropped the box by the anchor, not caring any more. What was the point? Sonny might as well go ahead and shoot us.

Mom stopped beside me. Tapped me on the arm, then faced Sonny. "The tide's turned. The boat has drifted a bit. We'll need to wade out."

Drifted? I looked across the water and froze. Wait a minute. The boat wasn't moored where we left it. It had been moved about twenty feet along the shore and now floated farther out in the cove. A boulder stood between the boat and us. We'd be in at least three feet of water when we grabbed the boat's ladder, and the railing would be high over our head.

I watched Sonny, wondering if he'd realize that a change in tide couldn't drop a boulder in our path the way Mom said. But he just grumbled about having to get wet. The change meant it would be impossible for him to climb the boat ladder one-handed while lugging such a heavy chest. It meant he still needed to keep us alive for a little while longer.

I looked into the woods and found Skagit in the bushes, his dark nose poking out at me, but he lay still like I'd taught him, quiet and waiting. No one else hid there.

That left only one possibility. Whoever had brought Skagit here had shifted the mooring lines, then hidden themselves on the boat.

Chapter Twenty-Six

Kenzie

I huddled in the stern of the camp boat, cold, wet, and tired. Jon sat across from me, looking equally miserable, our agreed-upon silence broken only by the sounds of the boat creaking on its mooring lines. Rain dripped off the canopy and trickled in meandering streams along the deck. The boat rocked in an occasional small wave. My butt grew numb from sitting on the hard surface.

Leah had moored the boat quite close to shore, and we quickly discovered that, no matter where we hid on board, anyone standing on land could see us. We shifted the boat farther out in the cove, with a towering boulder partially blocking the view. Hopefully, Sonny wouldn't see us until he climbed on board.

The list of risks grew longer the more I considered them. Had Skagit found Chris and raced out to greet him? Maybe Sonny would see him and figure out we were here? Or he would take one look at the boat and know we moved it? Even if he suspected nothing, I wasn't sure Jon and I could defeat him. His burned hand should slow him, but he was huge, well-fed, and well-rested. Our chances of success were slim.

I forced aside the worst scenario. If he killed Chris and Leah before he returned, this entire effort would be for nothing. I'd failed Tim. I couldn't fail Chris.

Exhaustion weighed my arms and legs, but the steady rain had defrosted one of Leah's casseroles, and Jon and I had gorged, scooping cold handfuls of broccoli-laced macaroni and cheese into our mouths like starving animals, topping it off with some fantastic pound cake we found in a tin. The food offered energy. Fear kept me alert.

Time passed. A voice, far in the distance, jerked me to attention.

Jon cautiously peered over the side railing, stared for a moment, then sank back to the deck. He held up three fingers. *Three.*

A surge of relief carried me on its crest for a moment, but then my eyes fell on the gun that rested in Jon's lap. Tremaine's gun with two bullets left. I couldn't afford a moment of celebration.

I strained to hear. Footsteps came closer, pebbles rolling beneath shoes. The sounds were uneven, stumbling, sure signs of fatigue. I heard a loud thump as something heavy dropped to the ground, and I jumped. Had they actually found something? The idea of treasure had been so far from my mind, it seemed outrageous to believe Allman's journal was more than a story.

I looked at Jon, but he just shrugged.

Leah's voice came, tired but determined. "The tide's turned. The boat has drifted. We'll need to wade out."

Yes, Leah, yes. She knew better than that. Her words were for Sonny. She must know we'd hidden here, and she'd make sure Chris knew too.

"We need to move the boat closer in." Sonny's voice shook, sounding weaker, less confident, less in charge. "It'll be too hard to get the box up the ladder in water that deep."

"Sorry. No way to get the boat in closer until the tide changes." Complete bullshit. "But if you want to wait for six hours ..."

"Shut up." Impatient. Irritated. *Good.* More likely he'd make mistakes.

A moment of silence stretched on, and I imagined Sonny thinking hard. He needed to keep his gun in play, or he risked attack from Leah and Chris. He'd be vulnerable trying to climb the boat's ladder one-handed. He had something to transport that sounded heavy, and he couldn't haul it up the ladder unassisted.

"You. Go over to that tree. Kid, take this rope and tie your mother's hands to the middle branch. Do it right. If I have to make you do it over, I shoot Mommy in the foot."

Jon flinched, and a wave of anger flitted over his face.

Sonny's voice came again a few minutes later. "Nice job. Now pick up the box. Both hands. Don't drop it. I'm going to back into the water, heading toward the boat, and you're going to wade out after me, staying ten feet away. Your mom is in range. If you drop the box or try to run, she's dead."

Splashing sounds moved closer to the boat. I clutched the canoe paddle that lay ready beside me, my hand slick with sudden sweat. My heart pummeled my ears. So loud, I worried Sonny might hear.

Jon scooted across to my side, whispering, "Sonny will come first. Get ready."

I gave him a shaky nod. When Sonny's head and chest appeared over the gunwale, Jon would shoot him. No warning. No argument. No hesitation.

Two bullets. Two shots. My paddle served as a desperate backup, and Jon's pocketknife sat ready beside him, the long primary blade gleaming. I shivered, and it wasn't from the cold.

Jon slid stealthily to sit opposite the ladder, bracing his back against the side of the boat. He flipped off the safety and gripped the gun in both hands. Despite everything that had happened, I had a hard time viewing a man's chest as a target.

"Stop right there, kid." Sonny's voice came from the base of the ladder. My mouth went bone dry, and I had to force every breath. "I'm going onboard, and you're going to stand there with the box. If I hear the least little bit of splashing, I'll have plenty of time to shoot. Don't try it."

Jon took a deep breath. Steadied the gun.

Sonny grunted. It couldn't be easy, climbing with one hand while trying to keep his gun from getting wet.

The metal ladder banged against the side of the boat. The top of Sonny's head appeared above the railing. One more step would bring him in range. I wanted to close my eyes and pretend I was somewhere else, but I forced myself to watch.

His next step thrust him another foot higher, exposing his head, shoulders, and upper chest. He was clenching the handgrip of his gun in his teeth, his jaw propped wide and his face distorted. His eyes widened as he saw us, and Jon fired twice. His arms jumped with the first recoil, then jumped again with the second.

One bullet hit the side of the boat, gouging a deep hole and spraying a mist of fiberglass. But the second bullet hit meat.

Blood spurted from Sonny's right shoulder, the same arm that had been burned, and when he yelled, his gun fell, dropping into the water with a reassuring splash. Jon scrambled to his feet and flipped his empty gun around to use as a club.

Panic overwhelmed me, my brain sending urgent commands to run even though I had nowhere to go. Sonny was alive, pissed, and lunging into the boat.

Blood streamed from his shoulder and profanity poured from his mouth. But his injuries did little to slow him. As soon as his feet hit the deck, he charged between the benches at Jon, his uninjured shoulder thrust in front of him the way a linebacker positions for a tackle.

Jon slammed the gun in a killing arc, but it slid off Sonny's arm without slowing his charge. I stood and swung the paddle with all the muscle power I possessed. It landed across his back with a bone-jarring crunch.

Sonny stumbled hard into Jon, his shoulder burying deep into Jon's stomach, slamming him against the side of the boat. He slumped there, dazed. I pulled the paddle back, but before I could swing again, Sonny seized Jon's injured leg, hoisted it up, and flung him over the railing. He landed with a splash.

Sonny pivoted to face me and lifted his bad arm, shoulder bleeding, hand crumpled against his chest. My next paddle blow landed on his forearm, and the impact tore the handle from my hand. The paddle landed out of reach. He groaned, took a step back, but then stood his ground.

I froze.

It was me and Sonny. Face-to-face.

I picked up the pocketknife, choked down a swallow, and tried to slow my out-of-control breathing.

"So, nurse-lady, here we are. One tied up and waiting, one down there drowning, one kid. And you. I'll take care of all of you, then I'm off to Canada with enough treasure to live like a king."

His eyes were crazed and his words were mocking, but his breath rasped as if each movement caused jolts of pain. A crimson stain covered the right side of his shirt and pants. His right shoe left bloody footprints. The muscles of his burned arm spasmed, jerking his ravaged hand in random movements. He talked that way to scare me, and it was working, but he was also giving himself a rest. He wasn't the man he'd been a few days ago. And he no longer had a gun.

I clutched my knife, gathered courage, and waited for my chance.

We stood six feet apart, a bench between us. He stepped portside, away from land. I stepped starboard, and when I reached the side, I headed for the stern, keeping benches between us.

He clenched his teeth, his eyes tight slits, and stepped in my direction along the starboard railing. "You can't hurt me. Not with that little knife. You don't have the nerve."

I stopped. There was nowhere else to go. He took his time, pausing with each step as if enjoying his anticipated victory.

I told myself to attack, but something moved behind Sonny. For an instant, my heart lifted. A hand reached for the railing. Jon had made it to the ladder.

But no. The hand was too small. Not Jon. It was Chris, climbing aboard with a swollen cheek and a blackened eye.

"No! Stop! Go back!"

Sonny thought I was talking to him. He smirked and took another step toward me.

Chris pulled himself up, swinging a leg over the railing, staring at Sonny's back with pure hatred. A small bit of silver glinted in his hand—the half-scissors Jon had carried, too small and silly to do much harm.

Chris had both feet on the deck now, water pouring from his clothing, mixing with Sonny's blood, creating puddles of pink. I stepped forward, holding my knife out front, hoping to keep Sonny focused on me. "What are you waiting for, Sonny?"

He took a slow step closer, still in no hurry, but behind him, Chris's foot slid on the slick deck. He teetered for an instant and grabbed hold of the railing with the hand that held the scissors.

The railing twanged. Gently. A tiny, musical note. The sort of sound no one would ever hear, much less pay attention to.

But Sonny heard and reacted with frightening speed. He whirled, spotted Chris, and lunged. In one swift blow, he smashed the boy's head against the railing. Chris's eyes rolled back. His body crumpled against the rail, his head and arms hanging over the side.

It took Sonny only seconds to hoist the rest of his body over the edge.

My scream coincided with the splash, and I raced to the side of the boat. Chris's body floated in the water. Unmoving. Unconscious. Face down. Looking the same way Tim had.

I lost it. I leaped toward Sonny, my paltry knife slashing. I might have sliced his side or maybe his arm, but he stuck his good arm in front of him like a battering ram and smashed into me. His fist slammed into my breastbone, and he pushed me back to the stern. My legs ended up pinned, my body forced backward into a painful arc against the engine cowling.

His chest pressed against mine, trapping my right hand and the knife between us, his body hot as a furnace against my frozen skin. My left arm flailed against his back, but his hand clamped hard around my throat, his thumb closing on my carotid. "Your turn, bitch."

My head spun. I couldn't draw air. I couldn't scream, couldn't breathe, couldn't escape. Black spots danced at the edge of my vision.

Fear hijacked my whole body, but every sense went into overdrive. The coppery scent of the blood saturating Sonny's shirt. The pulse beating at the side of his forehead. The rasp in his chest as he drew each breath.

Chris.

Panic rammed some sense home. Whether I lived or died was irrelevant, but I had to save Chris.

I twisted, my back screaming, and I slid my free hand down Sonny's blood-slick arm until I reached his injured hand. I curled my fingers into a claw and clutched hard. His burned flesh felt crisp in places, hot and wet in others. My fingernails dug in deep, scraping and tearing the raw, swollen flesh, ripping at hypersensitive nerve endings.

Sonny shrieked and curled inward, freeing my knife hand.

The knife ripped into his belly a little off midline, just below his ribcage. I angled it to avoid bone, and it tore through his diaphragm. The pulsing vibration of his heart passed through the knife and into my hand. I used my full strength to push and gave the handle a hard twist.

His body convulsed. I let go of the knife. The handle jerked twice as his heart gave two final spasms. He sagged to the deck. His eyes glazed. He was gone.

A microsecond of revulsion caught me in the gut and another split-second of guilt doubled me over. But *Chris, Chris, Chris* sent me hurtling to the railing. Leah was screaming, still tied on shore. Skagit was barking as if trying to alert the entire planet.

I had an instant glimpse of Chris's body, still suspended in the water, face down, then Jon arrived, having fought his way around the boat against both the current and the effects of Sonny's massive blow.

He seized Chris. Flipped him onto his back. He glanced toward shore, but it would take forever to drag him that far.

"Jon! Bring him here!" I hurried to the ladder and leaned far over the side.

Jon dragged him toward me. Lifted one flopping arm, then the other for me to grasp. He hoisted from below and I hauled from above, and Chris's body, too limp, too unresisting, slid over the edge and thudded to the deck. I jerked him onto his back.

He didn't move. My fingers on his neck felt no pulse. My palm on his chest found no heartbeat. A wicked bruise already discolored his forehead. For an instant, I was staring at Tim, pale and immobile on the concrete verge of a swimming pool.

Not again. Please, not again.

My training kicked in, and I leaned close over the small, sweet face. Tip the head back. Mouth-to-mouth, two smooth, steady breaths. Hands fisted together on his breastbone, ten sharp compressions. I pushed through my exhaustion, pushed past the shivers wracking my body, and started again. Jon materialized across from me and took over the breathing.

We counted together, our voices shaking. Two. Then ten. Two. Then ten. Start over. Repeat. A countdown toward another failure. Like Tim, Chris would die. Like Paige, Leah would lose her only child. *My fault. My fault. My fault.*

How long had it been since Chris fell in the water? Were my hands in the right place? Was I using the right pressure? Had the blow to his head done permanent damage? Was all this too late?

Leah's screams had shifted into a low-toned keening. Skagit had grown quiet, as if honoring yet another death. I kept the count going, tears dripping from my face and husky sobs choking every breath.

Then, Chris coughed. Took a wheezing, gurgling breath. Coughed again. Retched up seawater. Opened his eyes.

I slumped against a nearby bench. Jon yelled "He's responding" to Leah, then he took over, rubbing warmth into Chris's arms and legs, helping him sit, talking to him in a calm, soothing voice.

After a moment, Jon touched my shoulder. "You did it. He's alive."

I nodded, my throat so clogged, I could have been the one drowning.

Chris was alive.

But beyond him, in the stern of the boat, Sonny's corpse lay in an expanding pool of blood with Jon's pocketknife still sticking out of his chest.

I saved Chris. But I killed a man to do it.

Chapter Twenty-Seven

Jon

As soon as Chris looked like he was out of trouble, I hauled myself to my feet and called to Leah. "He's all right. I'll be there in a minute."

She folded as far forward as her tied hands would allow and let out a deep sob.

Chris kept clearing his throat and catching his breath. He looked around with a confused expression. The bruise on his head had taken on a purple tinge, but it wasn't swollen, and he didn't flinch when I poked around it. His pupils looked normal, but I was no expert.

"Give yourself a minute. Rest." I turned to Kenzie for help, but she sat slumped to one side with her eyes closed.

I rummaged through the stern locker, found an oil-stained sweatshirt, and used it to cover Sonny's face and chest. I rested a hand on Chris's shoulder, and he looked at me with more focused eyes. "I'm going to get your mom. Sit tight until I get back."

He spotted Sonny. "Is he dead?"

"Yeah."

He glanced toward Kenzie's huddled form. "She did it?"

"Yeah."

"I'm glad."

"And she's the one who brought you back to life. You almost drowned. Scared us silly."

"I don't remember." He gave a small grin.

The grin made things seem almost normal, and so did the lilt in his voice. The combination unraveled me. We'd come so close to losing him. Again. I leaned forward and kissed the top of his soaking wet head, so filled with gratitude I could think of no other way to express it. He pulled back a little, then looked me in the eye. "Thanks, man."

"No big deal." I tried to sound offhand, but it came out choked. "Let me go get your mom."

I swung my leg over the gunwale and found the top step of the ladder. Every movement triggered pain in my abdomen where Sonny had rammed into me, and the saltwater bit into the wound on my leg with a burning that made me gasp. I waded through the icy water toward shore, tripping on hidden rocks and stumbling into holes.

Skagit raced to meet me at the water's edge, his tail wagging at warp speed, but I headed straight for Leah.

"Is he okay? Is he really okay?" From where she sat, she could have seen Chris's floating body and me lifting him aboard, but not our attempts to resuscitate him.

"He's banged up and coughing but talking and alert. He's going to be fine." Fingers cold and awkward, I fumbled with the knots at her wrists. When I loosened the last one, she didn't even wait to rub life back into her hands but fell into my arms, burying her face in my chest, clinging as if I were the only solid thing in the universe.

I wrapped my arms around her and held her close, the warmth of her body spreading deep into mine, thawing parts I hadn't known were frozen. Every labored stroke of my canoe paddle, every taut, anxious minute of waiting while Sonny kept her and Chris captive, every shooting pain and exhausted muscle had been for Leah. Even if I never found the guts to tell her how I felt, it had all been worth it for this moment.

Over the years, when I'd let myself imagine holding her, I'd pictured a fireplace, a bottle of wine, soft music. Instead, we knelt on rocks and dirt, filthy, exhausted, and half-starved. It didn't matter. Leah nestled in my arms, and it was everything I'd ever wanted.

She pulled away before I was ready to let go. "Sonny?"

"Dead. Kenzie stabbed him with my pocketknife."

She nodded, a quick, sharp gesture of acceptance. "Good. Saves me the trouble. Erik and Bree?"

"Erik's got some bad burns, but he's alive. Bree's got a cracked shoulder blade."

"The cottage?"

"I'm sorry, Leah. It's gone."

She closed her eyes for a moment as if letting the news soak in, then got awkwardly to her feet. "I figured. Sonny threw around enough gasoline to take down five houses. I need to hug my son."

She scooped Skagit into her arms and waded toward the boat. I followed close, ready to steady her, but as always, she didn't need me.

"Chris!" She called from the base of the ladder, and his head popped over the side. "Take this wiggly dog of yours."

He reached down and seized Skagit, and she swarmed up the ladder. I reached up to follow, but Chris shook his head. "You have to get the box. I dropped it when I came after Sonny."

The water was too cloudy to see through, so, for the next ten minutes, I shuffled back and forth while Chris shouted instructions from the boat. "I think I stood closer to shore. No, maybe more this way. More to the right. Or I guess it could be more to the left."

My feet and legs had grown numb, dulling the pain of my throbbing bullet wound, and my patience was nearly exhausted when I finally tripped over the box and pitched face first into the water. I lugged it to the base of the ladder. Leah and Kenzie grabbed rope from the locker, and with the two of them pulling from above and me pushing from below, we hoisted the metal box on board.

I poked at its lid when I joined them on deck. "Rusted solid. No way to get into this without tools, and we can't keep Bree and Erik waiting any longer. Let's head for home."

"We need to get Chris to a doctor," Kenzie whispered, leaning in close. "His breathing is good so far, but his lungs need to be checked out. And his head got a hard knock."

She tapped into a reserve of energy and waded to shore to retrieve the anchor and untie the bow line, then she brought the canoe out of hiding and tied it to the stern of the larger boat. I took on the grisly task of searching Sonny's pockets and retrieving the boat keys. The engine purred to life at first touch, and we eased our way out of the cove and headed north toward the Point. Halfway there, we spotted a white boat roaring straight at us, and as it neared, I could make out the Sheriff's insignia on the side.

"Cut your engine, put your hands up, and prepare to be boarded!" A half-dozen armed men lined the boat's deck.

I killed the engine, and we all stood at the railing with our hands raised. Skagit barked like crazy. Uniformed men swarmed on board, found Sonny, and peppered us with questions, too many at the same time to answer. Once they assured us that officers were at the camp and medical help had already been dispatched for Erik and Bree, I cared little about the rest.

Wes, the tough-looking deputy in charge, took over. "You four, sit here." He pointed to two of the benches. "Kid, hang on to that dog. Who has the keys?" I handed them over. "We're going back to the camp and get everyone on shore, then we'll get the full story in an organized manner."

He sorted his men, some to return on the departmental boat, some to guard us. He selected a grey-haired veteran to skipper our boat.

I settled onto the nearest bench, relieved to hand over all responsibilities. To my surprise, Leah chose the seat beside me and sat close. I slipped my arm around her waist, and she snuggled in.

The trip home passed far too quickly.

Chapter Twenty-Eight

Kenzie

We returned to the camp, not quite prisoners but not treated as trustworthy either. After the traumas of the past few days, it felt unfair to be under guard, but I swallowed my indignation. I could hardly claim innocence. These cops had four dead bodies on their hands, including Sonny's bloody corpse lying right in front of them.

The journey was endless. Beside me, Chris clung to Skagit and leaned against my shoulder, worn out and half asleep. He wasn't coughing, but I wished for a stethoscope. If he'd inhaled water, pneumonia was a risk.

The deputy eased the boat onto the camp's beach, avoiding the rocks that had destroyed Sonny's craft only four days before. Two other boats were anchored offshore, and people in uniforms went in and out of the bathhouse. Others clustered around remnants of the cottage. Thin wisps of smoke still drifted from the ashes, but the rain had put out the worst of the fire. The back wall still stood. The rest looked like a collection of blackened lumps. Leah gasped when she saw it, and after that first look, she kept her eyes elsewhere.

Wes gave us no time to inspect anything further. "All of you, on shore. We came here to the camp first and found your two injured friends. They've already been evacuated by helicopter to Bellingham, but they were in rough shape and couldn't be questioned. The woman told us where to find you but nothing more. We need some information before we transfer you to the mainland."

"Chris needs medical care. He almost drowned." I snapped the words, fed up with the whole scene, and to Wes's credit, he called over a crewman with a medical kit to do a careful listen to Chris's lungs. He checked Jon's leg and bandaged Leah's wrists, raw from her attempts to escape at the cove. He nodded to Wes when he finished. "They all need evaluations at the hospital. The boy needs close observation for the next day or two, but right now he's in good shape."

"We've got time for questions?" When the crewman agreed, Wes ushered us on shore.

Two guards preceded us. Two followed. We ended up sitting in a tired row on one of the logs that lined the beach, the focus of all those eyes. Wes stepped aside for a phone call but first sent one of the men to their boat. He returned with a stack of blankets. A few minutes later, he brought hot chocolate for Chris, coffee for the rest of us, and a handful of power bars. Warmth and calories. A life-saving combination.

Every muscle ached, and what I wanted most was a bed and unlimited sleep, but for the first time in days, life did not feel hopeless.

I was alive, and that simple fact brought delight. I breathed fresh air. I savored a cup of coffee. I chewed food that actually tasted edible, a far cry from chopped cattail hearts. Flowers bloomed in riotous colors, water rocked the boats in the cove and lapped against the shore, and a break in the clouds let rays of sunshine through. I soaked in each detail, my senses on overdrive. I was safe. We were safe. We'd made it.

Wes returned to stand in front of us. He crossed his arms and opened his mouth, but a man ran down from the smoldering cottage and interrupted.

He wore workman's clothes, and he skidded to a halt in front of Leah and Chris. "Oh my god, they found you. Thank heavens. I was so worried." He hugged Chris and pulled a handful of dog biscuits from his pocket and began handing them one at a time to Skagit. "They wouldn't believe me when I called from the skiff. The 9-1-1 operator said a missing dog and a sloppy mooring knot didn't mean a thing, but I knew something was wrong."

Leah looked confused. "Knot? Jeff, what are you talking about?"

He explained what Chris had done, and I reached across to squeeze Chris's hand. "Nice job. Worthy of an Olympian."

He beamed, then looked down at his feet and patted Skagit. Tim would have reacted the same way, but this time, the thought caused no pain.

Jeff continued. "I called Marilyn after I got blown off by the operator, and she said *Jeff Watson, don't you dare come home. Those people are in trouble.* So, I went all the way into Anacortes. Got a lift to the Sheriff's office and raised hell. One of the deputies there pulled up a photo of the man who'd been with you—that Sonny guy—and said he was wanted in the murder of a night watchman. When I told him I'd seen him here, oh boy, that's when things started jumping. I insisted on coming along."

His story at least explained how the deputies had arrived when they did. A shame they hadn't been a bit faster. Leah hugged Jeff and showered him with thanks. He scuffed a boot through the beach pebbles and turned a brilliant pink.

Then, Wes's questions began.

Jon took the lead and told a concise version of the story from start to finish. The rest of us jumped in to contribute details along the way. Leah, Jon, and I had all witnessed Drake's death. Chris had been there when Sonny killed Tremaine and Ryan. No one else had seen my final struggle with Sonny, but Jon and Chris described his fury when they fought him. By the time we reached that part of the tale, Wes had relaxed, and the mood had shifted.

"We've got forensic people here. I'll send a diver back to the cove to retrieve Sonny's gun. We'll need more interviews and detailed statements from each of you, but I don't anticipate the DA will file charges. It appears Ms. Adams acted in self-defense." He cleared his throat. Shifted on his feet. "Give me another twenty minutes, and we'll get you out of here and to a hospital."

He walked uphill toward the bathhouse, and his deputies left with him.

Jon sighed. "Hard to believe it's over. I'm glad they're not giving you a hard time, Kenzie."

"So am I." But I kept replaying the moment when the knife stabbed through Sonny's skin. When the blade hit his heart. That memory would stay with me forever.

Chris gave me a long look, reading my face with the same skill he'd shown from day one. "If you hadn't stopped Sonny, I would've drowned."

The other two nodded, and I knew they were right. The alternative would have been worse.

Leah's quiet voice from days earlier echoed in my head, asking *would you judge a stranger as harshly as you're judging yourself?* I'd come to this island to escape bad memories, not add to them, but the things that had happened here couldn't be left behind. They were part of me now, and perhaps I could find peace with that someday.

Chris polished off his second granola bar, then sat up straight, as if something new had occurred to him. "What about the treasure? Can we open the box now?"

We all twisted around. One of the deputies had lugged the rusty box off the camp boat, and it sat behind us. Jon shrugged his blanket off his shoulders. "I don't see why not."

He limped up the hill, spoke to Wes for a moment, then disappeared into the storage shed. He returned a few minutes later with screwdrivers, a mallet, and a pry bar. Wes and a few others followed him down the hill.

After a fair amount of hammering and levering, Jon loosened the lid of the box on three slides. The hinges on the fourth side were rusty but intact. "Chris, want to do the honors?"

Chris knelt beside the box. He grabbed the locking handle and lifted it. The hinges creaked, and he forced the lid open. Flakes of rust rained down from all sides. He reached in and pulled out a thick, faded book and passed it to Jon.

Jon opened it carefully, the pages brown and brittle. "Looks like a ship's log. I can make out dates and longitude/latitude notations. I can't read the writing, though. I think it's in Russian."

Chris pulled out a leather bag, untied the leather strip that closed it, and reached inside. The gold coin he removed glowed and sparkled in the light. "Look! The bag is full of them!"

He passed the bag around, then pulled out a second bag, and a third. One was full of clear stones and the next held colored ones, some red, some green. Two more were packed full of coins.

"Are those actually gemstones?" I couldn't believe it. Treasure was the stuff of books, not real life.

Jon let the clear stones run through his fingers. "I think these are diamonds. And those others may be rubies? And emeralds? We'd have to get an expert to be sure."

The four of us looked at it all in amazement, but the deputies were even more excited than we were. "Holy cow! If it's real, it could be worth millions! You're rich!" They passed the bags around. Called their buddies over to see.

Wes shook his head. "I don't know whether this counts as evidence or not. I'll have to get advice on that. And does it even belong to you? You don't own this island, do you?"

Leah held a half-dozen gold coins, looking stunned. "The owner gave us permission to search, and he said anything we found is ours. It belongs to the three of us, plus the two people who were evacuated." She turned to Jon. "What do you think? Are they right? Could it be worth millions?"

Jon shrugged. "If these stones are real, then yes. And these gold rubles all date from the early 1800's. They may have historic value that's greater than the gold itself."

"Mom, we're rich!" Chris couldn't contain his glee. "I need a new Nintendo Switch. And a computer. And I have to replace all my books that burned."

"Slow down, kiddo. We don't know yet what we've got here," Jon said, laughing.

Leah smiled. "Well, it can't hurt to daydream. Kenzie, what will you do with your share?"

The question seemed unreal. "Good heavens, I don't know. I never believed in the treasure. I'll have to give it some thought." But Tim's stone still rested in my pocket, a steady comforting presence. I could use the money for something to honor him. An art scholarship. Or maybe some sort of program for young people interested in drawing. In the midst of my exhaustion, a small burst of enthusiasm flared. Maybe something good could come out of this after all. I turned to Leah. "What about you?"

She considered for a moment. "We need to set aside enough to pay off Drake's debts, so his parents don't get harassed." That got agreement from the rest of us. "Then with my share, a college fund for Chris. Some savings in the bank." Leah glanced at the ruins of the cottage. "And I think I'd like to rebuild here. This is home. It will depend on what Gordon plans to do with the camp and the island, but maybe this money will help." She faced Jon. "And you?"

"I'd like to buy this island from Gordon if there's enough money. Negotiate a long-term lease if there's not. Keep the camp going. Manage the island as a nature preserve like Vendovi. I'd rig some reliable internet service and build a house here. I can work from here as easily as from Seattle."

Leah looked at him as if he'd just proposed working from the moon, and he took her hand. "I can give you as much space as you need. I can build on the opposite side of the island if that's what you want. But I love you, Leah. I always have. You don't have to love me back, but I want to stay close here. Close to you and Chris."

I sucked in a deep breath. Jon said *I love you* as if taking an oath, a solemn declaration rooted in years of patient certainty. His eyes never left Leah's, and a flicker of cautious hope passed over his face.

Chris froze with a handful of gold coins in his hand, looking back and forth between them, his face a shifting mix of surprise and expectation.

Leah swallowed with a visible gulp, but she hung on tight to Jon's hand, and her smile grew from a glimmer to a full-fledged grin. "Took you long enough, didn't it?" The delight on Jon's face matched hers. "But it seems a shame to build two houses when one will do." Chris let out a cheer.

I figured the two of them would stay entwined forever, but Jon extricated himself after only a minute or two. "Okay, Kenzie. We had a deal. Your turn."

The others looked puzzled, but I knew all too well what he meant. "Later. I'll do it later. When I'm not so tired. When I know what to say."

"Nope. No excuses." He turned to Wes. "Can we borrow your phone for a call?"

Wes looked from Jon to me, but Jon stepped closer and held out his hand. "This is important."

Wes pulled out his cell, opened the phone app, and passed it over.

Jon stepped in front of me. I'd known him only days, but we'd been through hell together. He'd heard my confession. Knew things about me that nobody else did. Now, he forced the phone into my hand. "Call your sister."

My mouth dried, but my fingers closed on the phone. I knew it was the right choice. I wasn't the same person as I'd been when I arrived on this island. But I still hesitated. "I don't know phone numbers anymore—they're all stored on my cell."

"I think you know this number." He stared me down. Not just determined. He cared. "You can do it, Kenzie. You'll both have holes in your lives until you do." His voice was so quiet, nobody could hear but me.

A solid warmth started deep inside and spread outward. I closed my eyes. Concentrated. And he was right. I knew Paige's number by heart.

I lifted the phone, and with shaking fingers and a trembling heart, I punched in the digits.

Paige answered on the third ring. "Hello?"

The sound of her voice took my breath away.

"Hello? Is someone there?" Now she sounded impatient.

Of course she didn't recognize the number. I needed to say something but couldn't find words. She was going to hang up. I would lose my chance.

Instead, she spoke again. "Mackenzie, is that you? Could that really be you?" Not angry. Not accusing. She sounded on the edge of tears.

I choked down a swallow and clutched the phone hard. "It's me, Paige. I called to say I love you. And I have so much else to say."

And at last, I had the strength to say it.

Acknowledgements

It's been a few years since my last published novel, and the pause makes the arrival of ISLAND ENDGAME that much sweeter. Wow! It's here at last. Picture me floating at ceiling height as I type this. I'm proud of this book, and I hope you've enjoyed the story.

Writing is a solitary challenge at times, but no book reaches completion without plenty of support, and I've been blessed with more than my share. My heartfelt thanks go to the amazing Laura Drake and to the Iron Clay Writers: Agnieszka Stachura, Claire Hermann, and Barrie Trinkle, all of whom have nurtured this book chapter by chapter through months of creation.

Beta readers Sharon Kurtzman, Barbara Claypole White, and Bianca Hankinson provided invaluable insight into the draft manuscript, keeping me from straying too far off track.

Jodi Warshaw's keen editorial eye helped hone the final version, and Dione Benson provided a final copyedit. Margie Lawson helped boost that first chapter into proper order, constantly reminding me to *do better*. Thank you all.

My always-patient family provided constant support and encouragement, without which none of my books would be possible. I love you!

Last, but definitely not least, I want to thank you, my readers. I can't tell you how much your kind words have meant over the years. I treasure every email, every review, every social media post. It's an act of faith to fling words out into the world. Thank you for letting me know that sometimes they land with a positive impact.

About the Author

R ebecca Hodge is an author of fiction, a veterinarian, and a clinical research scientist who lives and writes in North Carolina. Fiction writing is the space where her creative side comes out to play, and her writing centers on characters who are forced to discover the best of themselves. She has three grown sons, one crazy dog, two delightful granddaughters, and one patient husband. When not writing on the back porch or brewing yet another mug of tea, she loves hiking, travel, and (of course) curling up with a good book.

If you'd like to receive news about Rebecca's next book, go to her website at https://www.rebeccahodgefiction.com/ and sign up for her newsletter, which offers a book giveaway in every issue. You can also follow her on Facebook, Instagram, BookBub, and Goodreads.

f facebook.com/rebeccahodgefiction

○ instagram.com/rhodge.fiction/

BB bookbub.com/profile/rebecca-hodge

g goodreads.com/author/show/15943839.Rebecca_Hodge

Other Books by Rebecca Hodge

WILDLAND

" Fans of Cheryl Strayed's *Wild* or Kristin Hannah's *The Great Alone* won't want to put down this nail-biter." –Booklist

She'll do anything to save them. But what will she do to save herself?

When Kat Jamison retreats to the Blue Ridge Mountains, she's counting on peace and solitude to help her make a difficult decision. Her breast cancer has returned, but after the death of her husband, her will to fight is dampened. Now she has a choice to make: face yet another round of chemotherapy or surrender gracefully. Self-reflection quickly proves impossible as her getaway is complicated by a pair of abandoned dogs and two friendly children staying nearby, Lily and Nirav. In no time at all, Kat's quiet seclusion is invaded by the happy confusion of children and pets.But when lightning ignites a deadly wildfire, Kat's cabin is cut off from the rest of the camp, separating Lily and Nirav from their parents. Left with no choice, Kat, the children, and the dogs must flee on foot through the drought-stricken forest, away from the ravenous flames. As a frantic rescue mission is launched below the fire line, Kat drives the party deeper into the mountains, determined to save four innocent lives. But when the moment comes to save her own, Kat will have to decide just how hard she's willing to fight to survive--and what's worth living for.A heart-pounding novel of bravery, sacrifice, and self-discovery, *Wildland* will keep you on the edge of your seat to the very last page.

OVER THE FALLS

"Rebecca Hodge is quickly becoming **the master of gripping, life altering, realistic action fiction.** In *Over the Falls*, she creates that perfect blend of physical and emotional survival that keeps the pages turning."—Diane Chamberlain, *New York Times* bestselling author of *Big Lies in a Small Town*

Bryn Collins moved to the Eastern Tennessee mountains and never looked back when, fourteen years ago, her fiancé, Sawyer, jilted her for her despised sister, Del. Sawyer was later killed in a plane crash, but Bryn has never been able to forgive her sister for what she did, and instead chooses to spend her days in the idyllic beauty of the rugged landscape. Although a life-threatening accident ended her days navigating the perils of whitewater, she still finds refuge kayaking in the local lakes.But Bryn's placid life hits the skids when an unwelcome cast of characters reenters her life. Del goes mysteriously missing, leading her fourteen-year-old son, Josh, to Bryn's doorstep for help. Then Carl, a trouble-making outcast the sisters knew years before, is desperate to find Del because she owes him money, pulling Bryn into the orbit of his schemes.On the hunt for Del, Bryn and Josh follow an ever-elusive trail to Colorado, and at the annual Mountain Games competition in Vail, they finally confront the truth. For Bryn, all roads lead to the river, and on vicious Colorado whitewater, she is forced to muster every ounce of courage and strength she has to piece her family back together again.